BLINDSIDE HIT

MICHAELA GREY

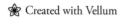

For Aaliya, who's Canadian but somehow knows almost nothing about hockey. I'm sorry for that time I said your brother was hot.

1

ETIENNE BRIDEAU WAS UGLY. He knew this fact, and most of the time he didn't think about it. He tried not to look in the mirror, to not catch a glimpse of his reflection in windows. He was good at what he did and that was what counted. He could out-skate anyone on his team and had the best plus/minus average in his minor league hockey team. The men he picked up in furtive encounters, safely away from the prying eyes of those who wouldn't approve, didn't seem to mind that his nose was too big and bony, his mouth was oddly shaped, and his smile showed too much gum, or maybe it was just that he never gave them the chance to see him in the light.

It didn't matter, he told himself. He'd helped his team win the Kelly Cup last year, for Christ's sakes. Who cared what he looked like? He was destined for the NHL, and nothing was going to get in the way of him getting there.

When he was traded to Toronto's minor league team, he knew in his heart he was on his way. He hugged his teammates, wished them well, and packed his bags for Ontario.

"CAPE BRETON, HUH?" Malcolm Kendricks was a big man, with a wide smile and booming voice. He'd introduced himself as the owner and general manager of the Thunder, his handshake hearty. "Good team. Defense a bit weak this year."

Etienne said nothing.

Malcolm glanced up, grin a flash of white against dark skin. "Relax, son. I've been watching tapes of you. You're a good left winger—potential to be great, I'd say. But you need to learn to play well with others. Your team is there to support you."

Etienne swallowed the retort. "Yes sir."

"You're not a puck hog, I'll give you that," Malcolm mused, looking through papers on his messy desk. "Rudy Wells is your team captain and first line center. He'll decide where he wants you."

"Isn't that usually the coach's decision, sir?"

"Ah well, you'll see," Malcolm said cryptically. "The team's on the ice, come meet them."

Etienne followed him down the hall and up the ramp to the rink. He could hear blades on ice, cheerful voices and the occasional thwack of sticks against pucks. His spirits rose, along with his nerves, as they emerged into the brightly lit space. Some fifteen players were milling around one end of the ice, a few others on the bench.

"Shootouts," Malcolm said unnecessarily. "Rudy! Over here!"

A figure split off the group and made for them.

Rudy was small, barely five foot nine, and lean, with dark skin and darker eyes. His smile was friendly, welcoming as he skidded to a stop beside them.

"Rudy, this is Etienne Brideau," Malcolm said. "He's all yours."

Rudy pulled off a glove and held out a hand. "Good to meet you, Etienne. Looking forward to seeing what you bring to the team. Got your gear?"

Etienne hefted his bag.

"Great. Let's get you a stall and on the ice." He led Etienne down the hall to the locker room, showing him the stall cleaned out and waiting. Etienne unpacked his gear as Rudy leaned against the stall next to him.

"Jackdaws have good things to say about you."

Etienne glanced up, halfway through stripping his clothes off. "They're a good team."

"Got family there?"

"No, actually." Etienne bent to pick up his chest guard. "My dad's in Brampton."

"Nice. I'm guessing we're a pit stop for you, am I right? Or is your dream to play for the ECHL until you retire?"

Etienne couldn't help the snort. "I want to play for the Seabirds, but I'll go to any NHL team that'll take me, to start."

"Fair enough. Well, I'll use you while I have you. I talked to Malcolm about your contract. Coach Hannity—the Freeze' head coach—may call you up occasionally, if they have a break in their line needing to be filled. Have you played in the AHL before?"

"Once or twice, with the Jackdaws," Etienne said, reaching for his skates.

"The Freeze are a good team. I'm friends with a few

of them, like Adam Caron and Li; I can give you some tips on how they operate."

"You know Adam Caron?"

Rudy shrugged. "Sure. Good guy."

"I've seen him skate in a call up for the Wolverines," Etienne said, trying not to sound starstruck. "His puck handling is ridiculous." *And he's hot as fuck. Probably best not to say that part out loud.*

"Taught him everything he knows," Rudy said with a wink.

"So where's *our* coach?"

"In his office, probably," Rudy said. "He spends most of his time there. You have a problem, bring it to me first." Something in Rudy's expression warned Etienne not to pry.

He finished lacing his skates and stood, towering over the much shorter center.

"Let's go meet the team," Rudy said, smiling up at him.

EVERYONE CROWDED around when he and Rudy came back up the tunnel, shaking Etienne's hand and slapping him on the back in friendly greeting. Most of the names Rudy tossed at him didn't stick, but a few stood out. Liam Thibault was a huge blond defenseman with a sunny smile. His shadow was a right winger named Johnny Girard, six inches shorter and fifty pounds lighter, as dark as Liam was bright. They never seemed far from each other and Etienne watched them curiously out of the corner of his eye as Rudy continued to introduce people. Were they together? Were they out? Did that mean he might have a chance to be out too?

"Logan Martel," Rudy said. "First line goalie. He doesn't speak, but he'll make himself understood."

Logan was tall and lanky, with olive skin and intense brown eyes. He had the goalie stare down cold, but his smile was friendly when he offered his hand.

"Theo Yoong and Robert Broussard," Rudy continued. "Theo's a D-man and Brewski's a left wing like you."

Theo was average height, spiky black hair standing up in sweaty clumps and golden skin gleaming from exertion. Beside him, Broussard scowled and didn't put out a hand. He was rangy and lean, with light brown hair and mistrustful green eyes that measured Etienne and found him wanting.

Etienne didn't offer to shake his hand, giving him a nod instead.

"Jax and Wyatt," Rudy said, pointing to two young men standing together a few feet away. "Wingers, fourth line. Let's do some shootouts!" he added, clapping his hands to draw attention. "Tenny, how about you go first?"

Tenny. His old teammates had called him Bridey, but Etienne found himself liking the way Tenny sounded. He nodded and gripped his stick as Logan skated for his crease.

He opted for an easy slalom toward the net, getting a feel for the ice—firmer than he was used to, sweet and clean beneath his blades—and watching Logan's reactions. He was going to be tough to get past, Etienne could already tell, keeping his movements to a minimum and not expending too much energy as he waited for Etienne to make his move.

Etienne sent a slapshot at Logan's left shoulder. Logan caught the puck and smacked it to the ice, and Etienne grinned, giving him a quick salute and circling back to the others. He watched as the rest of the team took their turns, cataloging Logan's reactions. When it was his turn again, he scooped up a puck and barreled straight for the goal.

Logan tensed, readying himself. Etienne sent the puck out in front of himself, aiming for Logan's left side, but at the last second he caught it with the tip of his stick, pulled it back as Logan lunged for it and sank it behind his skates.

Logan hit the ice and slid as the puck bounced off the back of the net. Etienne circled the goal and extended a hand to help him up. Logan accepted it, his eyes thoughtful and amused, and Etienne went back to the others.

"Nicely done," Rudy said, smiling at him. "Not often someone gets one over on Logan."

"Probably just lucky," Etienne said.

"Practice is at eleven every day," Rudy told him. "Strategy and planning sessions every Friday. Workout starts at eight—you don't have to be there but it's highly encouraged. Welcome to the team, Tenny."

2

THE THUNDER PUSHED Etienne to his limits physically, demanding more speed, more precise footwork, and better puck-handling.

Etienne took to it like a duck to water. His days were spent working out and on the ice, training until he could almost keep up with Rudy. Although in fairness, he told himself, *no one* could keep up with the captain. He was like smoke on the ice, vanishing when anyone got near. But Etienne kept trying, getting to the rink early and staying late, until one Friday night, two of his teammates descended on him.

Johnny and Liam each grabbed an arm as Etienne protested.

"Wait—what's going on?"

"Intervention," Johnny said. He and Liam dragged him off the ice as Etienne struggled in vain to free himself. "Stop fighting, Tenny," Johnny said, tightening his grip. "Look, you're a good winger, you *are*. You're almost as good as Rudy is. But if you don't lighten up, you're gonna burn out."

Etienne bristled. "I'm *just* as good as he is," he growled, knowing it for a lie even as he said it.

Liam snorted as they reached the locker room. "Sure, man. Say that where Logan can hear you. See how well you skate with bruised ribs and a black eye."

"Logan's biased," Etienne grumbled. He shook Liam's and Johnny's grips off his arms and bent to unlace his skates. "What are we doing, then?"

"Taking you out for drinks, and hopefully to get laid," Liam said cheerfully.

Etienne held in the snort at that. "*One* drink," he said instead.

"And lots of girls," Liam said.

Etienne sighed. "Not into girls." He froze. He really *was* tired, if he'd said that out loud.

"Lots of guys," Liam said, not missing a beat.

Etienne dragged his jersey off and eyed Liam warily. "That doesn't bother you?"

Liam slung an arm around Johnny's neck and pressed a messy kiss to his temple as Johnny rolled his eyes. "Be pretty fucking hypocritical if it did."

"You *are*—"

"Together?" Liam said helpfully. "Yep."

"Does Coach know?"

Johnny's and Liam's expressions darkened.

"Rephrase. Does the captain know?"

"Yeah," Liam said. "He's cool with it." He opened his mouth to add something but Johnny nudged him in the ribs.

"Fine," Etienne said abruptly. "Let me shower and we'll go."

Center Ice was a well-known gathering place for hockey players, and it catered to that demographic shamelessly, with signed pictures and jerseys of famous players on the walls and huge flat-screen TVs in every corner, playing whatever game was on. During the off-season, they played highlight reels, Liam told Etienne, towing him to a table in the back.

A cheer went up at the sight of the three of them and Etienne stopped dead in shock at the sight of most of his team gathered there, all grinning at him.

"*Why?*" he finally managed.

Liam clapped him on the back, hard enough to knock him forward a step. "Because you don't know how to have fun, and we're gonna help with that."

Rudy pointed to a chair, a smile on his dark features. "What are you drinking?" he asked as Etienne settled beside him with a nod to Logan.

Etienne shrugged. "I don't care."

"You may be a lost cause," Johnny said. "Tibs, get us a pitcher of beer, would you?"

Liam headed for the bar and Etienne looked around the table. Next to Logan was Broussard, and Theo, unfailingly as sunny as Broussard was sour. Jax and Wyatt were in the corner talking, but they spared a moment to wave at Etienne.

"You guys really all came out just to make sure I'd have a good time?"

Rudy gripped his shoulder, grinning at him. "You work too hard, Tenny. You need to relax."

"I can relax!" Etienne protested.

The faces around the table didn't look convinced. Liam returned with two pitchers of beer and flopped down beside Johnny, who absently curved his hand over the nape of Liam's neck.

Rudy followed Etienne's gaze to Johnny's hand and cleared his throat. "Ah, Tenny…."

"They told me before they press-ganged me," Etienne said.

"And you're okay with it?"

Etienne almost laughed at the echoing of his own question. "Seeing as I am too, yeah."

Rudy relaxed and glanced around the table, meeting everyone's eyes individually. Each in turn nodded as Etienne watched, confused. Finally Rudy turned back to Etienne.

"In that case, you should know most of us here aren't straight either."

Etienne's eyebrows shot up. "Sorry, what now?"

"Me, I'm bi," Rudy said.

"Knew I was gay when I was twelve," Johnny offered.

"I don't know what I am," Liam said. "I like hot people."

"Kinda ace," Theo said, shrugging. "But when I do feel… whatever, it's guys."

"Fuck off," Broussard snapped.

Theo sighed. "Robert."

Broussard glared. "Whatever. I'm gay, I guess. Probably."

Logan signed something. Rudy watched his hands and turned to Etienne.

"He says he's gay. Also, that reminds me, I need to get you and the rookies enrolled in the next sign language class at the university. Logan will go with you, give you some extra signs you'll need to know to be able to talk to him."

Etienne nodded and Logan gave him a smile surprising in its sweetness.

"Hey, so what's the deal with Coach?" Etienne asked Rudy.

Rudy's eyes tightened and he took a sip of beer.

"Come on," Etienne said. "He almost never comes out of his office unless it's to yell at us. You do all the actual play-making and strategy sessions. What's up with that? Why is he even employed?"

Rudy sighed and set his beer down. "It's not something I can talk about. Don't cross him, though."

A shiver of unease slid down Etienne's spine. "Why not?"

"Just trust me," Rudy said.

Someone roared with laughter from two tables away, making everyone turn and look. A group of men were clustered together around another, standing and holding his mug of beer in one unsteady hand.

"Hey," Johnny said, eyes narrowing. "Isn't that...."

"Adam Caron?" Etienne said. "Yeah, I think it is." He couldn't look away. Adam was even better looking in person than on the ice, his dark hair falling over a high forehead into big, dark blue eyes. He was grinning at something one of his companions had said, those full, kissable lips curving into an infectious smile that somehow lightened Etienne's mood just by looking at it.

"Is that—are those the fucking *Freeze*?" Broussard said, craning his neck to see.

"So it would appear," Theo said. He sounded faintly starstruck. Logan patted his shoulder, lips twitching. "I've only ever seen Adam skate," Theo said. "God*damn* he's hot. Ow!" He rubbed his thigh as Broussard glared at him. "I'm allowed to think other guys are hot, Rob. It doesn't mean I've suddenly stopped thinking *you're* hot."

"Speech, speech!" someone shouted.

Adam laughed and shook his head.

"Didn't he just get called up permanently by the Wolverines?" Johnny asked.

"That must be why they're celebrating," Liam said. "Let's invite them over." He was out of his chair and heading for the other table before anyone could stop him.

"Gosh, I love how impetuous he is," Johnny said into his beer. "That never backfires *ever*."

Liam was talking to the other group, which turned as one to inspect their table. Rudy and Johnny waved as Etienne tried to figure out how to make a run for it, but it was too late. All six men were on their feet and following Liam back over.

"Rudy!" Adam said, eyes sparkling. Rudy jumped to his feet to greet him.

"I honestly wasn't sure you'd remember me," he admitted.

"Have you *seen* you skate?" Adam demanded. "Of course I remember you!"

"Adam and I attended a training camp together last year," Rudy told the table.

"And you're just now telling us this?" Liam said, sounding betrayed.

"Join us?" Rudy asked Adam.

For several minutes, it was a mad scramble of finding chairs and rearranging to make sure everyone had room enough to sit down, and when the dust settled, Adam was sitting next to Etienne, crammed in so tight their legs were pressed together under the table.

"Hi," Adam said, offering a hand. "Adam Caron."

Etienne stifled a laugh. "I know who you are. Etienne Brideau. I play for the Thunder."

Adam nodded sagely. "I've heard your name."

"You have?"

Adam had clearly worked his way through more than a few beers. His eyes were glassy, cheeks flushed, and he swayed ever so slightly when he moved.

"Mm-hmm," he said, leaning toward Etienne. "The new left wing. Footwork like Astaire and a right hook like Ali. You're going places." He grinned. "Like me. I'm going places. I'm going to the Wolverines. Did you hear?"

"Yeah," Etienne said. His head spun, and he didn't think it was the beer he'd barely touched. Adam Caron —*the* Adam Caron—had heard of him. Had heard *good* things about him. He dragged himself together. "Sorry, uh—congratulations, man, that's amazing news."

Adam's smile widened. "Thanks. I'm celebrating."

"I can tell," Etienne said, fighting a smile.

Adam leaned in, lips to Etienne's ear. "I saw you watching me. Do you want to celebrate with me?"

Etienne froze. He hadn't heard right. There was no way Adam Caron had just hit on him. But Adam was smiling at him from an inch away, the intent clear in his eyes.

"Isn't there... someone else you'd rather, uh... celebrate with?" Etienne managed.

Adam pouted, pushing out that full lower lip. Etienne wanted to suck on it. He tore his eyes away, clearing his throat.

"You don't want to?" Adam was asking.

"Oh, I do," Etienne said, and Adam's smile returned,

bright enough to light the room. "But I just—" He gestured helplessly, at the people around them and then himself. *So many better options*, he was trying to say, but he couldn't figure out how to put it into words.

Adam put a hand on Etienne's thigh, making him jump. "My place is just a block away," he breathed.

Somehow, Etienne found himself following Adam from the bar as his friends laughed and shouted encouragement.

ON THE STREET, Etienne's common sense returned with a rush and he stopped.

"This is crazy," he said.

Adam was on him before Etienne could react, shoving him up against the wall and slamming their mouths together. He tasted like beer and peanuts, breath hot and tongue demanding. Etienne gasped and Adam pressed closer, hands roving across Etienne's chest and down toward his waist.

Etienne made a muffled noise of protest and caught Adam's hands before they could dip lower. Adam growled, fighting him, and they scuffled briefly before ending up with Adam's back pressed to the wall, wrists pinned to the brick.

Adam's eyes were huge, blown dark with lust, and he whimpered, twisting in Etienne's grip but not trying to break his hold.

"You like that?" Etienne said, squeezing his wrists harder.

Adam made a desperate, needy noise and nodded. "Please, I want—"

"You want to feel good?" Etienne murmured. He

leaned in and nipped sharply at Adam's earlobe, making him jerk.

"Want *you*," Adam panted.

You don't want me. Etienne was a convenient warm body, someone willing to give Adam pleasure. A sure thing. But right now, Etienne wasn't going to think about that. Not with Adam squirming against him, lips bitten red and eyes pleading for Etienne to do more.

"Not here," Etienne said. He took a step back, steadying Adam when he stumbled.

Adam straightened. "My place." He set off at a quick pace, realized Etienne wasn't beside him, and looped back to grab his wrist. "My place," he repeated, tugging.

"Okay," Etienne said. He didn't fight the smile as he fell into step beside Adam, who walked briskly despite his obvious inebriation.

Adam's "place" was a huge stone building with a doorman and gleaming marble floors.

"Good evening, Mr. Caron," the doorman said, pressing the elevator button and holding the doors open for them.

"Thanks, Bill," Adam said.

"Penthouse?" Etienne asked once the doors were shut.

"Not yet," Adam said. He was *looking* at Etienne, eyes raking up and down his body until Etienne felt laid bare, stripped naked standing there with all his clothes on.

"I've seen you play," Etienne said, in a desperate attempt to change the subject.

Adam didn't answer, leaning back against the mirrored wall and biting his lip.

"You're really good," Etienne said. The elevator was moving so *slowly*.

Adam raised an eyebrow. "Must be why I'm going to the Wolverines."

"Well no," Etienne said, unable to resist. "If you were *really* good, you'd be going to the Kingfishers, or maybe the Birds. Riptide, even. But the Wolverines?" He shook his head, grinning.

Adam burst out laughing. "Hey, fuck you, they're not that bad." He took a step forward, the intent in his eyes clear.

"You're weak on your left side though," Etienne said hurriedly.

Adam paused, brows drawing together.

"You shoot right," Etienne continued, "but you should strengthen your left side. You leave it open too much, and everyone knows it. How often do you get the puck stolen from that side?"

Something unreadable flickered through Adam's eyes. "I do okay." He took another step forward.

Etienne was saved by the elevator chiming and the doors sliding open. They stepped out into a dimly lit hall, Etienne's feet sinking soundlessly into the lush carpet. In front of a door with the number 501 on it, Adam fumbled with his keys, dragging them out and then dropping them. Etienne bent to retrieve them at the same time as Adam did, and froze, their faces an inch apart.

Adam licked his lips and leaned forward.

Etienne scooped the keys off the floor and straightened. "Which one is it?"

Adam straightened too, eyes narrowing. "What's going on with you?"

"Nothing. Which key is it?"

Adam indicated and Etienne somehow managed to get the door open. He held it for Adam to go through first, following him inside.

He stopped dead at the entrance to the living room.

"Not what you expected?" Adam inquired, tone dry.

Etienne glanced at him and then back at the living room, with its hardwood floors, the pinball machine in the corner, and the miniature golf course taking up most of the room.

"You have a golf course in your living room," he said blankly.

Adam came around the corner holding two beers. He held one out to Etienne, who took it dumbly. "I like golf," he said, shrugging.

"But in your *living room*," Etienne said.

"That just means you can fuck me on the green," Adam said innocently, and Etienne choked on his beer.

He coughed and spluttered, surfacing to the sight of Adam grinning at him and palming himself through his jeans. Heat shot through Etienne's groin and he set the beer down.

"Are you sure you want this?" he asked.

Adam tilted his head. "I said I did, didn't I?"

"Just making sure," Etienne said. "Take your shirt off."

Adam's smile was bright and happy. He pulled the shirt up over his head and dropped it on the floor. Etienne swore under his breath. Adam's abs were *obscene*, taut and defined under skin that looked satin-smooth and perfectly lickable. Etienne let his gaze wander, up over his firm pecs and the graceful wings of his collarbones and down, to the hair on Adam's belly that thickened where it disappeared under his waistband.

"Your turn," Adam said, but Etienne shook his head.

"Shoes."

Adam scowled but kicked them off.

"Now your pants, but not your underwear."

"You getting off on telling me what to do?" Adam asked, teetering dangerously on one foot as he tugged his jeans off.

"What do you think?" Etienne asked, knowing his voice had gone rough and low.

Adam swallowed and kicked the jeans into a heap. "Are you going to get naked too, or are you going to fuck me with all your clothes on?"

"Is that a kink of yours?" Etienne asked. He closed the distance between them, leaning into Adam's space without—quite—touching him.

Adam's eyes were wide and his mouth moved as if trying to remember words.

"Bedroom," Etienne said. "It's not a basketball court or something, is it?"

That surprised Adam into a laugh even as he turned to lead Etienne through the apartment. His bedroom was huge, a king-size bed dominating most of it. Adam flicked the lights on as they entered, and Etienne turned them right back off again, pushing him toward the bed when Adam protested.

"I can't see!"

"You don't need to see," Etienne growled. He shoved Adam onto the mattress and straddled him, hands already roving. In the dimly lit room, Adam's face was in shadow, but Etienne had always been good at seeing in the dark. He saw the moment Adam's eyes closed and his mouth opened when Etienne slipped a hand beneath the waistband of his boxers.

He wrapped his fingers around Adam's hard length, not stroking—just savoring the weight and feel of it. Adam hitched his hips up, making a frustrated noise.

"Come on," he hissed.

"Patience," Etienne murmured. He dropped his head and sucked a mark over Adam's collarbone, enjoying the way Adam writhed, one hand coming up to tangle in Etienne's hair. Etienne hummed happily when Adam pulled.

He took his time exploring Adam's chest with his mouth, tasting every inch of him and keeping Adam's shaft clasped loosely in one hand. He didn't let up until Adam was rolling his hips, breath stuttering as he looked for friction Etienne wasn't giving him.

"Please, please—" Adam's hands were roving over Etienne's shoulders, touching as much of him as he could as if mapping out his body with his fingers. It made Etienne shudder, the butterfly soft presses to his skin, and he sucked another mark into Adam's shoulder before he lifted his head.

"Supplies?" he asked.

"Drawer."

Etienne leaned across him, one hand on Adam's perfect chest to steady himself, and got the drawer open. He dropped the lube on the bedspread and tore the condom packet open with his teeth.

"I want to fuck you," he rasped.

Adam went very still, then nodded almost frantically. "Please, yes please, I want that too."

"On your stomach," Etienne ordered. He got off the bed to take off his clothes as Adam rolled over, pushing the boxers down. The pale globes of his ass glowed faintly in the light from the hallway. "You get told how beautiful you are a lot, don't you?" Etienne asked, pushing Adam's thighs apart so he could settle between them.

Adam had buried his face in a pillow, but Etienne caught the movement of his shoulders as he shrugged.

"I guess," he mumbled.

Etienne leaned down and nipped his shoulder, then licked the spot. Adam muffled a groan with the pillow.

Etienne couldn't help taking a few more minutes to explore Adam's body with hands and mouth, learning the curvature of his ribs, the way his muscles flexed and shifted under the skin as satin-soft as it had looked, the smell and taste of him as Adam writhed, begging wordlessly.

"C'mon," he said breathlessly when Etienne lifted his head. "Come *on*, I need your cock, I'm dying, please—"

Etienne muffled a laugh against Adam's ribs. "Are you saying my cock can save your life? Magical healing properties, maybe?"

"Won't know till we try," Adam shot back, pushing his hips up against Etienne's groin. "Fuck me already, would you?"

Etienne laughed out loud and went to his knees, retrieving the lube and coating two fingers.

"I don't need much," Adam husked, canting his hips.

"Do this a lot, do you?" Etienne asked, curious. He spread Adam's asscheeks apart with one hand and found his hole with slicked up fingers.

"Not in—ah—awhile," Adam managed as Etienne

pressed inside, gritting his teeth against the scorching heat that surrounded his fingers. "Busy training. I just like—oh *god* that feels good—I like the… come on, more, please—"

Etienne pumped in and out, taking his time and enjoying the curses that fell from Adam's mouth as he writhed back against him. He wanted to see how long it would take before Adam broke and begged for more.

Three minutes and forty-seven seconds, as it turned out.

Adam reached back with one hand, clamping down hard on Etienne's wrist and twisting enough to fix him with a glare.

"If I don't get your cock inside me now, I. Will. Die," he informed him.

Etienne couldn't remember the last time he'd laughed like this during sex. He pulled his hand out and leaned forward to kiss Adam, hard and rough and joyful. Then he broke away and went back to his knees. The first touch to his own neglected length had him hissing, fist tightening around himself to stave off the orgasm. *Not yet, not yet, not until I'm inside him—*

He rolled on the condom with shaking hands and dumped probably too much lube on his shaft, spreading the excess over Adam's hole. Then he lined up, pressing the head to Adam's entrance.

"Don't go slow," Adam begged.

Etienne could oblige. He shoved inside in one quick motion, burying himself deep.

Adam went rigid, spine bowing.

There was a breathless moment of silence as Etienne gave Adam's body time to adjust, running his hands up and down his ribs and over his shoulder blades as he luxuriated in the velvety tight grip around his cock.

Adam was breathing in short, sharp pants, shoulders shaking as he buried his face in the pillow.

"Okay?" Etienne asked. For him, it was better than okay. It was better than he could remember it ever feeling—Adam trembling beneath him, the sweet pliant feel of his body under Etienne's hands, the way every tiny movement he made sent sparks skittering down Etienne's backbone.

"*Fuck me already*," Adam snarled.

Etienne barked a laugh and obeyed, catching Adam's hips and tilting them for the right angle so he could pull out and drive home hard and fast.

Adam's strangled moans only added fuel to the fire kindling deep in Etienne's belly. He leaned forward, hips still working, one hand pressing Adam's chest into the mattress and the other snaking beneath Adam's stomach to find his cock.

Adam bucked against him, crying out when Etienne gripped him, body impossibly tightening even more.

"Make me come, please, make me come, I need to—"

"You say—*I'm* bossy," Etienne managed, but he changed his angle, slamming against Adam's prostate punishingly hard.

Adam's body locked up around him and he choked on a scream as he spilled over Etienne's fist, suddenly so tight Etienne could barely move.

Etienne drove deep one last time and filled the condom, sinking his teeth into Adam's shoulder as he shuddered through his ecstasy.

They collapsed to the bed in a limp, sweaty heap,

aftershocks shivering through both of them. It took Etienne several minutes to collect himself enough to pull out, petting Adam's flank soothingly when he moaned a protest.

He found washcloths in the bathroom and got one wet. Padding back to the bed, he rolled Adam gently onto his side and cleaned him up. Adam's eyes were closed, but he groped for Etienne's hand. When he found it, he tugged it to his mouth and kissed it clumsily.

Etienne suddenly found it hard to swallow. He cleared his throat and gently pulled his hand away, cupping Adam's cheek before tossing the used cloth in the hamper.

"You should sleep," he whispered.

"Will... y'stay?" Adam slurred.

God, Etienne wanted to. He wanted to crawl into the bed, pull the covers up over both of them and hold Adam for the rest of the night. But then morning would come, and Adam would be sober, and he'd get a good look at Etienne for the first time. And then there'd be regret, and embarrassment, and Adam wouldn't be able to look him in the eye, and Etienne would find himself outside Adam's door hating himself even more than he already did.

So…. "I can't," he whispered. He couldn't resist bending to drop a kiss on Adam's forehead, though, before straightening to pull the comforter at the end of the bed up and over his limp form. "Thank you. For— thank you."

Adam hummed, clearly mostly asleep, and Etienne smiled to himself as he picked up his clothes and tiptoed from the room.

Outside in the hallway, Etienne leaned against the

door for a minute. He hadn't expected to have so much *fun*. He wished, briefly, that he could have the opportunity to get to know Adam when he wasn't drunk and high on endorphins. He had the feeling Adam was worth knowing.

And then he put away that dream, tucked it in a drawer in his mind and turned the lock, and walked away, back to his own life.

3

THE WOLVERINES WERE on a whole different level from the Freeze. Adam had known this already, from being called up for a few games, but working with them on a daily basis had him dragging back to his apartment completely exhausted after practices, barely able to summon the energy to order food.

But even as tired as he was, he couldn't stop thinking about the man from that night. He hated that he couldn't remember his name. Edward? Ethan? It started with an E, he was pretty sure. His eyes had been such an unusual shade, a slate blue with glints of granite, and he'd fixed them on Adam as if nothing else in the world existed.

Adam had never felt so *seen*. He wanted more of that focus, more of those big hands all over his body, and more—if he was being honest—of being bossed around.

But with the intense training their coach was putting them through, Adam simply didn't have time to *find* the man from that night, no matter how much he wanted to. He fell onto his mattress, slept like the dead, and hauled himself to practice every day, usually cursing the day he'd decided to pursue a career in professional hockey instead of art.

It was working, though. He could *feel* himself getting faster, his reflexes sharpening, his awareness of the puck and ability to think several moves ahead increasing. Even his blind spot wasn't bothering him too much.

How had the man from that night picked up on that? No one else knew about the limited vision in Adam's left eye, not even the team doctor. *It wasn't that bad*, Adam told himself. After all, he could *mostly* see out of it. It was just that one area that was blurred, making him have to turn his head more to maintain his coverage.

His left winger was useless, though. Not only was he not fast enough, but he didn't pick up on Adam's cues and usually missed the shots Adam sent him.

"Get your head out of your ass and into the game, Jake!" Coach Benton roared at him after the umpteenth missed shot. "Cary's doing his best to give you goals and what are you doing? You off in fairyland? Dancing with the elves in the moonlight? Get it to-fucking-gether, you hear me?"

Jake hung his head. "Sorry, Coach," he mumbled. He glanced at Adam, wiping a drop of sweat off his nose. "Sorry, Cary."

"It's okay," Adam said. "Just *watch* me when I have the puck, okay? If you're open, I'm gonna send it to you, so be ready."

"And *you*," Coach said to Adam, who jerked.

"Me?"

"What do you think you were doing, going high

on that last shot? Hunt's never going to let you get a top-shelf goal. You gotta go low with him."

Adam scowled, gripping his stick. He *could* go high, he knew he could. He just had to catch Hunt off-guard.

"It's been a week, and I already know that look," Benton said. "Stop thinking you know better than me, buddy, because I'm here to tell you, ya don't."

"Yeah, you don't," Jake chimed in.

"*You* sure as shit don't either," Benton said, whirling on him. "So go sit down and practice your shutting-up face before I make you do a bag skate."

Jake snapped his mouth shut and scurried for the bench.

"You've got potential, kid," Benton said, more quietly. "But Hunty's going to stop every shot you make until you learn to quit telegraphing your moves."

Adam nodded.

"I want to start you on the third line our first game," Benton said, startling Adam into looking up. Benton raised his eyebrows. "Think you can handle it?"

"Against the Ravens?"

Benton nodded.

"Is Jake going to be my winger?"

Benton snorted. "Right now, I don't really have anyone else good enough to take his place. So yeah. You up to it?"

He'd have to skate twice as fast, watch for openings more closely than ever, and not rely on Jake for anything, Adam knew. He also knew he'd die before passing up this chance.

"Yes sir," he said.

"Of course you are," Benton said. "Shower and go home. Get some rest."

"I want to do some more drills," Adam protested.

"And I want a threesome with the Ice Girls," Benton said. "From the looks of you, you've forgotten what rest feels like. Go home and try to remember."

"Thanks, Coach," Adam said.

Benton smiled, transforming his somber face. "Looking forward to seeing what you can do, kiddo. Hey! What makes you think you've got the skills to pull off that move, Hunt?" He'd already forgotten about Adam, it was clear.

Adam skated to the bench and left the ice. A quick shower helped him clear his head and he found himself on the street a few minutes later with nothing to do.

He had no real friends in Toronto, unfortunately. Most of them were back in Seattle, and since he'd moved, the only people he'd really gotten to know were on his team or the training camp he'd attended that summer.

Adam straightened. Rudy would know who Adam's mystery man was. But he didn't answer when Adam called, the phone going straight to voicemail. Adam gnawed his lip briefly. He didn't know where Rudy lived. But he knew where he played.

Adam set off for the Thunder's practice rink, tugging his cap low to avoid being recognized. He was still new to the Wolverines, and the season hadn't even officially started, but the superfans were already posting sightings of him, along with speculation about his extracurricular activities.

The Thunder were in the middle of practice when Adam arrived, and he settled into a seat to watch. Rudy was every bit as good as he remembered from camp. *Thirty-two years old and faster than most of the twenty-two year olds on his team*, Adam thought, leaning forward to rest his forearms on the seat in front of him. He was wasted on the ECHL. Why was he still there?

Adam vaguely recognized the winger busy shouting at someone on his own team. Another player skated close and said something, and the man shut up, glowering at him. The player—he looked somewhat familiar too, and Adam thought he might have been at the bar that night—gave the winger a brilliant smile and touched his mouth with one finger before skating away.

The right winger was still glaring at the teammate who'd angered him, but he stopped yelling.

Interesting. Adam switched his focus to another pair.

This was… Johnny, he thought. He was only a little taller than Rudy, quick and sure on the ice and with a devastating slapshot. There was another player who appeared to be a defenseman, big and blond and not that great a skater, if Adam was being honest, and never far from Johnny. They'd been sitting together that night, he thought.

Another skater swung himself over the boards and hit the ice. Adam sat up suddenly, shock zinging through him. That was *him*. Adam would know that lean frame anywhere, those big hands that gripped his stick with the same surety as they'd mapped out Adam's body that night.

Adam watched intently as the man stole the puck from Johnny and proceeded to play a complicated game of keep-away. He didn't make for the goal. Instead, he skated in tight circles and intricate patterns, always whisking the puck out of Johnny's grasp just as he reached for it.

Adam could hear Johnny laughing and swearing in the same breath as the other man seemed to tire of the game and dodged around him, heading for the goal.

The goalie tensed, clearly dreading the winger's approach.

Relax, Adam urged him silently. *You'll never stop him if you're that locked up.*

Sure enough, the winger sank the puck between the goalie's legs with insulting ease, circling smoothly and skating away without looking back. The goalie yanked off a glove and shot him the finger, but he was laughing. Clearly, this man was liked and respected by his teammates.

Adam had to talk to him. *Had to.* He waited as Rudy gestured everyone around. He waved his arms a lot as he talked, and apparently had a lot to say. Finally, though, he dismissed the team, which headed for the locker room. Adam hurried after them.

"Rudy!" he said, and Rudy glanced up, surprised delight flashing across his face.

"Adam, what are you doing here?"

"Had a little spare time." Adam couldn't help looking for the winger, but he was already gone, vanished down the hall toward—presumably—the locker room.

"Wanna come back?" Rudy asked.

"Hell yeah." Adam followed Rudy through into the locker room, filled with rowdy men laughing and tossing things back and forth.

"You remember anyone I introduced you to that night?" Rudy asked, sounding amused.

"Not really," Adam admitted. "I'd put away a few by the time we joined you."

"Johnny," Rudy said, pointing. "Liam, defenseman and Johnny's boyfriend."

Rudy's casual acceptance of Adam's sexuality at training camp had been Adam's first clue that this was a man he could be friends with. He'd run into Adam in a little-known gay bar after practice one day, slid into the booth across from him, and given him that crooked smile. Adam, even taken aback, hadn't been able to help the smile in return.

Johnny waved and Liam flipped a salute at them.

"Theo," Rudy said, indicating the defenseman who'd talked the winger down. Theo smiled, making his eyes crinkle. His black hair stood up in sweaty tufts as if he'd just run his hand through it, and the winger beside him scowled.

"And that'd be Brewski," Rudy said. "Robert Broussard. Kind of a dick, but Theo usually manages to balance him out."

"Are *they* together?" Adam asked.

Rudy shrugged. "Getting there, I think. This is Logan, our goalie." His voice softened and Adam glanced at him curiously before looking where he'd pointed, to a tall, lean man with a hooked nose and sensitive lips, currently unlacing his skates. He glanced up when he heard his name, a smile curving his mouth. He didn't speak, though, just lifting a hand in greeting. "Logan doesn't talk," Rudy said to Adam in a low voice. "So don't ask him anything involving more than a yes or no question unless you know sign language."

Adam scanned the room, frowning. "One's missing." The tall winger was nowhere to be seen.

"What the hell," Rudy muttered. "Johnny, where did Tens go?"

Johnny shrugged. "Said he had something to do and took off."

"Etienne," Rudy told Adam. "But I guess you know *that* much, considering you left with him that night."

Etienne. Adam cleared his throat and Rudy snickered.

"I don't suppose you have his number, do you?" Adam asked.

Rudy regarded him. "So *that's* why you showed up, is it?"

Adam shifted his weight. "Look, I just—"

"I'm giving you shit, man," Rudy said. "Truth be told, I'm glad to see someone taking an interest in him. He doesn't...." He sighed. "I haven't known him long, so maybe I'm totally off-base, but if anyone deserves good things, it's Tenny. And from what I've gathered, he doesn't get them very often."

Adam left with Etienne's number—as well as Johnny's, Logan's, and a few others'—saved in his phone. He took a cab home, staring at Etienne's name on the screen and trying to figure out how best to open a conversation.

ETIENNE WASN'T proud of the way he'd fled after he'd caught sight of Adam Caron in the stands. *He and Rudy are friends,* he scolded himself on the way home as the subway car swayed. *He was just there to see Rudy, he probably doesn't even remember you.* But he hadn't been able to stop the jolt of sheer panic at the sight of him, sitting there watching them practice so intently. *Don't let him get close enough to reject you*, his heart whispered.

He was almost to his door when his phone buzzed. Etienne pulled it out and frowned at the unfamiliar number.

A little birdie gave me your number, the message read.

Etienne stared at the screen for a long minute before remembering to dig out his keys and unlock his door. *Who is this?* he typed back once he was inside, but he knew, and his traitorous heart jumped.

He dropped his keys on the hook and kicked off his shoes, waiting for the reply.

Call me Prince Charming.

Etienne snorted. *Why would I do that?*

Because you ran like Cinderella when you saw me.

Etienne stared at the screen for several long moments. Nothing else came through. Finally, he set his jaw and began to type.

Maybe I had things to do.

Unhitch your pumpkin?

Etienne bit back a laugh. *Two minutes in and we've already descended to euphemisms?*

Please, was the response. *If we were using euphemisms, I'd come up with better ones than that.*

Polishing my slippers, Etienne sent.

Good one. Cleaning the chimney.

Etienne bit his lip against the smile. *Emptying the gutters.* He flopped onto the couch, stretching his legs out.

Jerking off, Adam suggested.

Etienne burst out laughing. *What do you want, Adam?*

So you DO remember me!

Etienne rolled his eyes. *You're kind of hard to forget.*

:D was the reply this time. Etienne stared at it, unreasonably charmed, as Adam started typing again.

Was wondering if you wanted to get together.

That put the brakes on Etienne's good mood. *No,* he sent immediately.

Why not?

A beat of silence.

You didn't like me?

Another beat.

I did something wrong.

Etienne chewed his lip.

I made you uncomfortable. I'm sorry.

"Goddammit!" Etienne said aloud. He could almost *see* Adam's hangdog expression at the thought of upsetting him. *You didn't make me uncomfortable, you didn't do anything wrong. I liked you a lot, I'm just... really busy. I don't have time to hang out.*

He pressed Send and waited. It didn't take long for Adam to start typing again.

Lucky for me I'm a patient man.

Etienne blinked. *What does that mean?*

It means you won't be busy forever. And when you're free, I'm gonna...

Etienne waited but the sentence stayed unfinished. *You're gonna what?*

Romance the shit outta you, Adam replied promptly.

Etienne nearly dropped the phone. He hadn't really just said that, had he? But it was still there, blue on white, and Etienne couldn't *breathe*.

He leaned forward, putting his head between his knees and waiting for this fantasy to fade, the one where the star hockey player—the *gorgeous* star hockey player—was interested in *him*, Etienne Brideau, with his big nose and stupid gummy smile and gangly, rawboned awkwardness.

The phone buzzed again and Etienne scrambled for it.

Still there?

Yeah, Etienne sent. *Just swooning from how romantic you are.*

Oh, I've got better moves than that, Adam replied. *You sure you're too busy to go out? I can show you some of them in person.*

And *that* was the worst idea ever. Adam hadn't gotten an up-close look at him at the rink that afternoon—Etienne had made sure of that. And the night at the bar, Adam had been so drunk he was probably seeing triplicate of everything. He had no idea what Etienne really looked like, and when he *did?* He'd run. Politely, of course, because Etienne already knew Adam was nothing if not a well-mannered Canadian boy, but he'd find a reason to cut their date short, and there'd never be another one.

You're taking way too long to think about this, Adam sent. *I must be getting to you.*

Etienne shook his head. *You're persistent, I'll give you that.*

Thanks!

I wish I could say yes. God, how he wished he could say yes. It hurt, deep in his gut, to tell Adam no, to turn down the opportunity to see him again. To *touch* him again. But in the cold light of day, Adam wouldn't want him to anyway. *But I just can't.*

In that case, Adam replied, *I've got another question for you.*

Etienne braced himself. *Shoot.*

Wanna be friends?

Etienne *did* drop the phone that time, and it bounced off the hardwood floor as he scrambled to retrieve it.

Seriously? Are we twelve?

Don't hate, Adam responded. *I haven't been here long. My only friends are my teammates, and most of 'em are okay but I don't really want to be with them 24/7, you feel me? And I like talking to you.*

Etienne laughed helplessly, rubbing his face. What *was* it about this man that made him forget all his carefully constructed defenses? It didn't take him long to compose a reply.

As long as you don't mind that we can't hang out in person much (at all) *then yeah. I'd like to be your friend.*

:D

4

———

It didn't take long for Adam to worm his way into Etienne's life. Looking back, Etienne wasn't even really that surprised—that was just how Adam *was*. People let him in, gave him things, smiled instinctively at him. Part of it was because of how good-looking he was, but part of it was simply *Adam*, with his infectious smile that made deep dimples appear in his cheeks and his dark blue eyes light up. He made people want to be near him.

Even over text, Etienne wasn't immune to it. To *him*. He woke up most mornings to a text from Adam, usually complaining about bad coffee or his breakfast sandwich being made wrong or the bag skates his coach was going to make them do.

That was the thing about Adam—he complained a lot, but it never occurred to him to demand change. If the coffee was bad, he dumped it out and went somewhere else. If his sandwich was wrong, he ate it anyway. The bag skates—well, everyone complained about those. But Adam still did them, and Etienne did his best not to think about Adam bright-eyed and sweaty after practice.

Because as much as he complained, Adam also found joy in life. The very first morning after they started texting, Etienne woke up to a blurry, out-of-focus picture that appeared to be a small black cat, although the only thing of her in frame was her pink nose, one golden eye, and part of an ear.

Look at this precious girl! Adam had sent. *I want to take her home with me.*

Do it, Etienne replied.

No pet policy :(

A few hours later, Etienne got a picture of a butterfly perched on the brim of Adam's cap. It was, admittedly, lovely, but Etienne was more transfixed by the smile on Adam's face.

Is there a no butterfly policy in your building? he asked.

Maybe I should start a butterfly sanctuary where my golf course is! :D

Etienne set the picture of Adam with the butterfly as his lock screen.

SEVERAL TIMES A DAY, Adam sent Etienne pictures or links to funny or interesting things. He never seemed to expect a response, and he never seemed to care that he usually texted Etienne first and not the other way around.

Etienne began to look forward to checking his phone when he woke up and after practice. At first, he let Adam send the pictures, but when he saw a small, wiry-haired terrier out for a run with his owner on his morning jog, he couldn't resist.

!!!! Adam replied. *Did you pet him?*

Sadly, no, they were in a hurry. Maybe if I see them again.

After that, Etienne sent Adam pictures as well—of his food, of his skates, hanging up by the laces and waiting to be sharpened, of little things that occurred during his day. Adam always responded with delight, and usually a picture of whatever was happening with him at that time. Etienne got a *lot* of pictures—usually unfocused and clearly snapped on the sly—of Adam's teammates, both in the locker room and on the bench.

You know I could probably sell these for a lot of money somewhere, he pointed out.

Maybe you should, Adam responded. *Thunder don't get paid much, gotta supplement that income where you can. No shame, baby.*

Etienne sent him a picture of his hand, flipping him off.

AFTER A PARTICULARLY GRUELING PRACTICE, Etienne dragged himself home, thinking longingly of an ice bath and possibly a career as an accountant. He was locking the door behind him when his phone rang. Etienne answered without looking at it, juggling his gear and the phone and trying not to drop everything.

"Hey," Adam said, and Etienne *did* drop his gear, although thankfully not his phone.

"Um, hey," he said. Then Adam's tone registered and he frowned. "Are you okay?"

"Yeah." Adam sighed.

"You don't sound okay." Etienne kicked his shoes off and limped for the kitchen. "What happened?"

"Nothing," Adam said. "I mean. Not really."

Etienne found painkillers and cold water and settled himself gingerly on the couch, suppressing a groan. "You're gonna make me work for it?"

Adam sighed again. "My baby sister's getting married."

"Isn't that supposed to be good news?" Etienne asked. He trapped the phone between his ear and shoulder so he could down the pills in one quick gulp.

"Not when it comes with my mom hinting about when am *I* going to get married, who's going to my games, am I ever going to have babies she can spoil…."

Etienne winced. "Does she know?"

"No." Adam sounded morose.

"Would she care?"

"I don't know," Adam admitted. "She's set on me having kids, but she's also pretty liberal. She and Dad both are. She'd probably come around."

"So why not tell her?"

"And crush her hopes and dreams of me marrying a pretty blonde girl and having two perfect children and a picket fence?" Adam snapped. "I can't—I don't think I can face her putting on a brave face and telling me she loves me anyway."

Etienne grimaced. "Yeah, that would suck. But not telling her the truth's gotta suck more, doesn't it?"

Adam made a small, disgruntled noise that Etienne definitely didn't think was cute. "They're in Seattle, anyway. I'll have to fly out for the wedding, but at least they won't drop in on me."

"What about the team?"

Adam was silent.

"Ah." Etienne took a drink of water.

"I *want* to come out to them," Adam said. "I don't... I'm just...."

"Yeah, I get it. It's not an easy conversation to have."

"What if they don't want me around?" Adam sounded miserable. "Or make comments about me checking them out in the locker room or something. If my playing suffers because they don't trust me anymore, I don't think I—"

"Do you trust *them*?" Etienne interrupted, mostly to forestall the spiral of panic he could hear building in Adam's voice.

Adam subsided. "Yeah," he said after a minute. "I mean, I think I do. I don't know them all that well yet. Jake is great—I don't think he'd care. And Hideki is chill."

"Maybe you should come out to the two of them first," Etienne suggested. "See how they take it and go from there."

"That's an idea," Adam said. "I hate this."

"I know."

Adam sighed. "What are you up to?"

Etienne stretched his legs out, trying to suppress the groan.

"Are you hurt?" Adam asked, voice sharpening.

"Just sore," Etienne said through his teeth. "Tibs and Johnny had a fight. Tibby can't skate when he's in a *good* mood. When he's upset, he's basically a wrecking ball on razor blades."

"Do you want a massage?" Adam said, and Etienne's dick twitched at the thought of Adam's hands on him. "I give great ones, ask anyone on the team. I

41

can come over—"

"No," Etienne said hurriedly.

He told himself Adam's silence wasn't disappointed.

"I'm just… gonna go to bed," Etienne said. "Look, your mom loves you, right? You can still adopt, it's not like you're sentencing her to never being a grand-mother. And the team will accept you, I promise."

"Take a hot bath with Epsom salts," Adam said.

Etienne smiled. "I will. Talk to you later, Cary."

Rudy sat down beside him after practice a few weeks later and Etienne glanced at him, surprised.

"Help you?" He bent to untie his skates.

"You and Adam, huh?" Rudy said.

Etienne stiffened.

"Hey, whoa," Rudy said as Etienne straightened, turning to look at him. "You know we don't care about *that.*"

"Well, it's not like '*that*' anyway," Etienne said, bending back to his skate. "We're just friends. There's nothing… else."

"Sure," Rudy said. "Because I always smile like that when I get a text from a *platonic* pal."

Etienne yanked the skate off and dropped it to the side without answering.

"Look," Rudy said. "I'm the team captain, it's my job to keep an eye on you guys, make sure everything's okay."

"And there's something wrong with me texting a friend?" Etienne snapped as he pulled off his other skate.

"Just the opposite, actually."

Etienne glanced up. Rudy's eyes were sincere.

"He makes you laugh. You never laugh, Tenny. Ever since you guys started talking, you've been... lighter."

"What the fuck does that mean?"

"It means," Johnny said, dropping onto the bench on Etienne's other side, "you're skating better and smiling more. Both things we like and want to keep happening."

"I wasn't skating well before?" Etienne asked, bristling.

Johnny rolled his eyes. "Brewski's already got the 'prickly asshole' award, so don't bother trying. All we're saying is... we want you to be happy."

Etienne looked at his hands, trying to swallow the lump in his throat.

"Are you guys dating?" Johnny asked, nudging him gently.

Etienne shook his head. "No. He doesn't—it's not like that."

"Seemed like that at the bar," Johnny said, almost under his breath. Etienne shot him a dirty look and Johnny gave him an innocent one right back. "I'm just *saying*."

"Johnny, go check on Liam before he gets us into trouble. He's trying to talk to Kendricks."

"*Shit*." Johnny bolted.

Rudy laughed.

"Is he actually talking to Kendricks?" Etienne asked.

"Nah," Rudy said. "I just wanted to say, without witnesses because I know you hate showing emotion, that if you need anything at all, we've got your back."

Etienne nodded, the lump in his throat returned with a vengeance. "I—thanks."

AND SO IT went for another month, until the pre-season officially started. Texts and calls from Adam dropped sharply after that, which made sense, even though Etienne hated checking his phone and finding nothing there, but they still talked at least once a day.

When the Wolverines lost against the Senators, Adam sent one thing. *:(*

You'll get them next time, Etienne told him. *That was a dirty fucking hit Eckhart made on you.*

Hurts like hell, Adam admitted. *Banged up my knee, I'm icing it but can't get up to get food or piss or do anything, it sucks.*

Etienne stifled the urge to head for Adam's place. *You're a Leaf, can't you afford to hire someone to help?*

But then stranger in my house :(

So?

Adam's reply was quick. *Gives me heebie-jeebies. Can't stand it.*

Etienne snorted to himself. *You took me home after knowing me five minutes.*

You're different, Adam replied.

Etienne stared at his phone, and after a minute, it buzzed again.

Feel like I've known you forever.

Me too, Etienne admitted. His heart was in his throat as he pressed Send, but Adam just replied with a smiley face, and Etienne laughed, relaxing.

THE THUNDER WERE BUSY TOO. Their first few games were on home ice and they won two and lost the other by a narrow margin. Adam texted Etienne confetti and streamers after the first two, and a line of sad faces after the third.

Ref should have ruled that goal good, he said.

Etienne, sitting in the locker room sweaty and dejected, was inclined to agree.

Will you do some drills with me? Adam asked.

Etienne tensed.

Not now, Adam clarified. *Things are crazy for both of us. But when the season slows down? I've never seen footwork like yours. Like… you're not as fast as Rudy on a breakaway, maybe, but you SMOKE him when it comes to getting the puck and keeping it away. Do you think you could teach me?*

Could he? Etienne considered. Could he get face to face with Adam, risk Adam rejecting him? He wouldn't, Etienne thought. He *wouldn't.* After nearly three months of talking to him, he knew that much. Adam wouldn't push him away just because Etienne was ugly. But he also wouldn't *want* him.

Etienne suddenly didn't care, though. He wanted to get on the ice with Adam, face off against him and see who'd emerge victorious. He wanted to see Adam *smile* at him, goddammit.

Yeah, he sent back. *Once things settle down, sure.*

Adam sent him a string of happy face emojis and Etienne laughed, clutching his phone in the locker room, sitting there in all his gear, exhausted and drained but somehow lighter than ever.

5

THREE DAYS LATER, his phone rang with a number he didn't recognize. Etienne answered, and a polite female voice asked for Etienne Brideau.

"Speaking."

"Mr. Brideau, this is Toronto General."

Etienne blinked. "General what?"

"Hospital," the woman said. "Toronto General *Hospital*. My name is Alice, and you're listed as Adam Caron's emergency contact."

"His what? *What happened?*" Etienne demanded, already scrambling off the couch for his shoes.

"He's suffered a concussion," Alice said briskly. "It's not too serious, but we'd like you to come down to the hospital. He can't be released on his own recognizance yet and he says he has no other family in the area."

No other *family*. Etienne didn't look at that statement too closely as he dragged his shoes and a jacket on and bolted out the door.

He decided on a taxi, flagging down the first he saw and nearly falling into the back.

"Toronto General," he gasped. "*Hurry.*"

He tipped the driver extra when they made it there in record time and then charged through the hospital's sliding glass doors, making for the first official-looking person he saw, an older woman behind a desk.

"Adam Caron," he said, still out of breath. "Please, where is he?"

"Are you family?"

"I'm his emergency contact, they called me." Etienne showed her his ID, shifting his weight impatiently.

The woman typed for a minute. "Room 203, second floor, turn right out of the elev—"

But Etienne was already gone, running for the elevators. On the second floor, he found room 203 almost immediately. There were several men clustered outside, all of whom looked up at Etienne's approach. Etienne recognized several of them vaguely, but he didn't stop to talk. He pushed past, knocked, and shoved the door open.

Inside, a nurse gave him a dirty look, but Etienne's attention was on the bed. He approached, suddenly apprehensive. Adam looked pale and there was dried blood on his temple, stark rust against the whiteness of his skin. His eyelids fluttered as Etienne got close.

"Go 'way," he complained, batting ineffectually at the nurse's hands. "Where's Tenny? Want Tenny."

Etienne leaned over the hospital bed, fighting the temptation to take Adam's free hand. "I'm here, Cary. I'm right here. Let the nurse do her job, okay?"

Adam turned toward him, eyes unfocused. The dried blood streaking his temple made Etienne's chest ache.

"Tens," Adam mumbled.

48

"Yeah," Etienne said, bending closer to hear him. "What is it?"

"Saw a butterfly today."

Etienne shot the nurse a panicked glance. Was he hallucinating? Disassociating, or whatever they called it? But she smiled and shook her head.

Normal, she mouthed.

Relieved, Etienne took Adam's hand. "Yeah?" he managed. "Was it pretty?"

Adam nodded. He couldn't seem to focus on Etienne's face, his expression dazed. "Color... of your eyes," he slurred.

"If you'll move over to this side," the nurse said, oblivious to Etienne's inner turmoil, "I can get his head cleaned up."

"What *happened*?" Etienne asked her as they swapped positions.

The nurse shrugged. "You'll have to talk to his doctor."

"Jake," Adam said.

Etienne waited, but Adam's eyelids were drooping shut.

"Jake what?" Etienne asked gently, rubbing the back of Adam's hand. Jake had to be Jake Kano, Adam's left winger and subject of not a few rants on Adam's part, usually about how he never watched where he was going and couldn't read Adam's body language for love or money.

The door opened and a young Indian woman wearing a white lab coat walked in. Her thick hair was in a braid over her shoulder and there was a tiny stud in her nose.

"Dr. Khatri," she said, holding out her hand to Etienne. "Are you Mr. Caron's emergency contact?"

"I guess so," Etienne said, accepting it. "I mean, he doesn't... there's no one else."

Dr. Khatri just hummed, consulting the chart at the end of Adam's bed.

"Please, can you tell me what happened?" Etienne asked, a little desperately.

"The buckle on his helmet strap broke," Dr. Khatri said. "From what I understand, he was going for the puck and someone got in the way?"

Jake. Etienne tightened his grip on Adam's hand.

"He would have been fine, except for the helmet," Dr. Khatri continued. "Mr. Caron ricocheted off the boards at about twenty miles per hour, lost his helmet, and when he went down, his head bounced off the ice."

Etienne winced involuntarily.

"Yes," Dr. Khatri said, her tone dry. "He's suffered a grade two concussion, bordering on grade three. He needs to be kept on bed rest for at least three days, until he's able to function on his own. It's likely he's suffering short-term amnesia, meaning he'll forget conversations within seconds of having them. He'll also have balance issues, severe headaches, and probably a lot of irritability. That's common among athletes used to being in full control of their bodies and then losing that control. If he doesn't have family in the area, he'll need a home health care nurse until he's recovered."

"No," Etienne said instantly. "They're on the west coast. I'll do it."

Dr. Khatri looked skeptical. "You'll take care of his every need for three days, including using the bathroom, showering, and making sure he eats?"

Etienne swallowed hard but lifted his chin. "Yes."

"His vision is blurry right now," Dr. Khatri continued. "That's fairly common after a head injury, but I want him to go to his doctor in three days to make sure it clears up. It could be a sign of something worse."

Adam stirred. "Tenny. Want Tenny."

Etienne bent over, close to Adam's face. With the blood washed off, he was terrifyingly pale, his lips almost white.

"I'm here," he said. "You're okay, Cary, the hospital is going to take good care of you."

The nurse from earlier had left the room without Etienne noticing, but now she came back, alarm on her face.

"There are quite a few very large men in the hallway," she said. "And they all want to talk to you, Mr…?"

"Brideau," Etienne said, straightening. "They're the Toronto Wolverines. *This*—" indicating Adam in the bed— "is also a Wolverine, and they're worried about him."

"Maybe you should go talk to them," Dr. Khatri suggested, "before they disrupt the other patients."

So Etienne squeezed Adam's hand, disentangled himself gently, and headed for the door.

A big man with a sandy beard and rumpled hair met him first. "Coach Benton," he said. "You are?"

"Etienne Brideau, I play for the Thunder."

Benton's eyebrows went up. "And you're Adam's emergency contact?"

"Apparently," Etienne said, shifting his weight.

One by one, the others introduced themselves. Even worried about Adam, Etienne couldn't help feeling faintly starstruck. There was tall, imposing

Claude Latour, defenseman and enforcer, nothing short of a legend in his time. Next to him was short but almost as imposing Victor Yanovich, another defenseman. Hideki Matano, a center, was beside Victor, and then there was Jake, tall and blocky and with a miserable expression.

"How is he?" Jake asked.

"In and out," Etienne said. "Doctor said he's got a grade two concussion, bordering on grade three. He's going to need help at home for a few days."

"I'll do it," Jake said immediately, and Etienne warmed to him.

"Thanks," he said, "but I've got it."

"How do you know Cary, anyway?" Benton asked, eyes shrewd.

"Mutual friend introduced us and we've been talking ever since," Etienne said. He glanced at the door. "I should go back, unless there's something else?"

"Does he need us here?" Jake asked. He reminded Etienne of a golden retriever, big and sweet and a little clumsy.

"I don't think so," Etienne said, smiling at him. "I'll tell him you came, though."

He was back in the room before they reached the elevators. Adam was twisting restlessly on the bed, the nurse trying vainly to keep him still.

"Thank god," the nurse said when she saw him. "Make him stop *squirming*, would you?"

Etienne hurried to Adam's side. "Hey," he said, leaning over so he was in Adam's line of sight. "Be still, Cary, the nurse is trying to work."

Adam quieted, groping for Etienne's hand. "Saw a butterfly today," he murmured, eyelids drooping again.

"I know," Etienne said, gently brushing Adam's hair off his forehead.

"Was pretty. Like you." Adam's face relaxed.

"He's out," the nurse said. "You can have a seat if you want."

Pretty. Like you. Etienne groped for a chair, his mind spinning. Adam hadn't meant it *that* way, of course, but still he hugged the words close, watching Adam's face as he slept.

6

HE CALLED Rudy while Adam was asleep.

"Hey, Tenny, the team's coming to mine tonight, you in?"

"I can't," Etienne said, watching Adam's face. "Adam... he's in the hospital."

"He's *what*? What happened? Is he okay? Are you with him?"

"He's got a pretty bad concussion," Etienne said. He couldn't help taking Adam's hand again, limp in sleep, and brushing a thumb across his knuckles. "He'll be okay—yes, I'm with him. Apparently his winger ran into him and Adam's helmet strap broke, his head hit the ice."

Rudy sucked in a sympathetic breath. "And you? How are you?"

"Me?" Etienne said, startled. "I'm fine, why wouldn't I be?"

Rudy said nothing, but his silence said volumes.

"I'm *fine*," Etienne insisted. "I'm going to—look, Rudy, he needs someone with him for the next three days. The doctor suggested a home health nurse but Adam… he hates strangers in his house. I'm… I need to stay with him."

"For three days?" Rudy said.

"We don't have any games until this weekend," Etienne said. "It'll just be practice I'm missing, and I'll make up the time, I promise—"

"Relax," Rudy interrupted. "We'll cover for you with Coach. As much as you've been training lately, a break will do you good."

Etienne closed his eyes as relief swept over him. "Thank you," he whispered.

"Just… see if you can figure some stuff out while you're with him," Rudy said, and hung up before Etienne could protest that there was nothing *to* figure out.

THE HOSPITAL RELEASED Adam the next day and Etienne insisted on renting a wheelchair for him.

"I hit my head, not my leg," Adam complained, the drugs making his voice slow, but Etienne ignored him, bundling him in and making sure he was comfortable. Adam folded his arms, sulking, as Etienne pushed the chair through the halls and out to the waiting car and driver.

He swore under his breath as they came out the door and nearly ran into several people clustered together. They caught sight of Adam and converged on him, holding out recording devices.

"Adam, Adam Caron, are you okay? Can you give us a statement?"

Adam flinched, raising a hand, and Etienne

scowled thunderously at the journalists, startling them into stepping back.

"No comment," Etienne snapped.

He settled Adam in the back and ducked around to the other side without making eye contact with any of the reporters.

Doors closed behind him, he fussed with the seatbelt, checking and double-checking that Adam was comfortable, until Adam pushed weakly at him.

"I'm not *dying*."

"Sorry," Etienne muttered. The driver was careful, not braking or accelerating too quickly, and Adam rode quietly, his head back against the seat and his eyes closed as Etienne watched him.

When they arrived, Etienne had the driver double-park while he got the wheelchair out, unfolded, and Adam into it. Then he gave the driver the last of his cash and wheeled Adam through the doors.

Bill was on duty again, his eyes widening at the sight of Adam in the wheelchair.

"Mr. Caron, Mr. Caron, are you okay?"

Adam winced.

"Keep your voice down," Etienne said. "He's got a concussion."

"I'm fine, Bill," Adam said, voice faint. "Just need rest."

"It's that hockey, I've told you over and over it's too dangerous," Bill said, and the look on his face said he was gearing up for a rant.

Etienne made for the elevators. "Tell us about it another time," he suggested over his shoulder, and pushed Adam's chair into the cage.

The doors slid shut and Adam sighed gratefully, leaning back to rest his cheek against Etienne's stomach. Etienne caught his breath, reaching for the fifth floor button without dislodging him.

"Everything hurts," Adam said in a small voice. He rubbed his cheek against Etienne's shirt, brows knitted, and Etienne couldn't help cupping the back of his head, avoiding the bruise on his temple.

"You can take another pill when I get you upstairs," he murmured.

Adam didn't reply, face still buried in Etienne's stomach.

UPSTAIRS, Etienne wheeled him into the bedroom. "Do you need the bathroom before bed?"

Adam hesitated but finally nodded.

Etienne dithered for a minute about the best way to do it and finally got Adam to his feet, pulled the scrubs he'd been given down around his ankles, and eased him onto the toilet.

"Call me when you're done," he said, and bolted.

He found Gatorade in the fridge and grabbed a bottle. When he came back to the bedroom, he could hear noises from the bathroom.

"Cary? I'm coming in."

Adam was upright, pants halfway up his thighs as he clung to the sink and gasped for air.

"I told you to *call me*," Etienne said, diving to help him. "Put your arms around my neck."

Adam obeyed, trembling like a leaf in a high wind, as Etienne tugged the scrubs up into place and tied the waistband.

"You fucking idiot," he murmured, guiding him

back to the chair and rolling him out to the bed. "You allergic to asking for help?"

Adam didn't say anything. His lips were white again, color drained from his face, and he swayed, eyes unfocused.

"Okay, let's get you into bed before you pass out on me," Etienne said, alarmed.

Getting Adam up out of the wheelchair was tricky. His limbs were loose, head falling forward, and Etienne was left to wrestle two hundred pounds of large, semi-conscious hockey player into the bed by himself.

He just managed it, sitting down heavily beside Adam once he was tucked in.

Adam, on his side facing him, fumbled for Etienne's hand with his eyes closed.

Etienne was swamped with the memory of that night, of Adam kissing his hand and asking him to stay, and he laced their fingers together, holding on tight.

"We need to call your parents," he finally said.

"No."

"They deserve to know you got hurt, Cary."

"Coach called. Told them."

Etienne hesitated.

Adam opened his eyes, dark blue and miserable. "They'll fuss," he said. "Please, Tens. I can't—"

Etienne squeezed his hand gently. "Not yet, then. Do you want your pill now?"

Adam nodded and winced. He didn't sit up when Etienne offered it to him, opening his mouth instead, eyes still closed. His tongue was soft and wet, curling around Etienne's fingers when he placed the pill inside.

"Glad you're here," Adam whispered, face mostly smashed into the pillow.

Etienne smoothed the hair off his forehead, away from the horrible purple and green bruise that covered the left side of Adam's face. He said nothing, still stroking Adam's hair until his breathing slowed and evened out and he fell asleep.

ETIENNE INTENDED to sleep on the couch that night, but Adam had other ideas.

"What if I need you in the night? I still can't go to the bathroom on my own. I might fall and hit my head again and make it worse and it would be all your fault."

Etienne laughed and Adam smiled.

"The bed's big enough for both of us," he said. "It doesn't have to be weird. Please, Tenny?"

Etienne swore under his breath. "We're not having sex, Cary."

Adam mimed weak astonishment. "Who said anything about sex? You have a dirty mind, Etienne Brideau, and I'm a wounded man. For shame."

Etienne rubbed his face, trying to hide the laughter, but he knew he wasn't successful.

WHEN THEY GOT into bed that night, Adam wriggled backward until his hips were nestled in Etienne's groin.

"*Adam—*"

"I like to spoon," Adam said without looking at him. "Just fucking hold me already, would you?"

Etienne bit the inside of his cheek viciously. *You will not get hard*, he told himself, and slipped an arm around Adam's waist. Adam was soft and pliant against him, hair tickling Etienne's nose. He smelled like soap and hospital sanitizer.

"Sponge-bath tomorrow," Etienne murmured. "Wash the hospital off you. How's your head?"

"Hurts," Adam said. "Tenny—"

"Yeah?"

"Thank you," Adam said. He found Etienne's hand and twined their fingers. "I know... I know you're busy, and you didn't want to do this, but—"

"I *did*," Etienne said fiercely. *Just because I shouldn't be here doesn't mean there's anywhere I'd rather be.* He kept his mouth shut on the words.

"But you always have excuses when I try to hang out with you," Adam mumbled, pressing the good side of his face into the pillow. "You never—"

"Adam, stop," Etienne said. Adam shut up. Etienne sighed, the gust of his breath stirring the curls on Adam's nape. "I'll... look, I'll try to explain. Later. When you're not so doped up and hurting, okay? But it wasn't you. It was never you."

Adam said nothing, but he wriggled just a little closer and relaxed in Etienne's arms.

7

Etienne was up before the sun the next day. He wasn't sure what Adam would be able to keep down, so he made soft-scrambled eggs, toast, and added yogurt he found in the fridge to the tray before carrying it into the bedroom.

Adam stirred, groaning. He pushed himself to a sitting position, hand to his head. "Smells good," he mumbled.

"Think you can eat?" Etienne asked. He settled the tray across Adam's lap and leaned over to inspect the side of his face, taking Adam's chin in two fingers and turning his head gently to get a better look. The bruising was becoming a mottled green, yellow seeping in around the edges. "How's it feeling?"

"Still hurts," Adam said, letting Etienne move his head back and forth.

Etienne held up a finger, just out of Adam's line of sight.

Adam tensed. "What are you doing?"

"Making sure your vision's not compromised." Etienne moved his hand across Adam's field of vision. "Tell me when you see it."

Adam pushed his hand away. "I'm fine."

Etienne frowned. *Something* was wrong—Adam's shoulders were tense and hunched and he was looking anywhere but at Etienne.

He held up his hand again and Adam slapped it away.

"What the *fuck*," Etienne demanded.

"Just *leave it*," Adam snarled.

"No," Etienne snapped. "You wanted me here, you made me your official emergency contact, for Christ's sake—the least you can do is tell me what the *fuck* is going on with you right now."

Adam squeezed his eyes shut, tucking his chin to his chest. The gesture took years off his age, making him look young and vulnerable, and Etienne's heart clenched.

"Cary," he said gently. "Talk to me."

There was a beat of silence. Just as Etienne had decided Adam wasn't going to tell him, he reached for Etienne's hand, holding it up and opening his eyes. He fixed his gaze on Etienne's finger and Etienne got the message.

"Tell me when you see it," he said again, and moved his hand.

Adam said nothing, his mouth set and miserable, until Etienne's finger was well past where he should have been able to see it.

"There," he said, and he sounded resigned.

"*Adam*," Etienne said.

"I know!" Adam shouted. He flinched at the volume of his own voice and turned his face away.

"Dr. Khatri said you might have blurred vision for a couple of days, but this is more than that, isn't it?" Etienne asked. "How much can you see, Adam?"

The reply was a long time coming. "It's—I've always had a blind spot in my left eye. But now... I can only see about forty percent from it. Right is fine."

Forty percent. Etienne drew a breath and Adam hunched his shoulders.

"Leave me alone."

"Do you *want* me to leave you alone?" Etienne said, keeping his tone gentle. "Or do you want me to *not* ask you why your left eye is almost blind and stay with you while you eat breakfast?" *And how you managed to hide it from the team doctor?*

Adam turned back just enough to look at him. "That one," he said, almost inaudible.

ETIENNE SETTLED beside him on the bed, lying flat on his back and lacing his fingers across his stomach. He could hear clinking as Adam picked up the fork and began to eat.

A lot of things suddenly made more sense. The way Adam got pucks stolen more from his left side. How much he complained about his left winger and how Jake never seemed to read his cues. Etienne stiffened, a thought striking him. He'd been on Adam's left the night of the bar. No *wonder* Adam hadn't seemed bothered by Etienne's looks—he hadn't been able to *see* him.

In spite of everything, a tiny worm of disappointment twisted in his gut. He'd thought—he'd *hoped*—

Adam was different. But it had just been a combination of bad vision and alcohol, nothing more.

Adam set the tray on the floor and scooted down the bed, on his side next to Etienne. He said nothing, and after a minute, Etienne rolled sideways so they were facing. The morning sun crept over the bed, making Etienne blink in the light. He was exposed, vulnerable, laid bare for Adam's searching gaze.

Let him look. Etienne wasn't the only one who'd hidden, who'd kept a piece of themselves from view. He met Adam's eyes knowing there was defiance in his, waiting for the disappointment, the rejection.

But it wasn't there. Adam searched his face, his gaze so intent it felt like a finger brushing across Etienne's eyes, down his nose, up over his forehead and along his cheeks. And then he smiled.

"I know what would make me feel better," he said.

Etienne raised an eyebrow.

"If you kissed me," Adam said.

Startled, Etienne rolled off the bed so fast he nearly fell. When he made it to his feet, Adam was in the same position, looking very innocent. Had he really just said that?

"No," Etienne said, pointing at him. "We're not doing that."

Adam pouted. "I think it would help."

"Tough," Etienne said. He stalked around the bed, giving Adam a wide berth, picked up the tray, and headed for the kitchen.

He washed dishes with his head spinning. Adam hadn't. Adam *had*. Adam had looked straight at him and seemed to want, against all reason and logic, to kiss him. *Him.* The ugly duckling who'd never grown into a swan. *Why?* Even with a blind spot, Adam still knew, now, what Etienne looked like. It didn't make sense. He went around and around with it, not finding an answer, and when he was done with the dishes, headed back for the bedroom.

Adam wasn't on the bed. There was a noise from the bathroom and Etienne hurried that way. He knocked on the closed door.

"Adam?"

"I'm fine," Adam said, but his voice was faint.

"I'm coming in." Etienne pushed open the door, making Adam yelp weakly in protest even as he sat down hard on the closed toilet lid.

"I'm *naked*," he protested, both hands going to his groin. Behind him, water was running in the shower, filling the room with steam.

"I promised you a bath today," Etienne said, remorse prickling his skin. "I'm sorry. Let's get you clean."

Adam scowled ferociously but didn't argue as Etienne left, coming back with a stool from the bar.

"Water's not good for the wood," Adam pointed out.

Etienne gave him a look. "Would you rather collapse halfway through when your legs give out? I didn't think so. You're a fucking *Wolverine*, you can buy a new barstool."

"You're gonna have to get over this Wolverine thing," Adam muttered, but his lips were twitching. "Besides, I'm on IR for a month."

"Injured reserve doesn't make you less a Wolverine," Etienne said, softening his tone. He'd been put on IR before—they all had—and he'd hated every single minute of the enforced inactivity. Setting the stool in the shower, he pulled off his shirt.

Adam gasped. "What are you—"

"I'm getting you clean," Etienne said. He put his hands under Adam's elbows and hauled him upright, so they were face to face. "And before you get all maiden aunt on me again, let me remind you that I've seen it before." Adam perked up, opening his mouth, but Etienne beat him there. "I'm also not here for your spongebath fantasies, so save it."

He *hated* how attractive Adam's pout was, the way his full lower lip stuck out and his brow furrowed. Etienne looked away, clearing his throat, and stayed close as Adam made his shaky way into the shower and lowered himself onto the stool under the spray.

He tilted his head back, eyes fluttering shut. "God, that feels good."

"Think you can clean yourself?" Etienne offered the sponge.

Adam looked at it, then at him, and a calculating look crossed his face.

Etienne tossed the sponge at him, hitting him in the chest with unerring aim. "If you're well enough to *flirt*, you're well enough to wash yourself."

He stood by the open shower door, trying not to listen to the noises Adam made, the small grunts and sighs of appreciation as the hot water beat down on his knotted muscles.

Lost in a fantasy about him being the one to pull those noises from Adam's throat, he didn't realize something was wrong until he heard his name.

"Tens—" Adam sounded slightly panicked.

Etienne ducked into the shower. "What is it?"

Adam's face was white again, skin pale and waxy, and he clutched at Etienne's arm with trembling fingers. "'M gonna—"

Shit. Adam was swaying dangerously on the stool, still half-soaped up and with suds in his hair.

"Okay, put your arms around my neck," Etienne said. "Can you do that?" He helped Adam raise his arms and loop them loosely across Etienne's shoulders. "Just hold on," he murmured, and set to work rinsing the soap away.

Adam's damp cheek was pressed against Etienne's, his breathing harsh and rapid in Etienne's ear. Etienne used his cupped hands to wash away the soap with clean water, letting it swirl down the drain as Adam clung to him. Then he maneuvered them so that Adam's back was to the spray.

"Tilt your head back," he said, cupping Adam's skull in one hand as Adam obeyed. It didn't take long to get the shampoo out, leaving Etienne with the problem of how to get Adam back to the bed.

He eased away just enough to grab the huge towel next to the door and gave Adam the fastest drying-off in history. Adam was only semi-conscious by that point, head on his chest and eyes shut. There was no way he was walking back to the bed under his own power. Etienne swore under his breath and pulled Adam up off the stool over his shoulder into a fireman's hold, straightening his knees.

Adam jerked back to awareness and Etienne nearly dropped him as he flailed, trapping Adam's legs against his chest.

"*Stop*," he said through his teeth, maneuvering them out of the bathroom. "Just hold *still*, for God's sake."

Mercifully, the bed wasn't far. Etienne got Adam on it before his back gave out, collapsing next to him, shirtless and in his wet jeans, to wheeze for a minute.

Adam curled on his side, fingers finding Etienne's, a damp press of skin on skin.

"Okay," Etienne said as the burn in his lungs faded. "Okay." He turned his head to better see Adam's face. "We're going to talk soon, you and I."

Adam hummed and fell asleep.

ADAM WOKE UP CLEAN, dressed in his own clothes, and plastered against a large, warm, solid surface—Etienne, he deduced after a minute. His head still felt like rusty nails were being driven through it, but his eyes were focusing and he was reasonably sure he wasn't going to throw up.

Progress, then.

Etienne had used the time while Adam was asleep to not only dress Adam, but also himself, wearing an old Seabirds jersey and a pair of soft pants. His eyes were closed, his hand warm between Adam's shoulder blades.

Adam studied him for a minute, his too-big nose above that sensitive, oddly-shaped mouth that didn't smile enough, closed eyes Adam knew were slate-blue and breathtakingly intense.

Even with the concussion and headache from hell, Adam *wanted* him, with a desperation that bordered on insane. He wanted to make Etienne laugh more, break through that reserved shell to the man Adam knew was underneath. *Why* had he refused to hang out with Adam in person for so long? Why had he run from Adam at the rink, and yet over text and on the phone, he was warm and funny and kind? Adam didn't *get* it. He wanted to. He wanted to understand.

"You're being creepy," Etienne said without opening his eyes.

Adam huffed a laugh and ducked his head, rubbing his cheek against Etienne's chest.

"How are you feeling?" Etienne asked. He gently disentangled himself and sat up, searching Adam's face.

"Better, I think. Sorry about the… shower thing."

"Which part? Doing it without me, flirting with me during, or passing out and making me carry you back to bed?"

Adam gaped at him. "You *carried* me back to bed?"

"Fireman's hold and everything," Etienne said dryly, lips twitching.

"Then… all of that. Except the flirting. I'm not really sorry about that." Adam sat up too fast, wincing but holding out a hand to stop Etienne when he moved to help him. "I know we need to talk. But… can it wait?"

Etienne narrowed his eyes.

"Just until tomorrow," Adam said. "My head feels like it's going to split down the middle, man. Have mercy."

Etienne sighed. "Okay. I'm going to make lunch. Do you think you can eat?"

"I can try," Adam said.

"You don't have anything in your cupboards," Etienne told him later.

Adam had managed to eat the sandwich Etienne had put together and was lying down again, pain medication making him feel pleasantly swimmy. He made an agreeable noise.

"I'm not leaving you to go buy groceries, which means we'll have to order some," Etienne continued.

Adam hummed again, not really hearing what he was saying but enjoying the sound of his voice.

"What kind of vegetables do you like?"

Adam shrugged. Etienne's thigh was next to his face and Adam wanted to rub his cheek against it, so he did. "Donuts," he sighed, face mashed against Etienne's leg.

Etienne snorted. "I'm not buying you junk food," he warned. "You may be on IR but you still have to eat healthy. Donuts aren't a vegetable."

"But I want them."

"You were spoiled rotten as a kid, weren't you?"

Adam hummed agreement.

"Batted those big blue eyes and people just gave you everything you wanted," Etienne murmured, but he sounded amused. *Affectionate*, even, as he absently stroked the nape of Adam's neck.

"Donuts," Adam mumbled.

"Fuck off, I'm not buying you donuts."

"Glazed with strawberry icing," Adam slurred. His phone buzzed on the nightstand and he groaned. "Can you get that?"

Etienne leaned across and picked it up. "You have roughly a million messages from your team."

Adam whimpered. "I can't deal with them right now. Can you…." He rolled sideways, took the phone, and opened it. He found the group chat with his eyes half-closed and then pushed the phone back into Etienne's hands. "Tell them I'm okay, would you?"

Etienne huffed amusement and began to type. "Jesus," he said after a minute, sounding startled.

"Hm?"

"They're all talking at once," Etienne said. "Jake wants to know if he can bring you food. Hideki's offering his cleaning service. Hunt says you should have been more careful."

Adam smiled, pressing his face against Etienne's thigh. "They're good guys. Tell 'em I'll talk later."

Etienne touched his head, careful of the bruise, and then locked the phone and set it back on the nightstand. "All done. Take a nap."

"Okay," Adam said, and fell asleep.

THE DAY PASSED QUICKLY, with Adam waking only briefly a few times to use the bathroom and eat the food Etienne had made for him. Etienne stayed close, reading on his phone or using his laptop in the bed beside him as Adam rested.

He was feeling better, able to make it to and from the bathroom on his own and only a little shaky if he stayed upright for too long, but he still protested when Etienne tried to move to the couch that night.

"I'm injured," he said piteously, pushing his lower lip out and widening his eyes. "You can't leave me, I might be dying."

Etienne couldn't stop the laugh, one hand covering his mouth. "You're full of shit."

"Please?" Adam let the pout fall, letting Etienne see

the seriousness in his words. "Having you here… it helps. Helps me sleep."

Etienne rubbed his face, swearing under his breath. "Does *anyone* say no to you?"

"Lots of people," Adam said. He stopped and thought about it. "Okay, mostly just you. Although there was that one girl who laughed at me when I tried to flirt for extra sprinkles on my donut. She said her girlfriend thinks I'm cute, though." He grinned. "Got the sprinkles."

Etienne laughed again. "You're a menace. And I'm still not buying you donuts."

"But you'll sleep with me?"

"Key word being *sleep*, yes," Etienne said.

Adam smiled and Etienne shook his head, his answering smile bemused but that was definitely affection there, curving Etienne's lips and making his lovely eyes light up even as he brought his hand up to cover his mouth again. The motion seemed habitual, instinctive, like Etienne himself didn't realize he was doing it. Adam was determined to find out why, but it would have to wait until he could *think* again.

HE WOKE FEELING ALMOST HIMSELF, the headache retreating to a remnant of its former nasty self. Etienne brought him breakfast in bed again. Adam poked dubiously at the dark green leafy vegetable in his eggs.

"What is this shit?"

"You're a pro hockey player and you don't know what kale is?"

"That's what high-protein shakes and meal planners are for," Adam said. He took a bite and decided it wasn't bad. "Cooking is boring."

"Then you're not doing it right." Etienne settled beside him with his own plate. "How's your head?"

"Better," Adam said with his mouth full.

"Good. Then it's time to talk."

Adam froze. "Is it too late to change my answer?"

Etienne gave him an unimpressed look. "Yes. Does anyone on your team know?"

"No one knows," Adam said, hanging his head. "No one but you."

"So let's talk about it," Etienne said, his voice gentle. "How long have you been blind in your left eye?"

"I'm *not*," Adam protested, looking up. "I have a blind *spot*, and it's not usually even that bad—most of the time it's just sort of… blurred in that spot. I can still *see*. It's worse, since I hit my head, but I can't tell the doctor because she'll tell the team doctor and then I'll really be fucked. I'll be off the team, Tenny, I *can't*—"

Etienne's large hands covered his. "Breathe," he ordered.

Adam obeyed, focusing on Etienne's long fingers and the softly curling hair on the back of his hands. "All my life," he finally said.

"What? Oh."

"I've just always had it ever since I can remember," Adam said. He rubbed a thumb over Etienne's. "It's just… kinda blurry there. But I can *see*. I'm not—it's never been this bad before. What if—" He clamped his mouth shut against the panic.

"It'll come back," Etienne said, squeezing his

hands. "The concussion's probably just scrambled your brain a bit. Give it some time."

"Hockey's all I have," Adam whispered. His throat was tight. "It's all I've ever really wanted. What do I do if—"

"Stop," Etienne said. "You haven't lost it. You *won't* lose it. But Cary… you *should* have more than hockey. You know you can't play the game forever."

"I know," Adam said, blinking hard. "I want to coach, after. But I'm not ready to think about that yet. I just want to *play*."

"And you will." Etienne's voice left no room for doubt. "Tell me the second it clears up or gets better, okay?"

"If it does," Adam whispered.

"Wow, I had no idea you were such a negative Nellie," Etienne said, startling Adam into looking up. "What happened to your relentless positivity?"

Adam lifted a shoulder. "Kinda hard to be positive when you're looking at losing your career and what gets you out of bed in the morning."

"Well, you won't, so knock it off." Etienne let go of Adam's hands and rolled off the bed to pick up the plates. "I'm going to clean up."

"We still have to talk about you," Adam pointed out, and then his mouth fell open as Etienne *bolted* from the room. "What the *fuck*? Get back here!" He could hear Etienne in the kitchen, clattering and thumping as he started hot water running in the sink. Shouting hurt Adam's head, so he slid carefully off the mattress and made his way down the hall and into the kitchen, where Etienne was looking in the cupboards for dish soap. "You can't run away from talking about this," he said.

Etienne straightened with the soap in his hand, looking guilty. "You shouldn't be out of bed."

"*You* shouldn't have run away from me."

"I didn't, I'm washing dishes," Etienne protested, but he couldn't quite meet Adam's eyes.

Adam slid onto a barstool before he lost his balance. "I told you mine."

Etienne set the soap on the counter.

Adam took a deep breath and played his trump card. "If you're not going to tell me, I don't want you here."

Etienne's eyes snapped up to his, shock in them. "Cary—"

"You've dodged me for *months*," Adam said. Anger and hurt clogged his throat. "I know we're busy, but we've talked every single day for the past two months. You realize that? We haven't gone a day without at least texting each other once, even if it's stupid shit. But every time I've tried to see you, you've had some reason why you can't. So *why*? If you can't stand being around me, why do you talk to me on the phone? Why are we friends? *Are* we friends?"

"*Cary*—" Etienne sounded anguished. He flattened his hands on the counter between them, eyes pleading. "You're my best friend, you have to know that."

"Then *why*?"

"It's stupid."

"I don't care," Adam insisted. "We had an incredible night. Some of the best sex I've ever had. *The* best sex I've ever had, honestly. And you've been running from me ever since. Was I that bad in bed?"

Etienne laughed, but there was no humor in it. "I've never had a better night."

The raw honesty in his voice silenced Adam. He stared at Etienne, who rubbed his face.

"I—can I show you something?"

Adam nodded.

Etienne left the room, coming back with a laptop that he set on the counter in front of Adam. "I found your wifi password on the router while you were asleep," he said, busy typing in a website.

Adam was distracted by how close Etienne was and how good he smelled, and it took him a minute to look at the site that was loading. He blinked and looked closer. It seemed to be comprised of pictures of—

"Hockey players? Hey, there's Saint, I can't wait to play him. And Butterfly, I scored on him once, did I tell you that? Wait, hang on—that's *me*." Adam finally looked at the URL. "www.hockeyhotornot.com? Are you fucking kidding me right now?" He glanced back at his picture. "Oh, I'm number four. Wait, who's ahead of me?"

"You're not—" Etienne sounded frustrated. "*Look*." He leaned across Adam and scrolled down. And further down. And kept going, through pages that loaded endlessly and familiar faces that paraded past Adam until he *finally* stopped. "There."

"Hey, that's you." Etienne stared out at him from the screen in his draft picture, somber and closed-off. His striking eyes were hooded, their color barely visible in the picture. "You don't look happy." Adam twisted to look up at Etienne, beside him. "Don't like your picture taken? I've noticed that, you know—how you'll send me pictures of stuff, maybe your foot or your elbow might be in it, but never your face."

"Would you *look at the rating*?" Etienne

demanded. He sounded on the verge of ripping his own hair out, so Adam obediently swiveled back and looked.

"Rated #457," he read. "Well, that's dumb."

"Now click on my picture," Etienne ordered.

Adam obeyed.

"Read the comments."

Adam recoiled. "What's wrong with you? You *never* read the comments, man."

Etienne snatched the laptop and began to read. "'LOL he looks like a bushbaby got dropped in acid. Hope he's got a big dick to make up for that face.'"

Adam flinched.

"'Bet he's only had sex with the lights off,'" Etienne continued, voice hard and uncompromising.

He'd turned the light off that night, Adam remembered, and his stomach turned over.

"'Look at that nose,'" Etienne said. "'Wonder if he's got stock in paper bags to put over his head. Do they make bags big enough, you think?'"

"*Stop.*"

Etienne ignored him. "'Classic butterface.' Oh, here's a good one. 'He looks like a hillbilly fucked a pimple and he's the result.'"

"*Tenny.*" Adam put out a hand. "Stop it. *Stop it.*"

"You don't know," Etienne flung at him, slamming the laptop shut. Spots of color burned bright in his cheeks. "You don't know what it's *like.*"

"It's a stupid website!" Adam said. "You can't let something like this rule your life—"

"You get everything you want," Etienne interrupted. "And you want to know the sad truth of this shitty world? It's because you're pretty. Because you have big, blue eyes and perfect teeth and great hair and an even better body, and what's worse is you have a great *personality.*"

Adam blinked, confused. "Why is that worse?"

"Because I can't hate you for *getting* everything you want," Etienne snapped. He put the laptop down and took a step away. "You're kind and genuine and you've never once that I've seen used your looks to get perks or privileges. But you get them anyway. And you don't notice, do you? It's just part of being you. People give you things, and you accept them, and you smile and thank them and make their day, because *Adam Caron* just smiled at them, acknowledged their presence, and made their world a little brighter for one brief moment."

Adam opened his mouth but Etienne was on a roll.

"It's not like that for most of us," he said. "I'm invisible, Adam. No one sees me. No one gives me extra whipped cream on my coffee—"

"You wouldn't drink it anyway," Adam muttered.

"Not the point and don't interrupt me. No one *notices* me. No one flirts with me. No one goes out of their way to make me smile. I go through life and I scratch and claw and bleed for what I do and that's okay, I'm *okay* with that because that *is* life. I'm invisible." He took a shaky breath and pointed at the website. "Until I'm not."

Adam stared at him. "So you dodged me because... you think you're ugly?"

"I don't *think* I am, I *know* I am, but it sounds really stupid when you say it like that," Etienne said.

"Because it *is!*" Adam snapped, suddenly furious. "You thought I wouldn't want you because you're not, what, 'conventionally attractive'? You made that choice *for* me without giving me a chance. You just shut me down, even though I'd already seen you and *knew* what you looked like—"

"You were drunk and *you're half-blind!*" Etienne shouted. He clamped a hand over his mouth, clearly regretting the outburst, as Adam slowly stood.

"Fuck you," he said, very carefully. "Fuck you for thinking any of that makes the slightest bit of difference to me."

Etienne shook his head, dropping his hand. "I'm sorry," he whispered. "I didn't mean—"

"I didn't ask to look this way anymore than you did," Adam cut him off. "I know people are nicer to me because I'm attractive. I try not to take advantage of it. But *you* don't get to decide there's nothing between us when there clearly *is*, all because you think you…." He made a vague gesture. "You don't measure up, or something. It's bullshit, and it's not fair to either of us."

Etienne looked miserable, his shoulders slumped and head hanging. Adam wanted to shake him, or kiss him, or both. Shake him and then kiss him, he decided.

"I'll be out of your hair in five minutes," Etienne said, not looking up.

"You'll what now?"

"I don't have much to pack."

"Whoa, okay, I think this conversation has gone two very different ways for us," Adam said. "What did you get from everything I just said?"

"Fuck me, and I don't get to decide for you, and I took your choice away. You're obviously mad at me. So I'm going, okay?" Etienne took a step toward the bedroom.

"*Stop.*"

Etienne jerked to a stop and Adam blew out a half-laughing breath, raising his eyes to the ceiling.

"Lord give me patience," he muttered, took two quick steps, and hauled Etienne down into a hard, bruising kiss.

Etienne was completely still, frozen as if in shock. Adam growled and pressed closer, demanding entry, hands in Etienne's hair and bodies plastered together.

Just as he was about to give up and admit defeat, step back and gather his dignity up off the floor, Etienne groaned brokenly and snaked his arms around Adam's waist, yanking him even closer.

That was more like it. Etienne kissed like a man possessed, mouth devouring Adam's until Adam couldn't breathe, his head spinning and world swaying. Who needed oxygen anyway? He clung to Etienne's broad shoulders and let him take him apart, willingly giving up control.

When Etienne broke the kiss and eased away, Adam made a noise of complaint, trying to tug him back for more.

"Can't you see?" he said against Etienne's mouth. "How much it doesn't matter?"

"It only doesn't matter if you have it," Etienne said, sounding resigned. "But for the record, you noticed me. You flirted with me. And—" He swallowed hard. "You make me smile all the goddamn time."

"Uh, yeah," Adam said, tightening his grip. "Because I'm a delight."

He relished the laugh that burst from Etienne at that, pulling him back down into another kiss. But Etienne refused to let him deepen it that time, catching his hand when Adam tried to explore.

"Mm—no," he said, pulling free. "You're still

wounded, as you keep reminding me. No sex while you're on IR."

"*What*? But that's an entire *month*!"

Etienne doubled over with laughter, arms around his ribs. "Your *face*—" he sputtered when he was finally able to straighten. "Oh my god, Cary, you really think I'd make you wait a whole month for sex?"

Adam glared at him while Etienne wiped tears from his eyes.

"No, I won't make you wait a month," he finally said. "But I *do* think you need a few more days to recover."

"But—

"Nope." Etienne's voice was uncompromising but his eyes softened. "I'm your emergency contact, remember? I'm gonna take care of you." His lips twitched at Adam's expression. "Come here." He pulled him in, Adam going willingly, but didn't kiss him. Instead he wrapped his arms around Adam's waist and just held him.

"What are you doing?"

"Hugging you," Etienne said, lifting his head. "You do know what a hug is, right?"

"Fuck off," Adam said, shoving ineffectually at his shoulder.

"I'm just asking because you have a golf course in your living room," Etienne said, twisting away from the mock blow without letting go. "You're not what anyone would consider normal."

He let go but Adam protested wordlessly, catching at Etienne's shirt. Etienne stopped and tucked him back into his arms, his unhurt cheek on Etienne's shoulder.

Adam closed his eyes. "People don't hug me," he mumbled into Etienne's shirt.

"What?"

Adam lifted one shoulder. "They touch me, yeah, all the time. They never stop touching me. They fuck me if I let them. And sure, on the ice, my teammates if I score, that's to be expected. But outside of that, no one—besides my mom—ever hugs me. I don't know why."

Etienne's arms tightened. "Well, brace yourself, because I'm gonna hug the shit out of you." He paused. "I probably should've thought that wording through."

Adam tried to muffle the snicker. "Thank you," he whispered.

9

"I HAVE to go to practice today," Etienne said the next morning. Adam was propped at the bar, still half-asleep as Etienne made omelettes. "Will you be okay on your own?"

"Mm-hm," Adam said, good cheek on his fist.

"Also call your parents."

"Texted 'em," Adam said, his eyes closed. "'S fine. I'll call tonight."

Etienne frowned but didn't push. "Also I have a game this Saturday. And one on Sunday. So I'll be gone and pretty useless those days too."

"Mkay," Adam said. He blinked drowsily. "You have a game this weekend?"

"Two, yes, thanks for listening."

"I'm coming, right?"

Etienne nearly dropped the egg. Adam was sitting up, looking wide awake.

"You *want* to?"

"I might have moved up, but I still have friends

87

who play there," Adam pointed out. "You might even know some, there's this guy named Rudy—"

Etienne threw a stalk of kale at him. "Fine, yes, of course you can come. I'll get you a ticket."

"Oh, and the team doctor wants to see me this afternoon," Adam said. He sounded much less excited about that.

"Practice will be over by one, I'll take you."

"You don't have to, I know how to hail a cab."

"I'll take you," Etienne repeated. He loved the way Adam's eyes softened before he smiled, tiny lines fanning out and making him look young and sweet and impossibly beautiful.

"Eggs are burning," Adam commented, and laughed into his orange juice as Etienne swore and scrambled to rescue the situation.

RUDY TOOK one look at him when Etienne walked in the door and threw both hands in the air. "Praise *be*!"

"Oh, shut up," Etienne said, but he couldn't get the stupid smile off his face.

"Did you get laid, Tenny?" Liam demanded from across the room.

"None of your goddamn business," Etienne told him.

"How's Cary?" Rudy asked.

"He's better. Fast healer. IR for a month, but he's already fully mobile again."

Johnny and Theo joined them. "So are you guys like… together now?" Johnny asked.

Etienne shrugged, unsure what to say. He'd told the team. He knew, logically, that they had no problem with his sexuality, but still the old fear rushed back. Would he be ostracized? Reviled?

Theo just slapped him on the back. "Good job, man! Adam fucking Caron, *damn*, how the hell did you manage that?"

Etienne stiffened. That was somehow worse than the reaction he'd feared.

Rudy glared Theo back a step.

"Not that… he's not lucky… too," Theo stuttered. "I'm gonna stop talking now."

He scurried away and Rudy sighed.

"Don't take it personally," he said quietly.

Etienne rolled his shoulders, trying to dislodge the small bubble of hurt under his breastbone. "It's fine. Let's play some hockey."

Rudy checked Theo into the boards, which made Etienne feel a little better, and later, Theo skated by and offered to let Etienne do the same. Etienne was able to summon a smile as the hurt eased.

It felt good to be back on the ice again, stretching his muscles and pushing through the burn. Logan was in good form, but Etienne sank four shots on him, blowing him a kiss on the last one.

Still, the insecurity stayed with him, eating away at his insides, as he showered and changed and headed back to Adam's. He couldn't possibly be with someone like Adam. It was never going to work.

He knocked just as Adam yanked the door open and launched himself out it, tackling Etienne to the carpet. He landed with a hard thud, breath driven from his lungs, as Adam kissed his face over and over, up one side and down the other.

It took a minute for the roar in Etienne's ears to

subside enough for him to hear what Adam was saying.

"It's back, it's back, I can *see*, Tenny it's *back*—"

Relief swamped Etienne and he grabbed Adam and hugged him tight, lying there on the carpet in the hallway.

Adam tucked his face into Etienne's neck and hiccupped damply. "Hi," he said after a few minutes. "Um. Sorry."

Etienne rubbed his back. "No apologies necessary, but can we maybe go inside?"

Adam scrambled upright and held out a hand. Once inside and the door kicked closed, Etienne turned to him, cupping his face in both hands. Adam smiled up at him, tears in his beautiful eyes, lips a little tremulous.

"I told you," Etienne breathed, and kissed him. He could never get enough of this, he thought, the way Adam melted against him, ceding control instantly, going loose and pliant in Etienne's hands. They kissed slowly, tenderly, for several minutes before Etienne sighed and eased away. "What time is your appointment?"

"An hour," Adam said, looking faintly dazed. "Time enough to…."

"Nope," Etienne said, laughing and kissing his nose again because it was there and Adam was wrinkling it at him. "Have you showered?"

"Wanna help?"

"*Relentless*," Etienne said, and smacked his ass. "Get."

ETIENNE SAT in the waiting room while Adam went through the physical with his doctor. He picked up a magazine and absently flicked through it, not really paying attention. It was hockey-themed, because of course it was, and Etienne read up on a few players' stats, thinking about his game the next day. As he set the magazine down, the one beside it caught his eye and he found himself staring down at Adam's face, covered in blood.

"Oh *fuck*," he breathed.

UP-AND-COMING CENTER FOR THE TORONTO WOLVERINES INJURED DURING PRACTICE, RUSHED TO HOSPITAL WITH SEVERE CONCUSSION, the hysterical headline proclaimed.

"Fuck, fuck, *fuck*," Etienne chanted softly to himself, flipping the pages to read the story. It wasn't any less lurid than the cover, making it sound like Adam had been on death's doorstep and breathlessly speculating about the man who'd arrived to take him away but refused to give his name.

Adam came out of the back, smiling as he pulled his jacket on. The smile slipped when he got a look at Etienne's face.

"*What?*" he asked.

Etienne held up the magazine wordlessly.

Adam grabbed it, swearing under his breath as he read the story. "Okay, it's okay, it's just speculation, right? They made it sound worse than it is because that's what they *do*."

"Adam." Etienne wanted to shake him as Adam glanced up, clearly confused. "Do your parents subscribe to any hockey magazines? Because *we never called them*."

Adam's mouth fell open. "Oh fuck, oh fuck, oh *fuck me sideways—*" He pulled his phone out of his pocket and scrolled through the notifications with shaking hands. "They've been calling me since yesterday," he said, looking up with horror in his eyes. "They must not have gotten my text, Tenny, oh my god—"

"*Call them,*" Etienne ordered.

But neither Adam's mother nor his father answered, both going straight to voicemail. Etienne managed to get Adam out on the street as he tried again and again, getting steadily more worried.

"They're not there, they *always* answer, I fucked up, I fucked up so bad, what if something happened—"

"Nothing happened," Etienne cut him off. He flagged down a taxi and bundled Adam unceremoniously into the back. Inside, he gave the driver Adam's address and then turned back to face Adam, gripping his hand. "Nothing happened," he repeated. "Call your sister."

"Right, of course." Adam found the number, the phone still trembling in his grip. It was answered on the first ring and the tension drained from him at the sound of his sister's voice, loud enough for Etienne to hear.

"Adam? Adam, is that you? Are you okay?"

"I'm fine," Adam managed, sagging against Etienne's shoulder. "I'm so sorry, Noemi, I didn't realize that article was even a thing until five minutes ago, I'm *so sorry—*"

Etienne could hear Noemi crying, and Adam squeezed his eyes shut, a tear sliding down his cheek.

"*We thought you died,*" Noemi said, her voice thin. "Mom and Dad called Coach Benton and he said you'd suffered a concussion, t-that you needed s-someone with you because y-you couldn't be left alone, you hit your head on the *ice* and then you didn't answer your phone—"

"I didn't want to freak them out," Adam whispered miserably. "It wasn't even that big a deal, I knew they'd fuss and Mom would want to know who was taking care of me and be all nosy, didn't they get my text?"

"*No*, you asshole, or they wouldn't be on their way to you *right now!*"

Adam jerked upright, clearly horrified. "Please tell me you're joking."

"Oh, I'm not, and you deserve every inch of the tongue-lashing you're going to get," Noemi snapped. "I can't *believe* you didn't call us."

"I texted Mom!" Adam protested. "I *swear* I did, I told her I was fine and I'd call her tonight!" He pulled the phone away from his ear to look at the screen as Noemi said something. Adam glanced up at Etienne, mortification making his face slack. "I texted MOMA," he whispered.

Etienne's eyebrows went up. "The Museum of Modern Art? Is that a joke? Why do you even have them in your phone?"

Adam ignored him. "Noemi?" he said. "Have they left yet? Can you stop them?" Noemi's voice had quieted with her worries, and Etienne couldn't hear her response, but Adam sagged again, pressing his face into Etienne's shoulder. "I'm so fucked," he mumbled. "Noemi, I'll call you later."

"I'm guessing they're on their way?" Etienne said, resisting the impulse to pet his soft hair.

"Try 'just landed'," Adam said. He sighed and straightened. "We'll just barely beat them home."

"You texted MOMA," Etienne said. He couldn't— quite—stop his lips twitching.

"Shut up," Adam said. "It's so not funny."

"It's a little funny," Etienne protested, and caught the end of the death glare Adam leveled at him. "Okay, but it'll *be* funny. Twenty years from now, we can all have a good laugh about that time you texted MOMA instead of your mother and she thought you were dead and flew across two countries and then *actually* killed you."

Adam shoved at him and Etienne caught his hand, laughing, and pulled him into a kiss. Adam's mouth was still miserable, tight with unhappiness, and Etienne slid a hand into his hair, tugging gently until he heard the breath catch in Adam's throat.

"It'll be okay," he murmured, pressing their foreheads together. "They'll yell and get it out of their systems and you'll apologize and it'll. Be. Okay." He eased away enough to see Adam's face. "I'll get my stuff together and be gone before they get there, okay?"

Adam clutched at him. "No. *No.* If I have to do this, you are *not leaving me*, do you understand? Don't you fucking *dare* abandon me now, Etienne, or I swear to god I will *haunt* you when she kills me. Are we clear?"

"Okay, *Jesus*," Etienne said. "You're not coming out to them, though, right? Or are we doing that conversation too?"

Adam shook his head. "I don't think I can handle that right now."

"Then I'm just your friend who helped you out," Etienne said, patting his hand.

"You're so good to me," Adam said. "I'm gonna give you so much sex when they're gone, I swear."

Etienne snorted a laugh, cupping his good cheek. "Gonna hold you to that. Now for the real question. Why *do* you have the Museum of Modern Arts' number in your phone?"

Adam sighed. "I interned there in college, okay? I was an art major. And technically, I texted my old boss *at* MOMA, and she's very concerned, can I just go five minutes without fucking up, please?"

"An art major," Etienne said blankly. "And you became a pro hockey player because…?"

"Because I love the sport," Adam said. "I couldn't decide between hockey and art for awhile but ultimately I went with hockey because there's nothing like the rush I get from being on the ice."

"What kind of art?"

"Studies, actually. History and shit. I thought about teaching for awhile, but then I realized I just… I got more from hockey. I was happier in the rink. So I focused on that."

Etienne thought about Adam in a classroom, maybe wearing glasses and a cardigan as he lectured, and had to shift his weight.

"If you make a single 'hot for teacher' joke, I'm breaking up with you, I swear to God," Adam threatened.

Etienne went very still, hope and terror tumbling over each other in his chest. "Are we… are we together?"

Adam just looked confused. "I mean… I thought… you wanted to be?"

"We haven't talked about it," Etienne said. "You're doing that thing again, where you just assume. You do it kind of a lot."

"When have I *ever*—"

Etienne held up a finger to tick off a list. "You took me home five minutes after meeting me while drunk off your ass. You set up camp in my life as soon as you got my phone number. You made me your *emergency contact* without even asking me, for Christ's sake. And then you kissed me and it's like you've just decided we're together, but we haven't even *talked* about it, Cary."

Adam looked stunned and wounded, eyes dark and vulnerable. "I thought…." He swallowed hard. "I thought you wanted… me. And to be my friend."

"I did. I *do*. Christ, Adam, stop *looking* at me like that." Etienne captured Adam's hand as he tried to pull away. "I love being with you. Talking to you. You make me laugh so much. You're… you're so great, and I have such a good time with you, and dear *God* I want to fuck you into the mattress so hard. But I just… you can't just assume these things. Okay? I need to have input on this too."

Adam nodded silently.

Etienne cupped the back of his neck. "I want to be with you. I want to date you. If—" His turn to swallow. "If you want *me*."

Adam leaned forward into a kiss, teeth and tongues meeting wet and messy. "I want you so much," he whispered. "I didn't mean to bulldoze you. I'm sorry. The doctor was asking for a contact and I didn't have anyone here—it was a choice between you and *Jake*, I mean come on—and I meant to ask you after and make sure it was okay but I just forgot and then everything happened and…."

"Yeah, I get it," Etienne said. He rubbed the nape of Adam's neck with a thumb, making him shiver. "Did you ask the doctor when you can have sex?"

"He said non-strenuous activity is fine now, nothing too… athletic."

Etienne smiled, knowing it was dark and possessive and enjoying the way Adam's eyes widened. "I can work with that."

WHEN THE TAXI pulled up in front of Adam's building, Adam fumbled to pay the driver, looking slightly dazed. Etienne drew away, silently giving him space to pull himself together.

It was a good thing he did, because Adam's parents were knocking on his door when Adam and Etienne stepped out of the elevator.

"Mom!"

Adam's parents spun. His mother was tall and rangy like Adam, and Etienne could easily see where Adam had gotten his looks in her dark eyes and high cheekbones.

"Adam Alexis Noah Caron, you are in *so much trouble.*"

Etienne had to give Adam credit for not turning tail and running as she advanced on him, her dark blue eyes stormy with anger and worry. She cupped Adam's face, long fingers careful against the luridly purple and green bruise.

"What happened?" she demanded. "Why didn't you call me? Do you have *any idea*—"

"Yeah," Adam said, pulling away from her hands. "I *do*, Mom, I *do*. I saw my phone, I called Noemi, I'm so, so sorry, I know I fucked up. I thought I texted you but I was knocked out on painkillers and I sent it to someone else. I was going to call you tonight, I *swear*, but I knew you were going to fuss and I needed to not have a horrible headache when you were yelling at me. Speaking of, my head's still not great, so please don't actually yell?"

Adam's mother sagged and Etienne was struck with the sense memory of Adam doing that against him. "You're not out of the woods yet, young man," she warned him. "Hi," she said to Etienne. "I'm Colette, Adam's mother, and this is William. Are you a friend of Adam's he hasn't told us about?"

"Mom," Adam said warningly. "This is Etienne Brideau, he took care of me while I was recovering."

Colette ignored him, fixing her lovely eyes on Etienne and waiting intently.

Etienne took her hand. "It's very nice to meet you, although I'm sorry it's under these circumstances."

"Are you on the team, Etienne? I don't think I recognize your name."

"No ma'am, I'm a Thunder."

"Oh, the ECHL! Have you been friends with my son for long?"

"A few months," Etienne said, and Colette swiveled to Adam again, raising an eyebrow.

"How interesting that I've never heard his name before!"

Adam groaned, covering his eyes. "I don't tell you *everything*, Mom."

"Apparently you don't tell me *anything*," Colette said, and there was a definite thread of hurt in her voice that made Adam's head snap up.

"Maybe we should... go inside," Etienne suggested awkwardly. He held out his hand to William, who hadn't yet said a word. "Hello, sir. Etienne Brideau."

William shook his hand, smiling at him. Etienne

could see where Adam had gotten his smile, the way his eyes creased first and then his lips curved, sweet and slow.

"Thank you for taking care of our son," he said. His voice was deep and mellow, his brown eyes kind.

Adam dug his keys out and got the door unlocked as Etienne ducked his head.

"I was happy to be able to," he said.

They all filed inside and William took the bags to the guest room without prompting as Colette followed Adam to the kitchen, Etienne trailing behind.

"I really am sorry, Mom," Adam said. "I swear I thought I texted you."

"It was a miscommunication," Colette said. "One that will *never* happen again. And now that we're here and you're not dead, you can show us some of the city, maybe introduce us to your teammates!"

Adam shot Etienne a panicked look and Etienne coughed to cover his laugh.

"I should, um. Go."

"What? No!" Adam protested. "You can't leave, you just got here!"

"I'm sure your parents want to spend time with you alone," Etienne pointed out.

"We're not going to chase my son's friend away," Colette piped up. "Especially when he doesn't have that many to begin with."

"See?" Adam said, giving his mother a quick glare. "You can stay."

"I really shouldn't," Etienne said. "I have a game tomorrow, remember?"

"Oh, how wonderful!" Colette said. "Adam, were you planning on attending?"

Adam nodded, his face clearly saying he knew where this was going.

"Perfect, we'll come too," Colette announced.

Etienne suddenly understood Adam a little better, and he had to fight the laugh. She was a force of nature, sweeping everyone up in her path, but there was kindness and amusement in her dark eyes when she met Etienne's gaze.

"I'll get you some tickets," he said.

"You will *not*," Colette said as William came out of the guest bedroom. "We'll buy ours, but thank you for the offer."

"In that case—"

"Tenny, can I talk to you in private?" Adam asked abruptly.

Etienne blinked but nodded. Adam led him to his bedroom and shut the door behind them.

"Don't leave me with them," he said, his voice low.

"They seem very nice," Etienne said, no longer bothering to hide the smile. "I thought your mom was going to be a literal fire-breathing dragon but she's actually really lovely."

Adam clutched at his arm. "They're going to ask me questions about everything. Mom will make comments about how I need more friends and want to know why I don't have a girlfriend yet. Dad won't say much but he'll have opinions about how I'm playing, believe me. Please Tenny, I'm begging you."

Etienne ran his hands up Adam's arms. "Your parents love you, Cary. Are they going to morph into abusive monsters when I set foot outside your door?"

Adam shook his head miserably.

"Then I think I can safely leave you in their care." Etienne thumbed Adam's lower lip. "It's good for you to be told no," he said. Adam's scowl intensified but Etienne just grinned down at him. "Builds character."

"Fuck you," Adam grumbled, but he leaned into Etienne's body.

Etienne obeyed the unspoken request, gathering him close. He could easily get addicted to Adam's weight in his arms, he thought, how he fit perfectly under Etienne's chin and his breath tickled Etienne's collarbone.

After a few minutes, he tipped Adam's head up and sealed their mouths together. Adam opened to him willingly, letting Etienne plunder his mouth, huffing hot need across Etienne's cheek.

Etienne reached between them to rub Adam's shaft in his pants as he clung to him, making Adam whimper against his mouth, but finally he tore himself away.

"*God.*" He was gratified to see that Adam was as breathless as he was, debauched and panting. "Don't jack off without me," he ordered.

Adam opened and closed his mouth. "You have a control fetish," he finally said, sounding faintly accusing.

"And you like it," Etienne said. He winked at him, grabbed the laptop off the bed, and opened the door. "I'll see you at the game tomorrow."

HE ESCAPED with a quick wave to Colette and William in the kitchen, laptop strategically positioned across his groin, and took the subway home, where he spent the rest of the day in his own apartment, dealing with bills and grocery ordering.

That night, he was in bed, dozing off, when his phone buzzed.

It was Adam. *I'm so hard and it's your fault.*

Etienne was abruptly awake. *Show me.*

He waited breathlessly until his phone buzzed again with an attachment. Etienne opened it and groaned out loud at the sight of Adam's cock. It was just as beautiful as the rest of him, long and graceful, the head pearling pre-come at the tip.

Etienne got hard so fast his head swam.

Please can I do something about it, Adam's next text read.

Etienne rubbed himself absently through the flannel of his pajama pants.

No.

There was no reply for a long time, and Etienne began to wonder if he'd pushed him too far, if Adam was rebelling. The thought of him jacking off made him catch his breath.

Sunday night, he sent. He pushed down his pants and took a picture of his own cock, his hand loosely fisted around the base, then pressed Send. *Sunday night you can have this.*

Promise?

Yeah, Etienne replied.

Even if you lose?

Etienne's eyebrows went up and the bubble showing Adam typing popped into view.

Not saying you're gonna lose.

You're not.

You're gonna kill 'em.

But I mean...

Etienne could picture him, chewing on that sinful

lower lip, eyebrows drawn together as he tried to get his foot out of his mouth.

Sunday night, Etienne sent again. *No matter what. Goodnight, Adam.*

Night, Tenny.

10

ETIENNE WAS a mass of nerves in the locker room the next afternoon. Players jostled him, calling cheerful abuse back and forth, but Etienne barely heard them. Adam was in the stands. Adam was going to watch him play.

Logically, Etienne knew Adam had already *seen* him play, that he had nothing to prove. But that didn't stop his knee from jigging as he strapped his pads into place.

Rudy dropped onto the seat beside him and Etienne stifled a groan.

Rudy's grin was blinding. "Hi."

"Go away, Dad."

"Nope. Sorry." Rudy put a hand on Etienne's knee, stilling it. "We're gonna have a good game. Cary's gonna be impressed. Maybe you'll even get a hat trick."

"Don't *jinx* it, Jesus!"

"Fine, too far," Rudy said, holding up his hands in surrender. "But my point stands. So get out there and show him what you can do."

Etienne braced his elbows on his knees, staring at his skates. After a minute, he nodded. "Okay."

"Okay?"

"Yeah, okay. Let's do this."

ADAM SETTLED IN HIS SEAT, parents on either side of him, as the players hit the ice to warm up and pucks went flying. He wasn't usually on this side of the glass, but he liked it, finding Etienne's broad shoulders immediately. There was Rudy, quick and elegant as ever as he worked through a complicated footwork pattern. Liam and Johnny, never far from each other, were on the other side of the rink, and Logan was warming up in his crease.

"Excuse me," someone said from behind him.

Colette tapped Adam's shoulder and he looked up. A small girl with fair hair in pigtails stood there, wearing a green and white Wolverines jersey with his number on the sleeve, her mother hovering just behind her.

"Can I have your autograph?" the little girl asked.

Adam nodded, feeling in his pockets for anything to write on. The girl thrust a piece of paper and pen at him, and Adam accepted it.

"Who should I make it to?"

"Molly."

Dear Molly, you're the best part about playing hockey, Adam wrote, and signed his name in looping flourishes. When he handed it back, she read what he'd written, burst into giggles, and clutched it to her chest.

"Come back soon," she told him earnestly. "The Wolverines need you."

Adam laughed and waved goodbye to her before turning back to watch the players again.

His father nudged him. "Getting used to that yet?"

"Not really," Adam said, eyes on Etienne, who was talking to Rudy.

"Good," William said. "It's when you do get used to it that I'll need to worry about the size of your ego."

Adam glanced sideways at him, but William was watching Etienne as well.

"I like that friend of yours," he said. "Hey Col, let's invite Etienne out to dinner with us tonight."

"Perfect! Adam, does he have plans?"

"No," Adam said unthinkingly. "I mean. I don't know. I don't think so. I'm not his keeper, how would I know?"

Colette's gaze was a little too piercing, but she didn't challenge his stammering. "Text him so he'll know."

Adam scowled but dug out his phone. *Folks want you to come out with us tonight. Hope you don't have plans bc I already told them you were free. Sorry. (I'll make it up to you.)* He tapped Send and shoved the phone back in his pocket as the first line gathered on the ice for the puck drop.

THEY WERE PLAYING the Florida Everblades, a team known for its steady scoring and strong win/loss ratio. The Blades had gotten a new coach a few years before, and he'd turned their playing around, bringing them up through the standings until they had a real chance for the Kelly Cup.

The Blades were good, but so were the Thunder,

and Etienne.... Etienne was amazing. Adam had known it before he'd seen him at practice, had heard his name mentioned with favor by several people, but nothing had prepared him for the actuality of seeing Etienne in play. He was an up-and-comer, sharp and hungry and lethal. And—Adam couldn't help the bolt of lust that zinged through him as Etienne, challenged by an angry forward, dropped his gloves and swung—a good fighter, too.

The scrap was over quickly, Etienne taking his opponent to the ice and the linesmen immediately separating the two. Adam grinned when Etienne slapped the other man's back before heading for the box.

The Thunder won the game by a narrow margin, 3-2 in the last period. Etienne sank the winning goal, sending the puck winging gracefully topshelf over the goalie's shoulder. The goal horn sounded, Etienne's team mobbed him, and Adam cheered until his throat hurt. He couldn't remember the last time he'd had that much fun in the stands.

Etienne turned on the ice and found him, eyes locking unerring on Adam's form. He smiled, bright and sweet and exhausted, and Adam caught his breath, covering quickly with a cough. He had it bad for Etienne Brideau, he was beginning to realize.

He and his parents made it down to the tunnel and waited through the team handshakes, until the players shuffled off the ice. Adam leaned a hip against the barrier, signing autographs for the small crowd that had recognized him, while Etienne showered and changed.

His phone buzzed and Adam handed the last auto-graph off with a smile and turned to pull it out.

Are you serious right now?

Adam grimaced. *I'm sorry*, he sent back. *I wasn't assuming for you, I swear—she asked if you were busy and I said no and SHE just assumed... ugh okay I see what you mean.*

Etienne's reply didn't take long. *I'm taking this out on your ass, Caron.*

Heat lanced through Adam and he cleared his throat as Etienne sent another text.

I'm in the parking lot.

"He's outside," Adam told his parents, gathering them up and shooing them toward the exit. "And he's tired, so this is going to be a fast dinner."

SINCE HE HAD the dubious honor of knowing Toronto better than the others, Adam was left to choose the restaurant. He settled on a hole-in-the-wall Ethiopian place. Small, dimly lit, its interior barely visible through the smoke from both patrons and the grills in the kitchen—Adam had loved it from the first moment he'd stepped inside.

"I ate here a lot when I lived in the area," he said as he held the door open for them. "Their lamb tibs is incredible."

Etienne looked really good in his game day suit, the cut emphasizing the width of his shoulders and narrow waist, the silky fabric clinging to his muscled legs and outlining them tantalizingly. For all that he'd sounded irritated over text, the smile he gave Adam was sweet and private, just for him as they stepped into the restaurant and the proprietor hurried toward them.

She recognized Adam, greeting him with a hug and

concern over his bruises. Adam laughed it off, clasping her hands, and assured her he'd be fighting fit again in no time.

Settled at a table in the back, Etienne sitting beside Adam in a warm line from shoulder to hip to knee and Adam's parents across from them, Adam cleared his throat and picked up a menu.

"So what are we in the mood for?"

Etienne's knee nudged his but his face was nothing but calmly curious as he perused his own menu. "The tibs does sound good."

They placed their order and Colette fixed Etienne with a smile.

"That was a really good game. I had no idea how talented you were!"

Etienne ducked his head, the flush crawling up his throat visible even in the darkened room. "Thank you for saying so."

William leaned forward. "Where'd you learn puck-handling like that?"

"My father, ah… he taught me hand-eye coordination from an early age. I actually played lacrosse in high school and in the summers, but I liked being on the ice more, so…." Etienne shrugged.

"Where's your family now?" Colette asked.

"Gone," Etienne said bluntly. He winced as soon as he'd said it. "Sorry. Uh… yeah, they're not… around anymore. My mom took off early, my dad is—" He shot Adam a slightly panicked look.

"Mom, did you have plans for tomorrow?" Adam interrupted smoothly.

Colette took the offered out. "Yes, I thought we'd spend it sightseeing. I want to go to the aquarium, your father wants to go to the ROM."

"Cool, let me know when you're done," Adam said.

"Oh no, you're coming with us," Colette said.

Adam stiffened. "You're not serious."

Colette gave him a cool look. "I think you owe us a day of your time before we leave, don't you?" Her eyes softened. "We'll take it easy, since I know you're still injured. But we want to see you, honey."

But Etienne has a game tomorrow, Adam wanted to protest. *I promised him I'd be there*. Etienne's hand under the table caught and squeezed his warningly before Adam could say the words, and he swallowed them down with an effort.

"Sure," he managed. "Only fair, you're right."

"Etienne, how did you and Adam meet?" Colette asked.

Adam did his best to stay relaxed. Etienne could handle this.

"The day Adam signed with the Wolverines, my teammates shanghaied me to a bar not far from our rink," Etienne said. His voice sounded just like usual, deep and smooth, but Adam suppressed a shiver at the memory. "They said I didn't know how to have fun, so I got an impromptu lesson. Which mostly involved alcohol, obviously."

"Obviously," Colette said, lips twitching.

"Anyway, Adam was there, and he knows the captain of our team, so we all ended up sitting together. Adam and I hit it off and we've been talking ever since."

"And how—" Colette broke off as William jabbed her in the side with his elbow, sending him a wounded look.

Adam glanced at Etienne, who looked just as baffled.

"What's your plan for the future, Etienne?" William asked. "Do you have a specific team in mind you want to play for?"

"For now, I'd like to play for the Wolverines," Etienne said. "But in the future, I'm open to anything. There are a few teams I'd be honored to sign with. What about you, what do you do?"

"I do some coaching," William said. Adam managed to keep his face straight with an effort. "And Colette here is a surgeon. She makes the money."

Colette rolled her eyes. "If I'm the money-maker, how come you don't wash more dishes?"

Adam relaxed again, the conversation shifted to safer ground.

THE REST of the meal passed smoothly, Etienne answering more questions from Adam's parents while Adam tried not to watch Etienne's long fingers as he tore off pieces of the injera flatbread to roll the tibs in.

Etienne maintained the conversation easily, but Adam could see the lines of exhaustion setting in around his eyes and finally he'd had enough.

"Tenny, you really should go rest for your game tomorrow. Thank you for coming out with us."

Etienne nodded, wiping his hands. He gave Colette and William a smile.

"Thank you for having me, I had a good time."

"I'll call you a car," Adam said, but Etienne shook his head.

"I'll take the subway," Etienne said. "There's a stop just down the street."

He stood and the others followed suit.

"I'll settle the bill," William said. "Adam, you can walk Etienne out while I do that. Etienne, good luck tomorrow."

Adam followed Etienne outside and to the corner. Mindful of the public setting, he kept his hands in his pockets and a circumspect two feet between them.

"I'm sorry," he repeated.

Etienne slanted a smile at him. "I did have a good time."

"Does that mean you're not going to take it out on my ass?"

Etienne caught his breath sharply. "Do you want me to?"

Adam shrugged, pretending nonchalance, but couldn't quite hide the smile.

"Brat," Etienne muttered, his lips twitching. "Text me tomorrow?"

"I'll complain nonstop," Adam assured him.

"And let me know when you're free because I seem to recall promising you something tomorrow night."

It was Adam's turn to catch his breath. "Okay," he managed. "Really wanna kiss you."

Etienne's eyes darkened. "See you tomorrow, Cary."

11

Etienne woke up to texts from Adam.

Mom wants to go out for breakfast, save me.

Then a picture of Colette and William smiling for the camera.

Mom just asked if I was seeing anyone. I told her there was someone special but I wasn't ready to talk about it.

Etienne's chest bloomed with warmth. *Someone special.* He had no idea how to respond. Rolling upright, he scrubbed a hand through his hair.

How goes the parental torture?

We're heading for the aquarium, was Adam's reply. *This would be way better if you were here.*

Etienne smiled dopily at his phone. *Keep me posted and send me pictures of the octopuses.*

Got a thing for cephalopods? Adam asked.

Yeah, they remind me of you, you clingy bastard.

:D

Etienne laughed and got up to start his day.

THE GAME that afternoon was a sweep. The Thunder won 4-0, with Logan giving them their first shutout of the season.

Etienne returned to the locker room drunk on adrenaline and delight to a string of texts from Adam.

You're so fucking sexy on the ice.

Oh my god great stop, tell Logan he's a badass.

GOOOAAAAL THAT'S MY BOYFRIEND!!

Etienne burst into laughter, clutching his phone.

Seriously, you skate like a wet dream. Ya gotta teach me your footwork, man.

Rudy, undressing beside him, gave Etienne a grin. "We're going out to celebrate, Tens, you in?"

"Uh… I'm not sure," Etienne said. He scrolled through the texts.

The last one read, *Mom and Dad are taking me to dinner. Leaving in the morning. Are you going out with the team?* The time stamp said it had been sent a few minutes prior, so Etienne tapped out a quick response.

They want me to. Meet up after?

Sure, Adam replied. *Have fun, you earned it. Wish I could be there to celebrate with you.*

"I'm in," Etienne said to Rudy, who nodded approvingly.

THEY ENDED up at Center Ice, where they were greeted outside the door by cheers and backslaps and requests for autographs. Etienne got his share, signing his name with the same sense of unreality that always accompanied the realization that he had fans, people who followed his career and admired him no matter what he looked like.

Sandwiched in a booth between Theo and Logan, drinks ordered, Etienne leaned toward Logan.

"Adam said to tell you you were a badass tonight."

Logan flashed him a quick, delighted smile. *Thanks*, he signed. *So were you.*

"I had help."

Liam grinned at him from across the table. "How about that dangle of mine in the third period, huh? Goalie never saw it coming."

"You've been practicing your puck-handling, haven't you?" Etienne asked. "That was a great goal, man."

Liam's smile lit up the bar. Johnny cupped his neck briefly, looking proud, as the beers arrived and they settled in to do some drinking.

Etienne limited his alcohol intake, mindful of what he hoped the end of his evening would bring, and focused on enjoying the evening and his teammates. Liam, leaning down to whisper something in Johnny's ear. Logan, arguing vociferously with Broussard across the table, his hands moving so fast Etienne couldn't make out what he was saying. Theo laughing, slapping Etienne on the back. Bastien, Josef, Wyatt, and Jax crammed in the corner and talking above and under the noise of the bar. And Rudy, his dark eyes sparkling as he watched everyone, leaning against Logan's shoulder.

The only thing that would make it better was Adam being there too. Etienne was suddenly restless. He dug out his phone.

Ended up at Center Ice. How's dinner?

He didn't get an answer. Etienne downed another half a beer and tried to follow the argument between Logan and Broussard. As best he could tell from what Broussard was saying, it appeared to be about the plot of their favorite television show.

Etienne shook his head and checked his phone again. Still nothing. He told himself he wasn't disappointed, leaning around Logan's broad frame to talk to Rudy.

They were in the middle of a discussion about attack angle drills when the door swung open and Adam walked inside.

Etienne blinked, unsure if he'd somehow summoned a vision through sheer want or if Adam really was standing there smiling at him.

But then Rudy hailed him with delight and Adam headed toward them. Etienne straightened.

"Hey guys," Adam said. "That was a killer game. Mind if I join you?"

Everyone scrambled around to find room for him to squeeze in, Rudy and Logan sliding from the booth so Adam could slip in beside Etienne.

Up close, he looked incredible, wearing a long-sleeved T-shirt under a light jacket, soft hair falling in his eyes, and he smelled even better, a sweet-spicy aftershave that hinted of cloves and orange blossoms.

"Hey," he said, smiling at Etienne. "Is this okay?"

"Are you kidding?" Etienne said. "I thought I was hallucinating you just because I wanted to see you so badly."

Adam's smile widened but he turned away, leaning across the table. "Tibs, that dangle in the third was masterful."

Liam beamed again.

"And Logan," Adam continued, "your reflexes are *insane*. A shutout against the *Tigers* is no easy feat, man."

Logan signed *thank you*, smiling at him.

"Beer for Cary!" Liam shouted, waving at the waitress.

"No beer for Cary," Etienne said automatically. "Concussion, Tibs."

"Right." Liam looked chastened and then waved at the waitress again. "Beer for everyone else!"

Etienne winced. "We need to tip her a *lot*."

"I don't plan on staying long," Adam said, voice low so only Etienne could hear him. "And you're about done too, I think."

"One beer?" Etienne asked, blood heating at the promise in Adam's eyes.

"Sure."

When they arrived, Etienne knocked his back so fast his head swam.

Adam downed the Coke given him more sedately and then wiped his mouth. "Rudy, I think I'm gonna take this one off your hands for the evening," he said.

Rudy's smile was downright wicked. "Take good care of him."

"Oh, I intend to. Boys, it was a pleasure. Congrats again on the game and tip your waitress at least thirty percent, for the *love* of God."

Etienne followed Adam from the booth to the shouted cheers and laughter of his teammates. He flipped them all off, eliciting more laughter, and headed for the exit, Adam right beside him.

The night air was cool against Etienne's flushed skin as they stepped outside, and he was struck with the memory of the night he'd met Adam, how they'd kissed against the building.

Adam muscled in close, pushing Etienne back into the wall to kiss him hard and messy. Etienne laughed against his mouth. Apparently Adam remembered that night too.

He managed to break apart long enough to speak as Adam attacked his throat.

"You—*ah*—left your parents at your place?"

Adam lifted a shoulder. "They'd gone to bed. I snuck out."

"You snuck out," Etienne repeated, amusement building in his throat.

Adam looked up. "Yeah, why?"

"You snuck out of *your own place* to come see your secret boyfriend," Etienne said, and the giggle slipped free.

Adam scowled. "Would you rather I'd waited?"

"No, nope, absolutely not," Etienne said. He put his hands on Adam's waist and admired the way the moonlight silvered his cheekbones, leaving his eyes in shadow. "You're so beautiful," he said, almost to himself.

"So are you," Adam said.

That brought Etienne down to earth with a thump. He opened his mouth to argue and Adam stopped it with another kiss.

"Don't," he breathed. "Just once, don't. Okay? Can you do that?"

Etienne closed his eyes but the words ate at him, cutting through the pleasant buzz he'd had going. He wasn't beautiful. Would never *be* beautiful. Why did Adam insist on saying these things?

"Oh, Tenny," Adam said. He sounded despairing. "Why can't you take it? Do you hate yourself that much?"

Etienne opened his eyes and shook his head. "I— I'm sorry, Cary. I can't—I'm *not*. I don't understand why you say I am. I'm not like you, I can't be. And every time you say I am, it's like—it hurts. Because you're *wrong*. Why can't you see that?"

Adam sighed. "What I can't see is why you make it such a big deal."

"Spoken like someone who's never had to live with looking like this," Etienne flung at him, and instantly regretted it when Adam flinched.

"That's not fair." His voice was nearly inaudible.

Etienne knew he should apologize. The guilt choked him, and he opened his mouth but the words wouldn't come.

"Maybe I should just go home," Adam said quietly. His eyes were sad and Etienne's heart cracked down the middle. He couldn't breathe.

It was for the best. A clean cut, quick excision. Adam could find someone better than Etienne in a heartbeat, with a snap of his fingers.

When Etienne said nothing, Adam nodded.

"I'm so sorry," he said, and walked away.

Etienne watched him go, a dull, cold lump in his chest.

HE WENT HOME ALONE and curled up in cold sheets that didn't smell like Adam because Adam had never been to his apartment. Would *never* be at his apartment, because people like Adam didn't belong with people like Etienne.

It wasn't fair. It wasn't *fair*. Etienne pressed his face into the pillow, lonely, exhausted, and still half-drunk, and let the tears flow.

12

HE WAS ROUSED by knocking about thirty minutes later. Etienne lifted his head, blinking owlishly. Only Rudy knew his address, but he'd have called first.

He stumbled for the door, swinging it open to behold Adam on the other side, hand raised to knock again.

Etienne stared at him.

"I was thinking," Adam said urgently. "I was thinking about what you said, about how I assume things and don't talk about them. And I realized—do you think we just broke up, Etienne?"

Etienne couldn't remember how to speak. He brushed at his face, struggling to form a sentence.

"Tenny, please," Adam said. "Please answer the question."

"Yeah," Etienne finally managed, his voice rough. "I mean... yeah. Of c-course."

Adam stepped closer and Etienne drew back.

"That's not what happened," Adam said. "That's not—Tenny, I left to give you some room. To think about stuff. What I said. I was going to call you tomorrow and see how you were feeling and when I could see you again. But then I realized where your mind would go, and—I don't want to break up with you. I don't want to lose you, I've barely even *had* you yet. I'm not leaving unless you kick me out, tell me to my face you don't want me, and you'd better make it believable because I *know* you do." He set his mouth in a hard line, folding his arms as he waited for an answer.

Etienne fumbled through the haze of exhaustion and grief. "You… you're not?" *Not leaving me, not breaking up with me?* "Why not?"

Pain crossed Adam's face. "Because I don't see you the way *you* see you," he said. He took a step forward again and this time Etienne held his ground. "I see a man who's fought hard for what he's achieved, who's strong and tough and yet so surprisingly kind. A man who flips every single switch I possess and some I didn't *know* I possessed. How can you not see that I'm attracted to you, Tens, when half the time I forget what I'm going to say when you get close enough to touch me, or run into things because I'm distracted by you?" He stopped, frowning. "That last one happened when I wasn't with you. But my point stands."

"You ran into something? Because of *me?*"

Adam's eyes sparked with brief amusement. "Specifically, the wall after working out with Jake. I was thinking about you and high on endorphins and just—*smack*—head-first. He thought it was hilarious, of course."

Etienne didn't know what to say. He'd never been the sort of person who fogged others' minds with lust or want. He couldn't fathom it. But here Adam was, saying to his face that he'd gotten so turned on thinking about Etienne that he'd walked into a solid surface.

He reached out and hauled Adam through the door, kicking it shut behind them.

"Oh, thank Christ," Adam gasped. He hurled himself forward into Etienne's arms, shaking all over, pressing quick, desperate kisses up and down his throat. "I thought I'd lost you, I thought I'd been unbearably stupid *again* and you wouldn't take me back—"

Etienne caught his chin, mindful of the bruise, and slammed their lips together. It was rough and needy, hard enough to make Adam whimper, their tongues meeting and breath mingling as they gasped against each other's mouths.

Etienne stepped back, pulling Adam with him down the short hall and into the dark bedroom. He didn't stop when his legs hit the edge of the bed, tumbling over backward with Adam still in his arms.

They landed with a thump that strained the bedsprings and made Adam giggle before he resumed kissing Etienne's throat and up his jaw.

"You have such a lovely neck," he murmured between kisses.

"My Adam's apple is too prominent," Etienne said.

Adam laid a careful kiss on it. "I like it. And your jaw, and your mouth—"

"It's shaped funny," Etienne said, unable to stop prodding, like poking a bruise. "My upper lip is pointy but thin and my lower lip is fuller, it's *weird*, I have big teeth and my smile shows too much gum—"

Adam put a finger to his lips, shutting him up. "Stop it," he said. "I love your mouth, and your smile.

I *don't* love the way you put a hand over your mouth when you smile, though, because I'm betting someone somewhere made a jab about it and that's why you're so self-conscious."

Etienne lifted a shoulder, seeing no reason to argue.

"Your mouth is beautiful," Adam said. "And I want to see it wrapped around my cock."

Etienne sucked in a startled breath, hips bucking up involuntarily.

Adam lifted his head, suddenly serious. "I need to know something."

Etienne braced himself.

"Can you do this?"

"What, have sex with you?"

Adam coughed a laugh. "No. This. *Us.*" He rolled off Etienne's body and crossed his legs on the mattress as Etienne sat up slowly. "I need to know," Adam continued. "Are you going to carry this with you always, this self-hatred, the way you constantly compare yourself to me and come up short? Because I —" He faltered, rubbing his face. "I don't think I can do that. Even aside from the way it poisons you, I don't think I can live with the... the *guilt* of being 'the good-looking one' while you silently hate yourself. I know that sounds shallow, but—you'd end up resenting me, I think. Eventually."

Etienne swallowed hard. "I've never—" God, this was *stupid*-hard to say. "I've never f-found anyone worth putting it down for," he managed. "I don't—" Adam took his hand, eyes silently encouraging. "I don't know if I know *how.*"

"Will you try?" Adam whispered. "Will you let me help?"

Etienne's nod was the hardest thing he'd ever done, but the joy in Adam's eyes was worth the terror that clogged his throat, making it almost impossible to breathe.

"Tenny, please will you let me make love to you?"

Etienne took a shaky breath and nodded again.

"Lie back on the bed," Adam said. "Up against the pillows and take off your clothes."

Etienne moved to obey, tugging off his pants and socks and letting them drop off the side of the bed. His shirt followed and then he lay back as Adam… got off the bed?

He kicked off his shoes, then padded across the room. Etienne watched his dim form, wondering what he was doing, and then blinked in the light that flooded the room.

"Adam—"

"No arguing," Adam said flatly. "I know you like to be in control, but just this once we're doing it my way."

Etienne rubbed his arms, feeling exposed and vulnerable, his every flaw laid bare for Adam to examine. It took everything he had to not move as Adam came back to the bed and began to undress.

The jacket went first, then the shirt, revealing Adam's lightly-haired chest with the thicker treasure trail down those incredible abs. Then the pants and underwear at the same time, so he stood there as naked as Etienne, his cock already flushed and thickening rapidly.

Adam crawled onto the bed, fixing Etienne with a serious gaze. "This is what you do to me," he said, taking Etienne's hand and pulling it to his erection. "Do you feel it? How hard I am? I'm not thinking about anyone else right now. Only you. All of this—" His eyes fluttered shut as Etienne stroked him tentatively. "It's all you," Adam rasped, and bent to kiss him. When he pulled away, he kept a hand on Etienne's chest, pressing him down against the mattress. "Be still," he murmured, and proceeded to worship Etienne's body, one agonizing inch at a time.

He started at his collarbones, teeth grazing along them gently and making Etienne swear, then worked his way down. His mouth was warm and wet against Etienne's nipples, laving them and then sucking until they were rigid nubs and Etienne was panting at the unfamiliar sensation.

"Like that?" Adam said, pressing a kiss to one.

Etienne said something garbled and Adam laughed quietly. He picked up first Etienne's right, then his left arm, kissing down them, taking each finger in his mouth and sucking wetly before releasing with a *pop* that made Etienne shudder all over.

Then it was on to his torso, Adam rubbing his cheek against Etienne's abdomen and dragging his tongue through the hair there.

"*Fuck*, why is that hot," Etienne gasped, jamming a hand to his mouth.

"Because I want you," Adam said, and his eyes were blown dark with lust when he looked up. "Because you're beautiful."

Etienne's chest clenched with the familiar negation of the words, but he locked his mouth shut, refusing to let the counterargument escape. When he was able to focus again, Adam looked proud.

"You're already doing better," he said, and rewarded him with a bite to Etienne's hipbone.

Etienne made a strangled noise.

"Oh, I definitely found something you like," Adam said, eyes gleaming, and inched farther down. Etienne was aching hard, leaking in slow, heavy drops onto his stomach, but Adam ignored his erection, instead going down one leg and then the other.

Etienne made a protesting noise. Even with the muscle hockey had given him, his knees were bony, his feet knobby and long. But Adam reached up, resting a hand flat on Etienne's stomach, and kept moving down, pressing soft kisses to both kneecaps, then the delicate skin of his arches. Etienne twitched as Adam flicked a finger down his instep, fighting the slightly hysterical giggle.

"Got a foot fetish?" Adam asked.

"I... didn't *think* I did," Etienne said faintly, mesmerized by Adam's mouth hovering by his big toe.

Adam laughed and crawled back up his body. "I'm not finding out until after you're freshly showered," he said, then kissed him again. "Do you feel it yet, Tenny?"

"Feel... what?" Etienne managed. His veins were filled with sweet, liquid fire, weighing him down and burning him alive from the inside as Adam rocked against him, letting his length drag along Etienne's belly.

"How beautiful you are," Adam whispered.

Etienne swallowed hard. "I—I feel *you*," he said.

That seemed to be enough for Adam, who dipped his head to take another kiss. Then he slithered back down again, settling on Etienne's thighs. Bending, he blew lightly on the head of Etienne's cock.

Even that much made it jerk, spilling more pre-come on his belly, and Etienne had to bite down on his hand to hold himself still as Adam nosed along the base, breath hot on the sensitive skin, and then up, until finally, *finally*, his beautiful mouth closed over the tip.

Etienne choked on a moan, hips jolting, and Adam grabbed them in both hands, pressing Etienne back against the bed. His eyes were closed, expression serious, and his *mouth*—tight, wet, heat surrounded Etienne's cock, Adam's tongue working along the head and over the slit, then lowering, letting more and more of him in until the head was bumping the back of Adam's throat.

"Fuck, *fuck*, Adam, I can't—" He was on fire, burning up, every nerve trembling with unreleased energy and Adam hadn't even really *started*.

Adam let go of one of Etienne's hips to fist the base, working it in time with his mouth. It was wet and messy and Adam kept choking when the head of Etienne's cock hit the back of his throat and *fuck* that shouldn't have been sexy but Etienne wanted to hear more of it, wanted to make Adam take all of him, feel him take him all the way down. He got one hand off the bed and tangled it on Adam's hair.

Adam hummed, the vibrations shooting through Etienne's body, and covered Etienne's hand with his own.

Encouraged, Etienne put a little pressure into it, guiding Adam's mouth where he wanted it, pushing him down until Adam gagged and had to pull off, eyes watering. He dove right back down, though, face determined, trying again and again to deepthroat him as Etienne thrashed and moaned under him, hand tight on the back of Adam's neck.

"You look so hot choking on my cock," he panted.

Adam looked up, tears on his face from the effort,

mouth stuffed full, and his eyes filled with so much affection that Etienne's own eyes stung and he had to look away, overcome.

Instead he grasped the bedspread with his free hand, spreading his legs wider to give Adam better access. Adam took it, one finger tracing down the sensitive skin of Etienne's inner thigh, down under his balls, to press lightly against his hole.

He pulled off briefly, putting his finger in his own mouth and holding Etienne's eyes almost challengingly as he got it wet, then sucking him down again even as his now-slippery wet finger probed Etienne's entrance.

Etienne went rigid, sparks gathering under his skin in waves that threatened to tear him apart, as Adam began to pump in and out in time with his mouth.

"I'm gonna—Adam, I'm gonna come, pull off, *Adam*—"

Adam ignored him, taking him deep and crooking his finger sharply at the same time, and Etienne sobbed out loud as he erupted, spilling down Adam's throat, lost to everything in the fiery waves of ecstasy pulled from him with every movement Adam made.

Adam kept going, gentling his touches but still sucking until Etienne made a noise and tightened his hand in Adam's hair.

"Too much—"

Finally, Adam pulled off. His mouth was red, spit slicking his chin and hair standing on end. He was beautiful, wrecked and debauched and wanting, and Etienne sat up suddenly to kiss him, breathless and unable to say the words that crowded against each other in his chest.

Adam kissed back, one hand cupping the nape of Etienne's neck. He tasted like bitter salt, sharp on

Etienne's tongue, making him shiver as Adam opened so that Etienne could lick the taste of himself from Adam's mouth.

"*Jesus*," he managed when he tore away.

"Just Adam is fine," Adam said.

Etienne let out a yelp of laughter, falling backward onto the bed. "Come here," he finally said, but Adam shook his head.

"Not, ah… necessary."

"Seriously?"

Adam shrugged, looking briefly embarrassed. "You have no idea how hot you are. Literally, *no clue*. I thought I'd be able to hold on, but those noises were too much."

Etienne held out shaky arms. "Well, come here, then."

This time, Adam went willingly, fitting himself up against Etienne's side with his good cheek on his shoulder, one leg thrown over Etienne's thighs.

"I know you don't see it," he murmured. "But I need you to know I *do*, and sometimes I need to tell you. Okay?"

Etienne draped his free arm over his eyes, body still trembling with the last aftershocks of his orgasm. "Yeah," he rasped. He cleared his throat. "Adam. Thank you. I'm—"

"Don't say you're sorry," Adam interrupted. "Don't. Let's just… move on, okay?"

Etienne kissed the top of his head, closing his eyes. "Okay," he whispered. "How long can you stay?"

"I should probably go back," Adam said, sighing, but Etienne tightened his grip.

"Not yet, please? Just… a few more minutes."

"Okay, but if I'm gone when my parents wake up,

there *will* be hell to pay," Adam warned. He kissed Etienne's shoulder. "Sleep, baby."

Etienne was under before he fully registered the endearment, sinking below the waves with a contented sigh.

HE WOKE up to an empty bed and a text.

Accidentally slept almost all night with you. Didn't want to wake you.

Etienne yawned, stretching. *Did you make it back in without getting busted?*

Brought breakfast back with me, Adam replied. *Got "good son" points for that and no one's the wiser. We're at the airport now.*

Tell your parents it was nice meeting them and I hope they have a safe flight home, Etienne sent.

Can I come by later?

Etienne did a quick scan of his schedule for the day. *Gotta work out, and I have practice. Free this evening?*

See you then :)

13

————

Even with Adam on IR, their schedules didn't line up much. Adam still sat in on practices and attended planning and strategy sessions even though he wasn't allowed back on the ice yet. Added to that, his suddenly freer schedule meant the Wolverines planning coordinator promptly co-opted him for more community outreach.

Cleared for light, non-strenuous activity, Adam found himself coaching groups of kids, showing them moves, encouraging them to eat right—Etienne teased him endlessly about needing to learn that lesson himself—and exercise to maintain healthy bodies.

He enjoyed it, he told Etienne during one of their late night text sessions, but it was draining.

People feel... entitled to me, he admitted. *The kids are okay, mostly, but the parents—ugh.*

What do they do? Etienne asked.

Touch me, Adam replied.

Etienne tensed.

Not like that, Adam clarified before Etienne could

ask. *Sorry. Although I think some would if they thought they could get away with it. But like. They put their hands on me. My arms. Shoulders. Chest. Right up in my space. They never stop, and it's just. Idk.*

It had to be exhausting, Etienne thought. *You don't mind when I do?*

No!

Etienne relaxed as Adam kept typing.

YOU have permission. Free access, you could say. Touch me all you want, is what I'm saying.

Etienne grinned to himself in the quiet of his bedroom.

Since I'm not there, you think you could do that for me?

I'm way ahead of you, was Adam's prompt reply, and the next message was an attachment.

ADAM GOT a call one morning from the public outreach coordinator, Linda Rose Martinez.

"How are you recovering?" she asked, cheerful as ever.

"Better every day," Adam said. "Bored, though."

"Well, I might have something to help with that," Linda Rose said. "We're putting together a video for fans and I wondered if you might be interested in being in it."

Adam perked up. "What would it entail?"

A WEEK LATER, he seated himself in the makeup chair,

giving his artist a smile. She smiled back, looking slightly starstruck.

"Go easy on me," Adam told her. "It's my first time."

She giggled. "I'm Kelly. How ugly would you like to be?"

"Whole hog," Adam said cheerfully. "Do your worst."

He chatted with her as she laid out her tools, learning she was in school to be a cosmetologist, she was a Wolverines and a Habs fan, and she had a brother in the ECHL.

"So what exactly are you doing today?" she asked, selecting a foundation. "They said to make you ugly, but not why."

"I'm going undercover to talk to fans," Adam told her. "Give them a pop quiz about some of the players, find out who their favorites are and where they think we need to improve, all that good stuff. Then I'll pull off the wig and sign some autographs. The owner thinks it'll help with morale."

"To have you talking to people? Of course it will," Kelly said, then blushed fiercely. "Close your eyes and hold still."

Adam sat patiently through the process, offering the occasional suggestion as she put the prosthetic nose in place and fixed a wart with several wiry black hairs in place on his chin. She put fillers in his cheeks to round his face and blur the silhouette, then drew painstaking wrinkles around his mouth and eyes. Finally she produced a wig of coarse dishwater blond hair. It fell over Adam's forehead in a shaggy wave, and he blew the fringe out of his eyes as Kelly fussed with the back, making sure it was secure.

"Alright, take a look!" she said, spinning his chair to face the mirror.

A stranger stared back at Adam. His nose was big, with a prominent bump at the bridge. His round cheeks and wrinkles made him look fifteen years older, and the wig obscured his eyes, making him have to peer through the strands.

"The squint will help, that's good," Kelly said, patting his shoulder.

"You're a magician," Adam told her.

Kelly blushed again. "I'll be here all day to help you put it back together after you reveal your identity to people," she said. "Have fun!"

Out on the street in front of the arena, a cameraman hovering discreetly in the background, Adam took stock. Something felt... odd. It was several minutes of watching the people hurrying past before he was able to put a finger on what it was.

No one was looking at him. No semi-discreet sideways glances, no double-takes. No one seemed to even notice he was there other than to step around him and continue on their way. After a lifetime of being under the microscope, Adam didn't know what to think.

The cameraman cleared his throat and Adam twitched. Right, he had a job to do. He stepped forward at random, offering a passerby a smile.

"Excuse me—"

The woman looked him up and down, took a quick step sideways, and disappeared into the crowd.

Okay then.

Adam glanced around for his next target. "Hi there," he said to a middle-aged woman with a teenage boy beside her. "I'm with the Wolverines organization, we're conducting a public poll on recent changes in the team, would you like to answer a few questions?"

The woman's eyebrows went up. She glanced at her son, who shrugged.

"Sure," she said. "Clancy? He's the real hockey fan," she said to Adam.

The boy rolled his eyes but moved forward.

Adam gave him a smile. "Overall, how do you think the Wolverines are doing?"

"Could be better," Clancy said.

"How?"

"Their defense is weak," Clancy said. "You've got a couple of good ones, like that Kano kid—" *Who's ten years older than you*, Adam thought, amused. "—He's got talent but he needs seasoning. Experience. If it were me, I'd bust him back to the Freeze, let him get some conditioning with them for awhile."

"And what about their forwards?" Adam asked, nodding seriously.

Clancy's eyes lit up. "Hideki's incredible. He's got serious moves."

It was true, he did.

"What about the rookie, Caron?"

Clancy shrugged. "He's got potential. Needs to work on strength and endurance—he's fast, but his stamina's not great."

"Yeah, I need to work on that," Adam agreed, pulling off the wig. Mother and son's mouths fell open in an identical expression of shock as Adam grinned. "Thanks for your input. I'll put in some more time on building my endurance."

"You—you're—"

The cameraman hurried forward and held out a Wolverines shirt, which Adam took. Pulling the sharpie from his pocket, he signed the shirt and handed it to Clancy.

"See you at the next game?"

Clancy's mouth opened and closed. Adam couldn't help his laugh. "Take the shirt, kid. Go tell your friends about the time you told Adam Caron to up his game."

Clancy blushed fiery red. "I'm—I didn't mean—"

Adam waved that off, holding out a hand. Clearly dazed, Clancy took it.

"Good meeting you, Clancy," Adam said.

AFTER A QUICK MOMENT inside away from prying eyes to readjust his wig and make sure none of Kelly's hard work had been compromised, Adam went back to it.

He spent several hours getting footage with the cameraman, talking to as many people as he could. The moment when he revealed himself was fun the first few times, but then it began to pall, and then chafe. By the time he was done, he was irritable, frustration making his shoulders tight. He forced a smile for the last interviewee and went back to Kelly with relief. When she was done, he gave her a quick hug and a signed baseball cap but didn't linger.

He hadn't had time to text Etienne all day. There were several messages on his phone when he got in the car and gave the driver his address.

Eggy's in a mood about something. Rudy won't meet anyone's eyes and everyone's tense.

Adam scowled. Coach Eglanton didn't deserve the title, from what he'd heard about him.

You should have seen the save Logan just made. Thing of beauty.

Adam smiled. It had taken a while for Etienne to get to this point—where he'd text Adam random nonsense throughout the day simply for the joy of sharing his feelings about something. Adam loved it, seeing Etienne emerging from the careful shell he'd put up around himself.

I'm free, he sent back. *Have you eaten?*

Waiting for you, Etienne replied. *I'm on my way to your place now.*

AT HIS BUILDING, Adam tipped the driver and hurried for the stairs, unwilling to wait for the elevator.

Etienne was leaning against the wall when Adam appeared. He straightened, a smile blooming across his face. Adam caught his breath and walked into his arms. He put his head on Etienne's chest, listening to his heartbeat as Etienne held him.

"You okay?"

Adam shook his head and lifted a shoulder. "Yes. No. I don't—"

"Inside," Etienne said.

He shepherded Adam gently through the door and into the bedroom, settling him on the bed before sitting down facing him.

"What is it?"

Adam blew out a breath and held out his phone. "I did the thing."

Etienne inspected the selfie Adam had taken of himself in full makeup, his eyebrows rising. "This doesn't look like you at all," he said, smiling. "Did you have fun?"

"At first." Adam accepted the phone back and shoved it in his pocket. "But after a while, it kind of… I don't know. It started to grate."

"What did? Being ugly?"

"*No*," Adam said. "No, the way people treated me. They—" He hesitated. "It's going to sound really shallow."

Etienne squeezed his hand. "Say it anyway."

"They didn't see me," Adam said. "Not *me*. It was like—they'd look at me, realize I wasn't attractive, and immediately dismiss me as not worth their time."

"Not something you're used to, huh?" Etienne sounded sympathetic and a little amused.

"It's not that," Adam protested. "It's—this is what you meant, isn't it? You said… you said you're invisible, until you're not. Is this what you were talking about?"

"Yeah." Etienne no longer sounded amused.

"It's *stupid*," Adam burst out. "It's fucking awful, that people are this *shallow*. If anything, *you* should get mobbed every time you walk out the door, not me, because *you're* the beautiful one, goddammit!"

Etienne sighed and reached out, gathering Adam into his arms. "First of all, I'd hate that. Secondly, that's just how people are, Cary. We're shallow as shit."

"You're not," Adam said, pushing away enough to meet Etienne's eyes. "You see *me*. Not—" He gestured vaguely at himself. "Whatever this is, but *me*. You always have, ever since we met."

"Oh no," Etienne said, lips twitching. "I thought you were hot as fuck long before we met. Don't go thinking I'm not shallow."

"But you still—" Adam scowled, trying to find the words. "It's like you don't *care*. Like my outsides don't matter because you like my insides. That sounds weird but you know what I mean."

Etienne laughed and pulled him in again. "Yeah, I do. And you're right—your face and body are icing on the cake, for sure, but I'm not here for that. I'm here for *you*."

Adam closed his eyes. "I'm sorry people are shallow assholes. I'm sorry they don't see you properly."

Etienne kissed his hair. "You do. That's all that matters."

14

PRACTICES WERE GRUELING, and workouts almost as much so. Etienne went on the road with the Thunder two weeks after Adam's injury, riding the bus to the first of their away games.

Sure wish I had a private jet, he texted Adam. *Some people have the sweet life.*

If you were on the jet with me, I'd blow you in the bathroom, Adam replied.

Etienne smiled, the bus jostling and players talking around and over him. *Do you ever think about anything besides sex?*

I think about donuts, Adam responded. *Does that count?*

Depends. Are you thinking about having sex with the donuts?

Adam's reply was a long time coming. *Well, I WASN'T...*

Etienne couldn't stop the laugh, looking up to catch Rudy's eye as he turned in his seat. Rudy grinned at him and turned back around.

They lost their first two away games, the first by a narrow margin and the second to a shutout, which demoralized everyone.

Rudy stood up in the aisle between the seats after the second one, when it was clear Coach Eglanton had nothing to say.

"So that sucked," he said, drawing groans of agreement from everyone. "What'd we do wrong?"

"What *didn't* we do wrong," Johnny muttered.

"Okay, we'll start with you," Rudy said. "What should you have done differently?"

Johnny slouched in his seat. "I shouldn't have tried that drop pass."

Liam patted his knee. "You'll get it next time."

"So in practices, Johnny, that's what you're going to focus on," Rudy said. "Tibs, what about you?"

Liam glanced up. "Uh. I shouldn't have tried for that goal in the second?"

"No, you should not have," Rudy snapped. He swayed with the bus's motion as it rumbled around a corner but kept his balance effortlessly. "You should have sent it to me, because you were *covered* in players and I was open, I was waiting, I was *right there*, but you let that dangle go to your head and all of a sudden you're a rockstar. You're good at your job, Tibby, but your job is keeping the others off me and the wingers. Don't get me wrong—I *want* you to score. I'd love to see your numbers climb. But not when the team suffers as a result. Clear?"

Liam nodded, looking chagrined.

"Tenny, what did I do wrong?" Rudy asked.

Etienne jerked, startled. "What? You? Uh... nothing?"

"Not quite. I should have been more vigilant with

my forechecking, and I also let that center get by me to score on Logan. What did you do wrong?"

Etienne grimaced. "I wasn't in place for that pass you tried to send me."

Rudy just nodded. He surveyed the bus, the dejected faces surrounding him. "We played a subpar game. It happens. But even shitty games can help, because now we have a better idea of the weaknesses in our defense we need to shore up, and the drills we need to run to get faster and stronger. We'll do better next time. Right?"

The players mumbled.

Rudy's tone sharpened. "*Right?*"

"Right!" they chorused back to him.

Satisfied, Rudy nodded and sat down.

They won their next two games and sprayed Rudy with Gatorade after the second one as he spluttered and laughed.

15

BACK IN TORONTO, Adam was going out of his mind with boredom and frustration. He and Etienne texted constantly, but they couldn't easily talk on the phone, what with Etienne sharing a room with Josef, a Polish defenseman.

He's a decent guy, I guess, Etienne told him. *Doesn't pick up his stuff, though, I keep tripping over his shoes.*

Adam thought guiltily of the shoes he'd kicked off and left in the doorway. *When do you get back?*

Two more days.

It felt like a lifetime.

Last game tomorrow, then travel time home, Etienne sent. *How's your head?*

Fine, Adam sent. *Bruise is almost completely gone and everything. See?* He snapped a quick picture and sent it.

No headaches?

Nope. Just bored out of my skull. Training and practice are important, but I'm dying to get back on the ice.

What about your vision?

Adam rolled his eyes. *It's fine. Don't fuss.*

I'll fuss if I want to. Any changes at all to the blurred spot?

None, Adam sent, suppressing sudden irritation. *Do you want to check my blood sugar and potassium levels while you're at it?*

Etienne was silent for a long moment, and then the phone rang in Adam's hand.

He squeezed his eyes shut and answered it. "I'm sorry," he said.

"What's going on?" Etienne's voice was so deep and soothing, Adam could listen to him talk all day. He didn't sound angry—he sounded worried.

"Nothing." Adam sighed and flopped back onto the bed. "Josef doesn't care about you talking on the phone?"

"I went for a walk around the motel," Etienne said. "Talk to me, Cary."

Trust Etienne to know it was more than simple irritability. "Noemi called. They're working on scheduling the wedding, and they needed to know what dates I'd be available to fly out."

"And you don't want to go?"

Adam stared at the ceiling. "I do. I want to see them again. But…." He took a deep breath. "I'm gonna come out to them while I'm there."

"Okay," Etienne said, his tone warm and proud. "You can do this."

Adam scowled. "I shouldn't *have* to. It's fucking *stupid*. Straight people don't have to come out, why do we?"

"I know," Etienne said soothingly. "Things are changing, but it's slow. You'll still be okay. What dates do they have in mind?"

"Sometime in January, I think. I sent her my calendar and she's going to let me know. She said she's going to try to schedule it during our bye week."

"You'll be fine. They're not going to love you any less."

"Come with me," Adam said impulsively.

"I—what?"

Adam sat up. "Come with me to Seattle, Tenny. Please? I'll pay for your ticket and expenses, all of it. My parents have already met you and everything."

"So you want to just turn up with a boyfriend as the slideshow portion of your coming out presentation?" Etienne inquired.

"Exhibit A," Adam said brightly, and relished the sound of Etienne's soft chuckle.

"I don't know what the team has scheduled in January," Etienne said. "I'll look and see. *If* I'm free, I'll… think about it."

"I miss you," Adam said, lying back down. Maybe he should have felt embarrassed about admitting that, but he didn't. It was the truth, and he wanted Etienne to know it.

"I miss you too." Etienne sighed. "Just a couple more days, and then I have a few days off."

"We're going to spend at least one of them in bed, right?" Adam asked. "You, me, a dozen donuts…."

Etienne laughed but then sighed again. "I actually have to go see my dad."

"He's in Toronto?"

"Just outside, yeah." Etienne sounded distinctly unhappy.

"Do you want me to come with you?"

"You'd do that?"

"Of course. Anyway, it's only fair—you met *my* parents way before you expected to."

Etienne huffed amusement. "Yeah, but your parents are nice."

"Only on the outside," Adam said darkly.

That got more of a laugh, as intended.

"We'll talk about it when I get back," Etienne said. "There are some things you should know, but I don't want to do it over the phone. Speaking of which, I should go."

"Wait!" Adam said. He pulled his shirt up and took a picture of his abs and the semi he'd been sporting since Etienne had started talking.

Etienne caught his breath sharply. "Cary, *fuck*—"

"Use it tonight," Adam said, knowing his voice had gone husky. "Go in the bathroom or something."

Etienne groaned. "I'm standing in the middle of a motel with a boner, and it's all your fault."

Adam hummed. "Can I touch myself, please?"

"Yeah," Etienne rasped. "Get yourself off and show me the mess you made after. I'm going back to the room before I poke someone's eye out with this thing."

Adam was laughing as he disconnected, but it didn't last long. Neither did he. He sent Etienne a picture less than five minutes later of the cooling come splattered on his belly.

God, Etienne responded. *I can't wait to see you.*

16

————

ETIENNE TOOK the stairs up to Adam's apartment two at a time, too impatient to wait for the elevator. He was breathing hard but barely noticed as he topped the last riser and ran down the hall.

Adam jerked the door open and dragged him inside, wrapping himself around Etienne's form like a clinging vine. Etienne just managed to get the door kicked shut, staggering under his weight as he dropped his bag. His eyes prickled at the *rightness* of Adam in his arms, kissing his throat, stubble rasping against Etienne's skin.

"Hi," Adam said, going up on tiptoe to wrap his arms around Etienne's neck. He kissed him before Etienne could respond. "How are you? God, you smell like the bus. It's so good to see you—"

Etienne kissed him back, cutting off the flow of words, wet and hungry and possessive.

"Talking later," he growled, and muscled him toward the bedroom.

Adam went willingly, although he was so wrapped

up in Etienne's limbs that they nearly tripped several times. They toppled onto the bed and Etienne swarmed him, yanking Adam's pants down and shoving his shirt up.

"Fuck," he murmured, almost to himself. Adam was wide-eyed and panting underneath him, squirming but clearly struggling to be patient.

"*Tenny*," Adam said, nearly a whine.

Etienne took pity on him and swallowed him down, relishing the taste and feel of him on his tongue as Adam bucked and muffled a shout. Etienne set a brutally hard pace from the start, hand taking what his mouth couldn't, until Adam went tense as a bow string, hand tight to the point of pain in Etienne's hair as he spilled down his throat.

When he collapsed back to the bed, Etienne wiped his mouth, feeling immeasurably smug. Adam tugged on his hand.

"That's a good look on you," he said, words slurring slightly.

Etienne bent and kissed him, knowing how much Adam liked tasting himself in Etienne's mouth. "I'm gonna come on your face," he informed him, and Adam groaned and nodded.

It was a handful of minutes, his breathing harsh and unsteady and heartbeat thundering in his own ears, before he felt the familiar tingling sensation, the pressure building in his gut. His hand sped up and Adam closed his eyes, tilting his face as Etienne hunched forward and came, creamy spurts hitting Adam's cheek and jaw to slide down onto his throat.

Etienne caught himself on one hand, gasping for air. Adam looked deliciously debauched, hair on end, lips red with kisses and skin streaked with Etienne's come. He stretched, smiling, and opened his eyes.

"Welcome home," he murmured.

Etienne bent and kissed him again. "Thank you. Shower?"

"Mm." Instead, Adam tried to pull him down to the bed.

Etienne resisted, wanting to get the smell of the road off, but Adam blinked up at him pleadingly. He needed this, Etienne remembered, the physical intimacy with nothing being asked of him. Feeling like an asshole, he leaned over for a tissue, wiped Adam's face off, and then lay down, gathering him into his arms. Adam's breath was warm on his collarbone, hair soft where it tickled Etienne's nose, and he made a contented noise, burrowing closer.

I could spend years doing this and never get tired of it, Etienne thought.

THEY SHARED a lazy shower and even lazier handjobs, the edge of need blunted. Adam fell apart so beautifully in Etienne's arms, shuddering through orgasm with his head tilted back and mouth open, that it drove Etienne over the edge too, until they were panting and clinging to each other to stay upright.

Adam started laughing first, pulling away and turning to rinse off his front half. "Can you imagine if we'd been separated for a month?"

Etienne nipped his shoulder. "Don't even say it."

LATER, they lay in bed, Adam tucked against Etienne's side, quietly enjoying each other's company.

Finally, Etienne stirred. "I have to go see my father tomorrow."

Adam made an encouraging noise.

"Do you... did you still want to come?"

"Absolutely," Adam said. "If you want me there."

"It might make it easier," Etienne admitted. "Might make it worse. I don't know."

"You said, at dinner with my parents, that your mom left?"

"When I was six, yeah."

"Oh, Tens."

Etienne lifted a shoulder. "I barely remember her." A feeling of warmth, like being in her arms, a snatch of song he could never quite catch the thread of, and hot tears falling on his face. He closed his eyes, banishing the memory. "She had issues, I guess. Didn't want to be a mother."

Adam swung a leg over Etienne's thighs as if holding him to the mattress but said nothing.

Etienne stroked his arm, lying across his chest. "My dad... tried. But he had a full time job and a six year old kid and no idea what to do with him."

"What did he do?"

"He had a garage. He used to park me in the corner with a pair of rubber balls and make me do drills with them for hours after school. When it was cold enough, I'd do drills on the pond outside our back door. Summer was lacrosse, which was only an interim for hockey and a way to keep my hand-eye coordination up to par in the off months."

"He sounds... tough," Adam said carefully.

"Yeah. Anyway, I should tell you, before you

decide about tomorrow, that he's in a home. He has dementia and it makes him say some… shitty things. I'm used to it, but it's okay if you'd rather stay behind."

"No way," Adam said. "No fucking way. I'm coming with you."

Relief made Etienne's head swim. He pressed a kiss to Adam's hair.

"Stay with me tonight?" Adam murmured.

"I've got my bag," Etienne said. "If you're sure?" The thought of his cold, dreary apartment made him shiver.

"How else am I going to wake you with a blowjob?"

Etienne laughed and rolled on top of him to kiss him.

17

ETIENNE WAS nervous the next day, it was obvious. He'd kissed Adam good morning willingly, but in the car on the way to the facility, his eyes darted this way and that, fingers tapping against the gift-box of chocolates for his father and his knee jittering.

Adam touched his leg. "Breathe."

Etienne slouched, grumbling.

"You look nice," Adam said, trying to distract him.

It almost worked. Etienne glanced at him, eyes narrowing. Adam raised an eyebrow, daring him to argue. It was true, in any case—he'd shaved extra closely that morning and meticulously styled his dark hair so it was swept back in a sleek wave. Half-asleep in the bed, Adam had heard him talking to himself under his breath as he dithered over what to wear. In the end, he'd decided on a shirt the color of his eyes that he'd carefully ironed first and a pair of softly faded jeans.

Etienne finally glowered and muttered, "Thanks."

Adam rewarded him with a pat on the knee.

Four Winds Nursing Home was a sprawling facility that covered most of a city block. Low to the ground and blocky, it made no presumptions toward gracious living or state of the art facilities, but inside it was spotless, neat, and quiet.

The receptionist smiled brightly at Etienne when they approached. "Mr. Brideau, how nice to see you! Your father's just finished his breakfast and is in the common room, would you like to go through?"

Etienne led Adam through halls that smelled like antiseptic and cleaning solution, to a huge area filled with light from floor-to-ceiling windows and sunroofs overhead. Adam blinked, startled. It wasn't what he'd expected, somehow. The room was spacious, welcoming, with gracefully arching beams overhead and thick carpet underfoot. Several elderly people huddled over a puzzle in the corner, talking quietly. A few more were scattered throughout, one reading, others watching the television in another corner. A tiny old woman, face wrinkled and eyes sweet, waved at Adam as he passed and he waved back.

"Apparently sunlight is really good for a lot of different issues," Etienne said under his breath as he threaded his way across the room, Adam on his heels. "They spent most of their budget on this room because they saw a drastic improvement in both physical and mental health after just an hour spent resting in sunlight." He stopped in front of the windows and a man in a wheelchair. "Hey Dad," he said. He sounded wary.

The man lifted his head, blinking. He looked almost nothing like Etienne, Adam realized, vaguely surprised. His hair was the same color, as were his eyes, but the similarities ended there. This man's nose was straight and his mouth was full and perfectly shaped, even with age pulling at it. He'd clearly been a strikingly handsome man in his prime.

"Who are you?" he asked, staring at Etienne.

"It's me," Etienne said, summoning a smile that looked forced. "Etienne. Your son. This is my friend Adam. Adam, this is my father, Pierre Brideau."

Adam held out a hand but Pierre ignored it, focusing on Adam's face. His eyes lit up. "Etienne!"

Adam glanced at Etienne, who looked startled.

"Dad, this is Adam. I'm Etienne."

Pierre ignored him. "Etienne," he repeated, smiling at Adam. "So good of you to come see this old man, son. How have you been?"

Etienne swore under his breath and pulled up two chairs. Sitting, he leaned forward. "Dad. *I'm* Etienne. This is my friend Adam."

Pierre didn't seem to have heard him. "Where's your mother? She was just here. Did you bring me anything?"

Etienne leaned forward and placed the small white box of chocolates in his father's hand. "The kind you like," he said.

Pierre looked at him and frowned. "Who are you? Why are you talking to me like I know you? Etienne, who is this man?"

Adam didn't know what to say. He glanced at Etienne again, who looked frustrated and confused. Etienne caught his eye and shrugged helplessly. *Roll with it*, he seemed to be saying.

Pierre was still talking. "Look at you, all grown up." He laughed, a sudden sharp cackle that made Adam jerk. "You were the *ugliest* kid. No one believed you were mine, you know that? Have to admit I wondered a few times myself."

Etienne went very still beside Adam.

"I was embarrassed to take you places, I don't mind telling you," Pierre continued. "People wondering how I was so handsome and had such a homely kid. But I did my duty by you anyway, and I guess you turned out alright, didn't you? Downright good-looking, in fact." He examined Adam again, frowning. "Where's your mother?"

"She left," Etienne said, and Adam had never heard him sound like that, choked and deadly quiet. "She walked out when I was six, Dad."

"Tenny," Adam whispered, but Etienne shook his head, sharp and vicious, and Adam shut up. Worry ate at him with needle-sharp teeth, but there was nothing he could do here, not in front of the man who was *still* talking, this time recounting the time Etienne had asked someone to a school dance and been publicly rejected. He was *laughing*, the bastard, and Adam wanted to hit him suddenly, wanted to shake him and demand to know how he couldn't see the beauty in his own child, how he could have let him grow up with that poisonous worm festering at his core.

It wouldn't do any good. The man sitting in front of them didn't know what he was saying. They were years too late to stop the harm he'd already caused, but that didn't stop the tears from gathering in Adam's eyes as Pierre launched into another story of Etienne being rejected as Etienne sat beside Adam, still as stone.

Adam wanted to flee but he made himself take it, forced himself to stay in his chair, aching to touch Etienne but unable to. He wasn't leaving this room without Etienne by his side. When an attendant appeared to take Pierre for a massage, Adam couldn't hide the relief as he stood. Etienne followed suit silently.

"Come back soon," Pierre told Adam. He didn't look at Etienne as he was wheeled away.

Adam said nothing as they left the building. Etienne had the look of a bomb about to blow, his shoulders tight and his mouth set. Adam requested a car, careful not to touch him. He didn't know how to fix this. What was he supposed to say? What should he *do*? An idea occurred to him and he edited the destination request in the app, still silent. When the car arrived, they slid into the backseat, Etienne keeping his hands folded in his lap as he stared straight ahead.

But Adam hadn't given his home address to the driver. Instead, they pulled up in front of the practice rink. Etienne shot him a look as Adam tipped the driver.

"Adam—"

"No," Adam interrupted. "Get out of the car."

Etienne's mouth tightened but he did as he was told. Adam took him around the side, to the players' entrance, and Etienne followed him inside to the Wolverines' locker room, dim and quiet now in the middle of the day.

Adam flicked the switch. "You can use Barlowe's skates—he's about your size and he always leaves a pair here. That's his locker there."

"What are you doing," Etienne said very carefully.

"*We* are skating," Adam said. "Put them on."

He pulled out his skates as Etienne stood in the middle of the room, watching him. Adam pretended not to notice, lacing the skates up carefully and blessing the fact that he was wearing comfortable clothes he could move in.

Finally, Etienne pulled the skates out of the trunk Adam had indicated and sat down. His movements were stiff, uncoordinated, as if he'd forgotten how his joints worked. Adam's heart ached for him but he set his jaw and tied his skates. It wasn't the time for sympathy. Not yet.

He waited until Etienne stood, then tossed him a helmet. "Try that on."

Etienne obeyed. The helmet fit and Adam nodded, pleased.

"Had a hunch Woz's head was about your size. Let's go." He grabbed two sticks and a bucket of pucks and headed for the ice without looking back to see if Etienne was following, making a quick detour to the bank of switches that controlled the lighting.

Then he went up the tunnel and dumped the pucks out, tossing the bucket onto the bench before stepping onto the ice. He turned, skating backward, to watch as Etienne stepped out more slowly.

"Warmups, let's go," he ordered.

They warmed up slowly, careful not to stretch cold muscles too quickly, doing easy drills and exercises until Adam felt loose and tingly, his breathing comfortable in his chest.

"Passing drill," he said. "This end to that." He pointed.

Etienne grabbed a puck and sent it to him, and they were off. They traded the puck back and forth between them as they raced down the ice, and Adam wanted to shout with glee at how easy it was, the movement as natural as breathing to catch what Etienne batted to him and send it right back. He did a quick drop pass and Etienne caught it without hesitation, sending the puck ricocheting off the wall straight for Adam, who stopped it with his stick as they reached the other end.

"Again," Adam said. "Keep away now."

They switched it up, trying different maneuvers. Adam began testing him, curious to see how well Etienne could read his body language. He tried a dangle, faking an attempt to dodge around him, but nearly ran straight into him instead when Etienne didn't fall for it, his eyes intent but not as grim as they had been. Backhand, drop, and saucer pass, Etienne kept up with him through every trick Adam tried, but he couldn't get the puck from him, either.

Adam sent him the puck and then went after it. Etienne was every bit as fast as Adam, and his footwork was pushing Adam to the limits of his skill, but Adam's puck-handling was just slightly better. He made a lunge but Etienne was there before him, vanishing around him with the puck on his stick to sink it into the open net. Then it was back to the bench to grab another puck and repeat the process.

They matched like two pieces of a puzzle, knowing instinctively which way the other would go and working together seamlessly to support a play if they were teamed up or blocking each other's passes if they were facing off.

Adam got the puck away, raced down the ice, and sank it, Etienne on his heels. He threw his arms up in victory as Etienne tackled him to the ice, twisting so Adam landed on top of him. They landed in a flurry of limbs and skidded across it in a laughing tangle, fetching up against the boards.

Etienne's cheeks had bright spots of color, the

worst of the misery in his eyes swept away like cobwebs. He blinked up at Adam as if seeing him for the first time.

Adam tugged off a glove to cup his jaw. "Do you see it? How we fit?"

Etienne swallowed hard and nodded.

"Fuck him," Adam said, holding Etienne's eyes. "*Fuck* him, and anyone else who says you're not good enough, not perfect exactly as you are. It's you and me. Hear me? You and me. We're a team, and there's not a single thing I would change about you. *Nothing*. You are *perfect*."

Etienne's mouth worked and Adam bent to kiss him, fierce and hurting.

After a minute, Etienne's hand came up to grip the back of Adam's neck as his lips parted and he slipped his tongue into Adam's mouth.

Adam made a noise of encouragement, wriggling closer. They kissed for several long minutes until Etienne broke away, half-laughing, hair mussed and cheeks pink.

"I'm freezing my ass off," he said.

Adam scrambled upright, grinning at him, and extended a hand. On their feet, Etienne reached out and tugged Adam into a hug.

"You and me," he said, voice deep in his chest where Adam's ear was pressed. "Adam—"

"Let's go home," Adam interrupted. "I want to spend the rest of the day in bed. Think you can handle that?"

Etienne pinched his ass, grinning when Adam yelped. "Fine, but no donuts."

18

A MONTH LATER, Etienne got called up to the Freeze. He stared at the phone for a few minutes in shock before calling Adam, who had just gotten back from his own set of away games.

"Fuck yeah!" Adam shouted, making Etienne giggle almost hysterically.

"This weekend," Etienne said. "Can you come?"

"Oh, like anything would keep me away," Adam retorted. Something in Etienne's chest eased.

He spent Thursday and Friday practicing with Rudy and Adam, focusing on his puck handling.

"Don't be intimidated," Adam told him the night before the game. "This is my old team. They'll take care of you. Watch for Li when he gets jammed up. He's wicked fast but he gets stressed when too many people are on him. If he knows you'll take the heat off when he needs you, he'll pass you the puck all day long."

Etienne nodded silently.

"And Jetty will probably be your D-man. He's a

better skater than Tibby but he goes offside sometimes if things get fast—he tries too hard to anticipate where the puck will be. Gretzky he's not."

Etienne almost smiled.

"You're gonna do great," Adam said.

Etienne rolled on top of him.

"Whoa, hey, what happened to no sex before a game?"

Etienne smiled down at him, dark and full of promise. "*You* don't have a game tomorrow."

Adam gulped loudly enough to be heard in the suddenly quiet room as Etienne slid down his body. "I'm going to come out to my coach," he said.

Etienne stopped dead. "When?"

"When the moment's right?" Adam shrugged, going for unconcern, but Etienne wasn't fooled.

"You're sure?"

"Yeah." Adam ran a thumb down Etienne's jaw. "It's time. Now what were we talking about?"

Etienne huffed a laugh and pulled Adam's pants off.

THE FREEZE WERE everything Adam had prepped Etienne for. They were also raucously welcoming, loud and friendly as they warmed up before the game. Etienne found himself relaxing almost immediately, settling into his groove and finding his rhythm.

He meshed well with Li, slim-framed, dark eyed and unsmiling until Etienne sank a puck five-hole on the goalie, Shannon. Li's grin lit up his face and Etienne grinned back as he circled behind the net.

They won the game 7-3 and Etienne managed a goal and an assist to loud cheers from the stands.

He went home drunk on success and adrenaline, fucked Adam on his ridiculous golf course, and woke up to a message from his agent.

"Their left winger is going to be out the rest of the season, and their coach loves the way you fit into the third line," she informed him. "How'd you like to finish your season as a Freeze?"

Etienne blinked a few times. Was he hallucinating? Adam looked at him, eyes wide and questioning.

"I—yes," Etienne finally managed. "I'd like that."

Adam threw his arms in the air silently and fell over backward on the bed as Etienne hung up. "You're on your *way*, baby!"

Etienne laughed and crawled on top of him. Adam grinned up at him, hair rumpled and love bites on his neck from the night before stark against his fair skin. Etienne was hit by a sudden rush of emotion that roared through him, leaving him shaking.

"Tenny?" Adam sounded worried.

Etienne closed his mouth, shuddering. He couldn't say it, couldn't give words to this new feeling that was still so young and tender in his chest. It was too fragile, and he wanted to cherish it a little longer. "I wouldn't be here if it weren't for you," he finally said.

Adam poked him in the ribs. "You're here because of *you*. But maybe I helped your confidence a little. I'm okay with that."

"You and me," Etienne said, and kissed him.

19

ADAM FOUND his moment two weeks later, when Coach Benton called him into his office.

"Just wanted to go over a few things," Coach said cheerfully. "The community outreach coordinator says you've been instrumental in boosting both ticket sales and attendance in the events she's scheduled. She wants to know if you're willing to host a camp next summer for kids in underprivileged areas."

"Yeah, actually," Adam said, perking up. "That sounds awesome."

"Good, good. You're settling in well," Coach said. He glanced through papers. "I may shuffle the lines around a bit, but you're a solid addition to the team and I'm glad we have you."

Adam ducked his head. "Thank you, Coach."

"That's all, you can go."

Adam hesitated. "Actually, there was something I wanted to talk to you about."

Coach lifted his heavy eyebrows.

Adam opened and closed his mouth. The words wouldn't come at first.

Coach Benton waited.

"Um. I'm gay," Adam blurted.

Coach Benton said nothing, folding his hands on the desk.

Adam fidgeted. "Need you to say something, Coach."

"Well, I'm glad you felt you could tell me," Coach said. "Are you going to come out to the team?"

"I—yes. I want to. I think. Do you—" Adam snapped his mouth shut.

"Do I what?"

"Do you think they'll be okay with it? Are *you* okay with it?"

"My son is gay," Coach said. His eyes creased with his smile and Adam sagged with relief. "Yeah, Cary, I'm fine with it. What about the NHL? Are you thinking of coming out to the organization or just the team?"

"I... don't want the publicity but I also don't want to hide anymore," Adam admitted. "Everyone will look at me different and I just want to play hockey. But—"

Coach picked up a pen, twirling it idly between his thick fingers. "Let's start with the team," he suggested. "I'll get with our PR contact, let her draft something up for when you're ready. In the meantime—stay out of the headlines unless it's for good things, you got it? Rescue a little old lady or a kid from a burning building, fine. But no wild parties, no picking up random guys who turn out to be underage or packing cocaine, *nothing* that could smear your image and the team's."

"I won't," Adam said earnestly. "I'm—I have a boyfriend. No wild partying for me, I promise."

"Okay, good. Is it that kid Etienne?"

Adam blinked. "How—"

Coach laughed. "I met him when we were at the hospital. You made him your emergency contact, Cary. That kind of thing tends to be a giveaway. He's a good guy. I liked him."

"Well yeah, it's him."

"And he knows you're doing this?"

"Yes sir. He understands the ramifications."

"How do you want to tell the team? You want me to do it or you?"

Adam considered. The idea of telling everyone individually was exhausting. "I'd like to tell my line and a couple of others, I think. Once I do that, you can tell the rest of the team for me, if you don't mind."

"Fine by me," Coach said. "Let me know when you're done. Now get out of here, you're missing practice."

"Yes sir," Adam said, and escaped gratefully.

He took Jake, Victor, Hideki, and Hunt out for lunch after practice the same day, too nervous to wait any longer. Jake, always delighted by the prospect of food, buried himself in a giant milkshake and several oversized steak wraps as Adam tried to keep from squirming.

Hunt fixed him with cool, dark eyes. "Everything okay, Cary?"

"Yeah. Um. There was something I wanted to tell

you guys." Adam tore his napkin into shreds as Jake nudged him with a meaty shoulder.

"You're not leaving the team, are you?"

"Nah," Adam said, relaxing enough to smile at him. "I just—I have some news, and I wanted you guys to be the first to know, because you're my closest friends on the team."

"Are you pregnant?" Jake asked, and laughed at his own joke.

Adam gave him a mock-glare. "No, but I *am* seeing someone."

Jake and Victor exclaimed with delight. Hideki and Hunt traded glances and said nothing.

"What's her name?" Jake demanded. "What's she look like? Show us a picture, man, I'm sure you've got a thousand of them."

This was it. Moment of truth. Adam dug his phone out and unlocked it. He'd caught a rare picture of Etienne in bed one day, early in the morning when Etienne was too sleepy to protest. His eyes were half-closed against the sunlight, mouth curving up in a laughing objection as he reached out one hand to stop Adam from taking the picture, but Adam had been too quick for him.

It was his lockscreen. He set the phone on the table and slid it across to Jake.

Jake choked on his milkshake, spraying strawberry ice cream onto the tabletop, and Adam snatched the phone away before it could get ruined.

"Idiot," he said, wiping the screen.

"You can't just—" Jake heaved for air and gestured at the phone. "*Spring* it on a guy like that, Jesus!"

Adam glared at him and handed the phone to

Hideki, who showed it to Hunt. Neither of them said anything as Hideki handed the phone back.

Jake was still talking. "Isn't that the guy from the hospital? Weird name, starts with an E, I think?"

"Etienne," Hunt supplied.

"Yeah, yeah, him," Jake said. "You're with him? Like… *with* him?"

Adam rubbed his face. "Is it a problem?"

"No!" Jake looked at Hunt, then Hideki, and finally back to Adam. "I just—I assumed you were, you know…." He gestured vaguely.

"Everyone does," Adam said. He couldn't help the bitterness in his tone. "Doesn't fit the narrative for the star hockey player to also be queer. Makes people question his manhood."

Jake leaned forward. "You're a great center, Cary, and a good friend. That's all I care about."

Adam gave him a grateful smile and glanced at Hunt and Hideki.

Victor nodded. "Makes no difference to me. You're still a good hockey player. Just don't check out the guys' asses in the locker room."

Adam scowled. "I'm not suicidal, and besides, even if I *wasn't* taken, is that the kind of thing you think gay guys do?"

Victor blinked, looking thrown. "I mean—"

"You mean you bought into the stereotype that all gay men are horndogs and a locker room full of players is just so much fresh meat, right? Who cares about little things like basic respect and human decency?"

Hideki put a hand on Adam's arm. "Cary. Breathe."

Adam obeyed, throttling back the fury until he could meet Victor's eyes calmly.

To his credit, Victor looked ashamed. "I didn't mean—I'm sorry, Cary."

Hideki tightened his grip on Adam's arm but said nothing.

Finally, Adam nodded. "Apology accepted."

Hideki picked up his chicken wrap and took a bite. "Anything else to discuss?"

"That's not enough?"

Hideki smiled at him. "You're paying for lunch, right?"

"Yeah," Adam said, relief infusing him. "Of course I'm paying."

"Then that's enough."

20

ADAM COULDN'T REMEMBER the last time he'd been so stressed. He packed and repacked his bags, muttering under his breath as he pulled out and discarded outfits until his bedroom was strewn with clothes. He was crouched over his suitcase, deliberating over the fawn suit or the light blue, when Etienne walked in and blinked.

"Whoa. Did your closet explode?" His lips twitched. "There are easier ways to come out of it, you know."

Adam glared at him. "Stop making jokes and help me decide what suit to bring."

Instead, Etienne bent and kissed him. His mouth was warm and sweet, and he tasted like orange juice. "The fawn," he murmured. "It looks good with your coloring."

Adam slumped. "I hate this."

"I know." Etienne rubbed a thumb over Adam's lower lip. "You'll be fine. *We'll* be fine. Have you figured out how you're going to do it yet?"

"I think I'll let the moment decide," Adam said.

"Alone, or do you want me with you?"

Adam considered. "I think… my parents alone, and then with you for Noemi and Eli."

Etienne kissed him again. "They love you. It's going to be fine."

"Ugh." Adam sighed and rested his forehead against Etienne's shoulder. "Are you packed?"

"Finished last night," Etienne said. "The car will be here in twenty, are you going to be ready?"

"Yeah, yeah." Adam went back to work, sorting and folding until everything fit neatly into his suitcase. Then he straightened and dragged the luggage out of the bedroom and down the hall to where Etienne was waiting by the door. Maybe he could find something to do on the plane to distract himself.

"No, I do *not* want to join the Mile-High Club."

"But—"

"Stop it before we get this plane grounded and our asses thrown off."

"Killjoy."

21

THE FLIGHT WAS long and boring, with what felt like an endless layover, but Etienne was unsurprised to find that Adam was a lot of fun as a traveling companion. He didn't harp endlessly on delays, never grumbled about needing more leg room, and handled every instance of being recognized with grace, signing autographs and gravely discussing strategy with fans. Etienne hung back when that happened, not wanting to intrude, but every so often Adam would look up and find him, as if reassuring himself he was still there.

Before their connecting flight came in, though, Etienne could see the nerves creeping back. It manifested in the fingers Adam drummed against his thigh, the tense lines of his jaw, and the way he stared at the floor, baseball cap pulled low to minimize the chances of being approached.

With an hour before boarding left, Etienne couldn't stand it anymore. He put his book away, picked up his bag, and motioned for Adam to follow him.

He'd intended to take him for a sandwich, maybe a drink, something to soothe the tension strumming through Adam's body, but the bathroom sign caught his eye and another idea occurred to him.

Adam followed him inside, a question in his eyes. Etienne took his wrist and pulled him to the handicapped stall on the far end, locking the door behind them. The divider was set flush to the floor, so Etienne didn't even hesitate before pushing Adam into the corner and dropping to his knees on the—thankfully clean—floor in front of him.

"*Tenny*—" Adam's voice was strangled, but he was already hardening, a noticeable bulge in his pants.

"You have to be very quiet," Etienne said, looking up at him. "Can you do that, Cary?" He was working at Adam's waistband without waiting for a response. He got Adam's pants unzipped and pulled him out, enjoying the silken weight and glide as he pumped him a few times.

Adam's head fell back against the wall and he shoved a hand in his mouth.

Etienne smiled to himself and went to work.

He loved blowing Adam. It was one of his favorite things to do, he'd decided early on. Adam was so responsive, shuddering and twitching with every movement of Etienne's tongue, his hands coming to rest on Etienne's head—not to guide or demand, but simply to have a connection.

Adam was so obedient during sex, most of the time. Etienne suspected it had something to do with his position on the ice. He was seen as a leader, looked to for guidance during his shifts, even as a rookie. It made sense that he'd want to give up that control in bed, let someone else take over, even briefly. Etienne was happy to assume that responsibility. There were few things, not even sinking an impossible shot, that thrilled him the way Adam's utter surrender did.

He sped up, jacking him faster, until Adam's hands went tight in his hair and he stiffened, shaking as he emptied silently down Etienne's throat.

Etienne took it all, swallowing until Adam twitched and pushed weakly at his shoulder. Then he pulled off, tucking Adam's shaft away with gentle hands and zipping him up before standing.

Adam looked *wrecked*, sagging against the wall with bright spots of color in his cheeks and his lips bitten red, eyes dazed as he panted soundlessly.

Etienne moved in, pulling Adam against him and tucking his face into his throat. He could feel tiny puffs of air on his skin as Adam trembled in his arms.

"Breathe," he murmured. "Breathe, baby. Reel it in, you're okay. You're going to be fine. Your parents will still love you. Everything's okay."

Adam got his arms around Etienne's neck and held on tight. "It's so stupid," he mumbled into Etienne's throat. "Logically I know they won't, like... disown me or even be *bothered* by it. But I just—"

"I know," Etienne said, pressing a kiss to the side of Adam's head. "It feels like letting them down, like you're not 'living up to' whatever they had in mind because society has programmed you—and them—to get married to a pretty girl and have two perfect children and live a delightfully normal heterosexual life. It's fucking *stupid*, but that doesn't make it feel less real." He leaned back enough to meet Adam's eyes. "You're an incredible person, Adam Alexis Noah Caron," he said, and relished the scowl that covered Adam's face at that.

"You've been waiting to use that," Adam accused him, and Etienne laughed, not denying it.

He dropped a kiss on his nose and stepped back, assessing Adam's appearance. His color had returned to normal, eyes alert and no longer unfocused.

"Perfect," Etienne declared. "You no longer look like someone who had sex in a public bathroom." The outer door opened and Etienne cut himself off as Adam slapped a hand over his own mouth, eyes dancing with amusement. They waited in silence until the other man had left and then went out, discreetly washing their hands before reemerging into public.

22

THEY STEPPED off the plane in Seattle and a resounding cheer went up. Adam stopped so fast Etienne ran into him from behind, and they both stared at the crowd of people clustered around the gate, shouting Adam's name, beckoning to him, and holding out things for him to autograph.

Front and center was a curvy dark-haired young woman, holding a huge sign that read WELCOME ADAM CARON, TORONTO WOLVERINES SUPERSTAR, her dark blue eyes sparkling with glee.

"I'm going to *kill* her," Adam said under his breath, fixed a smile on his face, and walked over to greet the crowd, Etienne on his heels.

He spent thirty minutes signing autographs and enduring all the handshakes, hugs, and discreet gropes from fans before turning to glare at Noemi, who looked demurely innocent.

"Was that really necessary?"

"After the shit you pulled in May?" Noemi retorted. "Uh, yeah."

"Fine. Are we even now?"

Noemi pretended to think about it. "Introduce me to your friend and I'll let you know."

"Etienne, Noemi, my sister, nefarious mastermind and chaotic evil personified. Noemi, this is Etienne Brideau, and you are not allowed to prank him or in any other way inconvenience him when he's flown *all the way across the country* for your dumb wedding."

"As if I would," Noemi pouted. She took Etienne's hand, smiling up at him. "You're even taller than Adam, wow! Do you play hockey too?"

Adam rolled his eyes, hitching his bag up over his shoulder. "Can you please stop pretending Mom and Dad didn't already tell you everything that happened when they flew out?"

"Worth a try," Noemi said, and winked at Etienne.

Etienne's return smile was slow but said he was clearly charmed. Adam wanted to take his hand, just barely repressing the urge and clearing his throat.

"Baggage claim," he said. "Let's get out of here before Dr. Doom here decides to organize a flash mob or something."

"That was only a contingency plan in case the plane was late," Noemi protested, hurrying to catch up as Adam and Etienne set out for the carousels.

"Where are Mom and Dad?"

"Mom's in the car, I have to text her so she can bring it around, and Dad's at work." Noemi, barely five foot two, was nearly running to keep up with their much longer legs, and out of pure impish spite, Adam lengthened his stride. He should have remembered her trick from years past, but it was too late as she broke into an actual run and leaped onto his back with a thud.

Adam staggered, nearly dropping his bag, and Noemi locked her heels around his waist, one elbow on his shoulder.

"Asshole," she said triumphantly in his ear.

Etienne's eyes were wide as he stared at them and Adam wheezed for breath.

"'S fine," he managed. "Brought that—literally—on myself." He started walking again, Noemi piggyback, attracting more than a few startled and curious stares. Adam had learned early on that trying to make Noemi do something that wasn't her idea was nearly impossible. If he tried to get rid of her, she'd cling tighter. So he smiled at the gawkers and kept walking.

Halfway there, Noemi loosened her grip and slid to the ground. Her dark hair was still perfectly in place, eyes bright as she arched a challenging brow.

"Lesson firmly relearned," Adam said. He laughed out loud suddenly and hugged her. "Hi, Nomes. Are you excited to get married?"

Noemi hugged him back. "So damn excited," she said against his shirt. "I can't wait for you to meet him. Let's get your bags so we can go."

Adam grinned at Etienne over her head and Etienne smiled back, his eyes warm but with a lingering sadness in them. He'd never had an annoying little sister and a family that loved him, Adam remembered with a pang.

Well, he did now. He fell into step beside Etienne as Noemi dashed ahead and took his hand for one brief, stolen moment, trying to convey everything he was feeling with a single touch. Etienne squeezed back and then let go, a split-second before Noemi turned to urge them on.

COLETTE HAD the Range Rover pulled up when they got outside, and she hopped out to greet them, hugging Adam fiercely and kissing both his cheeks before turning to give the same treatment to Etienne, who looked bemused as she went up on tiptoe to hug him.

Noemi elbowed Adam in the ribs, making him grunt. "Help me with the bags."

He followed her around to the back while Colette talked to Etienne and heaved the luggage inside.

"Is he always this quiet?" Noemi asked.

"Like he could get a word in edgewise around you," Adam retorted. He slung the last bag in and went back around to where Etienne was saying something that made Colette laugh. "Let's go, I'm starving."

"You're always starving," Etienne said.

"How many times a day does he try to eat donuts?" Noemi piped up, grinning.

Adam sighed loudly. "*Please* can we go? I've got muscle mass to maintain here, and so does Tenny."

They piled into the car, Adam and Etienne in the backseat and Colette and Noemi in the front.

Noemi twisted and shoved several sheets of paper at Adam. "Your itinerary."

Adam scanned it and groaned out loud. "Suit fittings? Oh, hang on, waterskiing—that I can do. Wedding rehearsal and then rehearsal dinner. Jesus, Nomes, this sounds so boring I already want to die."

"I did my best to balance the tedious activities with fun ones," Noemi said. She fixed him with a sudden glare. "But make no mistake, you *are* doing them, boring or not."

Adam slouched in his seat, scowling. "So when do we get to meet this guy? I still haven't signed off on him, you know."

Noemi's nose went in the air. "As if I need your permission. Tonight, at dinner."

"What does he do?" Etienne asked.

Noemi glanced at him and smiled. "He's a goalie for the Kingfishers. We believe in keeping it in the family."

"In the family?"

"Oh, didn't I mention?" Adam said. "Dad was the assistant coach for the Kingfishers—he just got promoted. He's the head coach now."

Etienne's mouth fell open. "He—and you—" He punched Adam in the arm—*ow*—as Noemi giggled. "I can't *believe* you didn't tell me, you asshole!"

Adam shrugged, rubbing his shoulder, and slanted a grin at him. "Like you needed more stress before you stepped on the ice."

"Etienne, honey, how's your season going?" Colette asked.

"It's going well, ma'am," Etienne said, giving Adam a glare that said *this isn't over*. Adam looked forward to resuming the discussion. "I actually got called up to the Freeze and I'm finishing the season there."

"So Adam told us," Colette said, smiling at him in the mirror. "Congratulations, you deserve it. And getting close to the playoffs?"

"What line do you play?" Noemi wanted to know.

"Third, but I've been put on the second line several times," Etienne told her. "It's a lot harder than being a Thunder, but I'm hanging in there."

"He's killing it," Adam corrected. "His fanbase is

growing steadily and he gets writer's cramp signing autographs."

Etienne snorted. "One website does not a fanbase make."

"We all started somewhere, grasshopper," Adam said sagely.

Etienne shoved him and Adam shoved back. They scuffled for a minute, trapped in place by their seatbelts, pushing and tussling until Adam's head ended up somehow wedged under Etienne's arm.

"Tap out," Etienne told him.

Breathless with laughter, Adam struggled to get free, but Etienne's arm would not be budged.

"Boys," Colette said mildly, and Etienne let go like he'd been burned.

"Sorry," he said.

Colette smiled at him again. "I'm glad you and Adam are friends, Etienne."

The tips of Etienne's ears pinkened. "You can call me Tenny."

23

ADAM'S PARENTS' house was about what Etienne had expected. Three stories, dark-shingled, with a wide veranda that wrapped around most of the building and a turret room on one corner, it was warm and welcoming, with a lush green lawn and several huge trees drooping protectively over the house.

Adam nudged Etienne with an elbow. "Five bucks they put you in the turret room," he said out of the corner of his mouth as they lifted the bags out of the bag.

"Is that a good thing?" Etienne followed Adam up the flagstone path to the front door, where Noemi was waiting for them.

Adam just grinned at him and poked Noemi in the ribs as he passed her, dodging the punch she threw in retaliation.

Inside were hardwood floors, scuffed and worn with age but gleaming with a soft shine, and a wide hall filled with sunlight. Pictures hung on the walls, of Adam and Noemi at various ages, staged family portraits and candids hanging side by side. Etienne wanted to linger, see what Adam had looked like as a little boy, but Noemi was already ushering them upstairs, so Etienne reluctantly pulled himself away and followed her and Adam up the circular staircase to the second floor.

The middle space was open so Etienne could see to the entryway below them, doors standing open to his right. Noemi led them to the end of the hallway and pushed open another door as Adam laughed.

"Told you," he said.

Etienne stepped into the turret room, looking around in awe. It was perfectly circular, the walls a silvery brown and hung with tapestries and vibrant artwork in rich reds and golds. On one side was a full-size bed, heaped high with crimson and golden pillows and looking deliciously comfortable, if slightly too short for Etienne's height.

"Make yourself at home," Noemi said cheerfully. "Adam, you're in your old room."

Adam saluted and then shoved her out the door as Etienne ran a finger along the bedframe. He shut the door before turning to Etienne and leaning up against it.

"What do you think?"

Etienne smiled at him and sat down on the bed. "It's beautiful."

Adam crossed to stand above him. Etienne tipped his head back to look up at him and Adam ran a thumb along his jaw, making him shiver.

"I wish you could sleep with me," he murmured. "Maybe after I tell my parents."

Etienne laughed soundlessly up at him. "Are you

just going to barge in and tell them, all so you don't have to sleep away from me?"

Adam's answering grin was wicked, eyes dancing. "You underestimate just how much I like sleeping *with* you, pal."

Etienne caught Adam's hips and pulled until Adam slid onto his lap, straddling him, chest to chest. Adam looped his arms around Etienne's shoulders and bent to kiss him. He tasted like the apple juice he'd been drinking on the plane, sweet and tart. Etienne squeezed his hip but pushed him away enough to break the kiss.

"Don't you dare make me hard," he warned, and Adam laughed, but then sobered.

"I probably won't tell them tonight," he admitted.

"Okay," Etienne said.

"I'm gonna," Adam said.

"I know," Etienne said.

"I just... I need to make sure the time is right." Adam leaned forward and pressed their foreheads together and Etienne closed his eyes, reveling in the smell and feel of him.

"You'll be fine," he murmured. "Who else is up here with me?"

"I'm two doors down," Adam said, resettling his weight more firmly across Etienne's thighs. "Not sure who else will be up here. Great-aunt Hen, maybe?"

"Hen?"

"Henrietta," Adam clarified. "Ninety if she's a day and crazy as a squirrel in winter. She'll probably pinch your ass, be warned."

Etienne laughed quietly.

"Boys!" Colette's voice floated up from downstairs.

Adam scrambled off Etienne's lap and Etienne

followed him onto the landing. Colette smiled up at them.

"Adam, honey, your father will be here in a few minutes. When you're done showing Etienne the house and you're settled in, come on downstairs so we can visit."

Adam fired off a snappy salute, making her laugh, and jerked his head at Etienne. "Wanna see my room?"

"Hell yeah," Etienne said, following him down the hall. A bathroom separated his turret room from the room Adam was currently entering, and Etienne's stomach eased. It… helped, knowing Adam was only two doors away.

Inside, Adam had flung himself on a twin-size bed, arms and legs splayed. Etienne looked around at the posters on the walls, amusement welling.

"Beliveau, Crosby, Lemieux, Datsyuk… how long have you been building this collection?"

"Since I was old enough to handle a puck," Adam said, flat on his back.

Etienne stepped farther into the room. On one wall was a shelf holding trophies and ribbons. He'd led his minor and major junior teams in points and assists, named captain several times, and MVP even more. Next to the trophies was a shadow box with several pucks mounted inside. Etienne looked more closely at the signatures scrawled across them.

"Seriously, you got Gretzky to sign a puck for you?"

Adam propped himself on his elbows, looking pleased. "My parents took us to LA when Gretzky was still on the ice—I was just a kid. My dad knows their coach, of course, so we got to meet the players. He's really nice, by the way."

"That's fucking *awesome*," Etienne said, running a reverent finger down the maplewood.

Adam beckoned with one finger but Etienne laughed, shaking his head.

"I'm not making out with you in your childhood room, Cary."

Adam pouted.

"Bed would probably collapse anyway," Etienne pointed out.

Adam grinned at him, dark and wicked, and heat curled through Etienne's belly.

"I know how to get you over here," Adam said, and put a hand down his pants.

Etienne choked on his tongue and nearly brained himself on the door escaping the room. Adam's laughter floated after him as Etienne dashed down the stairs. He stopped at the bottom, took a deep breath to compose himself, and followed the sound of voices.

Colette and Noemi were in the kitchen. They looked up and smiled at the sight of him, and Etienne smiled back.

"Where's Adam?" Colette asked.

"Putting his stuff away," Etienne said, suppressing amusement. "He'll be right down. Can I help?"

"Check out the manners," Noemi said admiringly. "Etienne, any chance you can teach my brother a thing or two?"

"Pretty sure no one alive can do that. Although maybe if Lemieux tried, he'd listen," Etienne told her, and she dissolved in giggles.

"Tenny, would you chop carrots for me?" Colette asked, pushing a cutting board and knife toward him. "You can wash your hands in the sink here."

"So, Noemi," Etienne said, settling in with the

knife and vegetables. "Adam's told me a little about you. Tell me about your fiance."

Noemi's face lit up. "His name is Eli. He's a goalie for the Kingfishers. He got traded here two years ago from the Ravens, and he's got a five year contract here, so we'll be in the area at least a while longer, I hope."

"And what do you do?" Etienne asked.

"I'm an assistant coach for a private Seattle college hockey team," Noemi said.

Etienne blinked. Whatever he'd expected to hear, it hadn't been that. Noemi blinked at him demurely as if knowing what was going through his head, and he laughed to himself.

"That's amazing. Do you get a lot of crap for being a woman coaching men?"

"My fair share," Noemi said. "I'm taking my time. It's not easy for women in sports in general— convincing a bunch of very large men on knife shoes that I can look like this and still know more about the sport than they do takes some doing."

Etienne hesitated. "Sorry, 'look like this'?"

Noemi gestured to her figure but there was something like approval in her eyes.

"But… why does it matter if you're…." Etienne chewed his lip, looking for the word.

"Zaftig," Noemi said helpfully. "Curvy, if you want. Plus-size, although I hate that term and will punch you if you use it."

"Be nice," Colette murmured without looking up.

"The *point*," Noemi said, "is my ability to perform my job well and my knowledge of said job is constantly questioned due to my appearance *and* gender. It makes me a little twitchy, so thank you for not being a douche."

Etienne shrugged uncomfortably. "You're welcome?"

Noemi smiled brilliantly at him. "I like you," she announced.

Etienne returned the smile. "Likewise."

Adam clattered down the stairs and into the kitchen, dropping a kiss on his mother's cheek and stealing a carrot from Etienne.

"What's for dinner?" he asked, mouth full.

"Adam, wash your hands and start slicing bread," Colette ordered. "Butter and garlic, please."

ETIENNE WATCHED Adam and his family as they moved around each other in the kitchen, movements easy and comfortable. They'd clearly done this dance a thousand times, Etienne thought, smiling as Adam caught Noemi and spun her on the spot before dipping her into a backbend that had her sputtering laughter and threats.

Adam set her back on her feet and caught Etienne's eye. His smile widened and Etienne cleared his throat, looking away hastily before he did something stupid like kissing him and blew the story open.

Thankfully, the door opened just then.

"We're home!" William called. He appeared in the doorway as Etienne shot upright.

Head fucking coach for the Kingfishers, he thought. He was *definitely* taking this out on Adam's ass later.

William smiled, that same slow, lovely smile Adam had, and held out his hand. "Etienne, how was your flight?"

"Good, sir," Etienne said, accepting the hand. "Adam is a good traveling companion."

"Hey Dad," Adam said, putting the bread down to give him a hug. "He's lying, I complained the entire time."

"Of course you did," William said, lips twitching. "Adam, Etienne, this is Eli McKenna."

Eli was small and slimly built for a goalie, not even six feet tall, with piercing gray eyes and sandy blond hair. His smile was friendly as he held out a hand to Etienne and then Adam.

"Nice to meet you both," he said, his voice measured and calm. "Adam, you're doing some great things out there, and Etienne, I hope you don't mind—I looked up game tapes of you. Your footwork is incredible."

"Uh, I'm here too?" Noemi said, popping up beside Eli's elbow.

Eli laughed and put an arm around her, dropping a kiss on her upturned nose. "Hey there, bad penny."

Noemi grinned, wriggling as if it was a compliment.

24

THERE WAS something odd about Eli and Noemi, Etienne thought, but he couldn't put his finger on it. He watched them at dinner, curious, as Eli said something to Adam. The affection between him and Noemi was easy and comfortable, their hands laced together on the table. Colette leaned forward and asked Etienne a question.

"I'm sorry, what?" Etienne said.

Colette's eyes crinkled like her son's. "I said, the Freeze are close to the playoffs, right? How are you meshing with the team?"

"Pretty well, I think," Etienne said, uneasily aware that everyone was looking at him. "Li and Jetty are great, and we've even started on the second line a few times."

"He's leading the team for assists," Adam said, and there was no mistaking the pride in his voice.

"We should get on the ice while you're here," Eli said, raising his eyebrows.

"What are we doing tomorrow?" Adam asked Noemi.

"Suit-fitting and waterskiing."

"Perfect, let's hit the rink after," Adam said.

That settled, the conversation turned to general topics. Etienne watched the family dynamics, hiding his amusement as Noemi teased Adam, who pretended to be wounded, and William and Colette exchanged fond smiles.

Finally, comfortably full, Colette mustered help getting the table cleared. She shooed Etienne away when he tried to wash dishes, though.

"You get points for trying," she told him, "but that's why I had children."

"Shameless exploitation of our free labor," Adam complained. "Go in the den with Dad and Eli, Tens. I'll be there soon."

As IT TURNED OUT, Eli stayed to help with cleanup too, leaving Etienne alone with William.

"I earned my freedom the hard way," William told him, eyes creased with amusement. "Thirty years of marriage, fifteen years of washing dishes right alongside her until Adam was old enough to take over—now I only have to help if neither kid is home. We've been watching your playing. You're filling in that second and third line well."

Etienne ducked his head. "Thank you, sir."

William eyed him. "I'm not gonna be able to stop you from calling me that, am I?"

Etienne laughed. "Probably not, sir. Even if you

weren't the head coach for the Kingfishers, you're still Adam's father."

William nodded as if to himself. "You should know, Etienne, that Adam has our full support unconditionally."

Etienne stiffened. *Unconditionally.* Did he mean what Etienne *thought* he meant?

"Even if he quit hockey and decided to teach art or something, we'd back him a hundred percent," William continued.

Etienne forced himself to relax. "That's... a lot of hockey parents aren't that understanding."

"We taught our kids from an early age that happiness was important, and not chasing a dream we imposed on them. They both chose some form of hockey and I'm glad they did, but nothing they do could alter how much we love them."

Was it Etienne's imagination or did William look particularly intense, like he was trying to say something else? He was saved by Adam bursting into the room and flinging himself on the couch beside Etienne.

"Hi," he said. "What are you guys talking about?"

"You," Etienne said, fighting the urge to smile fondly as Adam preened.

"A worthy topic," Adam agreed. "How's the team this year, Dad?"

They began to discuss prospects as Etienne watched them. Adam and his father had an easy chemistry that spoke of a strong bond and mutual respect. Etienne both envied Adam that and was happy, deep in his bones, that Adam had it. He reached for him and stopped himself just in time, jerking his hand back.

Adam sent him an inquiring look and Etienne shook his head. Adam's eyes narrowed.

"Oh, fuck it," he said clearly. "Dad, I—"

The door opened and the rest of the family appeared. William gestured furiously at Colette as Adam snapped his mouth shut.

"Goddammit Colette, I was about to—I mean, Adam was trying to tell me something."

Colette's eyebrows shot up. "Adam, wouldn't you rather tell me?"

William shot Colette a dirty look. Etienne glanced at Adam, who appeared faintly horrified. He racked his brain for a rescue as Colette sat beside William and Noemi and Eli settled on the far divan.

"He was just gonna tell him what a good season he's been having," Etienne said desperately.

But Adam shook his head. His nostrils were pinched, his mouth set, but he faced his parents with his head up and shoulders back. "No," he said. "No. I'm—" He sucked in air. "I'm gay," he said, the words dropping into quiet air like a stone.

Etienne held his breath, watching Adam's parents, who were utterly still for one long moment. Then Colette turned to William.

"This doesn't mean you won."

"Excuse me, that's exactly what it means," William sputtered.

Etienne blinked. He met Adam's eyes, just as confused as he felt.

"He was trying to tell Dad first," Noemi said, sounding delighted. "Dad definitely won."

William punched the air as Adam looked between him and Colette, his mouth hanging open.

"You—you…."

"Oh honey." Colette stood and pulled Adam to his feet and into her arms. Over her shoulder, Adam looked poleaxed, and Etienne fought a sudden hysterical giggle. "We love you so much, darling boy."

Adam clutched at her shirt. "You're—you're not disappointed?"

William stood and joined them, wrapping his arms around both of them. "It'll take more than who you love to disappoint us, son." The deep affection in his voice made tears prick Etienne's eyes.

Adam choked on a laugh that sounded suspiciously like a sob. "Good, because he's o-on the couch."

Etienne froze. Adam hadn't meant it that way. It had been a figurative thing, using Etienne as an example of loving a man and not a woman. Adam tore away from his parents, reaching for Etienne, the apologies already spilling from his lips.

"I'm sorry, I'm so sorry, I didn't mean to put you on the spot, Tenny, please don't be mad, it just popped out—"

Etienne shook his head to dispel the dizziness, gripping Adam's hands but watching William and Colette smiling at each other behind Adam's back.

"I think they already knew," he said carefully. "About us—all of it. Didn't you?"

Colette's smile was brilliant. "Well, obviously. Oh, come here."

Etienne scrambled to his feet and Colette cupped his face in both cool hands. Her eyes were warm with sincerity.

"You are so good for my son," she told him. "And I am so, so glad he has you."

Etienne's throat was suddenly tight. "He's good for

me too," he managed, and Colette pulled him into a hug.

It took awhile to sort out the embraces and tearful declarations, but finally Etienne and Adam found themselves back on the couch. This time, though, Adam was tucked in under Etienne's arm, head on Etienne's shoulder, and their hands were twined together between them.

Etienne caught Eli's eye over Adam's head. Eli smiled at him, but there was something in his expression that looked almost wistful. But then Noemi tugged on his shoulder and Eli bent so she could whisper in his ear, and the moment was gone, affection replacing the odd expression.

"So how long have you known?" Adam asked his mother.

Colette snorted. "Please. What kind of friend drops everything to nurse you for three days? Not to mention the way you were glued to your phone every second you were apart."

"Grinning like a doofus," William added, a smile on his own face.

"And you really don't... care?" Adam said, sounding tentative. "You always talked about kids—"

"Well, of course I want grandchildren," Colette said. "But you're both—" indicating Noemi "—too young still anyway. Besides, you can adopt or use a surrogate when it's time."

Adam relaxed more into Etienne's side. Etienne couldn't resist dropping a kiss on his hair.

"Now that that's out of the way," Noemi said, "the

suit fitting is tomorrow at ten. Daved and Morgan are meeting us there. Then brunch and waterskiing after."

"Dav and Morgan are Kingfishers," Adam told Etienne.

"My groomsmen," Eli added.

The conversation turned to wedding plans and Etienne tuned it out, concentrating on Adam tucked against him, the soft hair tickling his nose and his cheek on Etienne's shoulder. He glanced up and caught Colette's eye.

She smiled at him and it held a wealth of emotion. *I'm glad it's you,* her smile said. *Take care of him.*

I will, Etienne told her silently, and Colette smiled wider, dabbing surreptitiously at her eyes.

25

THEY WENT upstairs hand in hand, Etienne yawning. Adam felt weightless with relief, delirious joy threatening to carry him into the air and only Etienne's firm grip keeping him on the ground.

At the top of the stairs, Etienne squeezed Adam's hand before letting go. "I'll see you in the morning."

Adam was brought back to earth with a thump. "Wait, what? But—"

Etienne put a finger over Adam's mouth. "If we fall into bed together five minutes after telling them we're a couple, everyone downstairs is going to know exactly what we're doing. I'm sorry, Cary, but that makes me uncomfortable."

Adam grimaced. Etienne looked unhappy too, but his jaw was set.

"Why do you always say no to me?" Adam said, keeping his tone teasing. He leaned in, hoping Etienne would get the hint, and he did, gathering Adam into his arms.

"Because someone has to keep your ego in check,"

he rumbled, voice deep against Adam's ear where it was pressed to his chest.

Adam smiled to himself. "Will you at least kiss me?"

Etienne put a finger under his chin and tipped his head back. Adam closed his eyes as their lips met. He loved kissing Etienne, the way he devoted himself to the task with single-minded focus. Adam was used to being noticed, but he was never *seen*, not the way Etienne saw him. Etienne looked past the surface, past Adam's appearance to who he truly was beneath.

They were both breathing unsteadily when they finally broke apart. Etienne smiled down at him.

"Goodnight, Cary," he murmured.

ADAM CRAWLED into his too-small bed, twisting to make himself fit without hanging over the edges. The house creaked and whispered around him, the usual nightly ritual of settling in for the night. When he was a kid, Adam had pretended the house was talking to him, telling him what it had seen that day. He closed his eyes, putting a hand against the wall. Etienne was so close, just two doors away. It would be the work of a moment to slip down there, no one the wiser, but Etienne had asked him not to. Adam would respect his wishes even if it killed him.

His phone buzzed. Etienne had sent him a Snapchat. Adam opened it and gulped at the sight of Etienne's abs, with their light dusting of hair that thickened on his stomach. Another picture came through as Adam was looking at the first. This one was of Etienne's hand down his pants.

Adam covered his mouth to muffle the groan as he went from semi- to *very* hard in record time. He fumbled one-handed with his shirt and managed to snap a picture of his own chest and abs, which he sent back.

Nice, Etienne replied. *Show me more.*

Adam pushed his pants down just enough to expose the vee of his hip. He knew just how much Etienne loved that part of his body.

Sure enough, another message came through. It was Etienne's cock, flushed and hard. *I'm so hard and it's all your fault.*

Adam laughed soundlessly, muffling the noise in his elbow. His phone buzzed again.

Come here, dammit.

Adam was up and out the door in a flash. He soft-footed it down the hall, avoiding the boards that always creaked, to ease Etienne's door open.

Etienne was sitting up in bed waiting for him. He held out a hand and Adam shut the door before crossing the room on silent feet to crawl on top of him.

"Hi," he whispered.

"Shh," Etienne murmured, tugging him down into a kiss.

There was no rush, no urgency, despite the illicit thrill of what they were doing. Etienne's tongue met and tangled with Adam's, his fingers reverent on Adam's shoulders, skimming down his spine and under the waistband of his pajamas. He squeezed and kneaded Adam's buttocks, deepening the kiss until Adam was gasping against Etienne's mouth, grinding down into his body and silently begging for more.

"You have to be quiet," Etienne whispered in

Adam's ear. "Can you do that?" One finger ghosted over Adam's hole, pressing lightly before disappearing again.

Adam shuddered. "You can—*ah*—make me," he managed.

Etienne's grin was wolfish, teeth glinting in the moonlight. "On your back."

Adam scrambled to obey, kicking and tugging his pants and shirt off as he went. Etienne moved more slowly, bending to rummage in the luggage beside the bed before turning back.

"You packed lube?" Adam whispered. "You Boy Scout, you."

"Hush," Etienne ordered, but Adam could hear the laughter threatening in his voice. He grinned, crossing his arms behind his head and arching his back in the moonlight dappling his skin.

Etienne's breath caught and he pulled his clothes off quickly before covering Adam's body with his own.

"You're the most beautiful thing I've ever seen," he growled in Adam's ear.

Adam preened. It was different when Etienne said it, somehow. It meant more, in a way that Adam was almost afraid to look at head-on. Instead he wrapped his arms around Etienne's neck and tugged at his hair.

"So are you."

It was a challenge of sorts. Would Etienne argue, like he had last time? Was he learning to accept it, or would he fight it again?

Etienne was very still, above him. Adam leaned back to see his face. Etienne opened his mouth. Closed it again. Dropped a quick kiss on Adam's lips, and whispered, "Thank you."

Adam smiled radiantly up at him. "Are you going to fuck me or not?"

Etienne caught his mouth in a ravenous kiss this time, teeth and tongue and devouring breath. A bottle cap clicked and then slick fingers probed Adam's entrance. He clenched up instinctively as they nudged inside, forcing himself to relax on a deep sigh.

Etienne rewarded him with another kiss, breath hot on Adam's face, even as he pushed in farther. Adam moaned softly against his mouth and Etienne bit at his lip sharply, a reminder to keep quiet.

"Can't," Adam managed. "Feels too good, Tens—"

Etienne hissed under his breath, planted one more kiss on Adam's lips, and went to his elbow, covering Adam's mouth with one big palm.

Adam made a grateful involuntary noise, muffled against Etienne's skin, and bucked up into the hand over his mouth even as he tried to grind down on the fingers in his ass. Etienne's hand over his mouth tightened as he added a third finger and Adam's eyes rolled back in his head.

He was a raw, aching nerve, strung breathlessly tight with want and need, every inch of his skin an instrument for Etienne to play. And play it he did, with nips and licks and quick, hard sucks until Adam was thrashing, pinned down by Etienne's uncompromising grip. He'd never felt safer, held so punishingly tight, and he whimpered into Etienne's hand, begging wordlessly.

Etienne withdrew his fingers and went to his knees between Adam's spread legs. His eyes glinted in the moonlight. "I can't fuck you hard," he whispered. "They *will* hear us."

Adam tried to catch his breath as Etienne lifted his

thighs and slung them over his arms. "Not gonna last anyway," he managed.

"Be quiet," Etienne said, and that was his only warning before he slid home.

Adam arched off the bed, mouth falling open, and Etienne slammed a hand down over his mouth again, folding forward and tucking his other arm under Adam's neck so they were joined from head to hip, Etienne's chest pressing Adam into the mattress and his breath rocky and harsh in Adam's ear.

Adam panted rapidly, turning his face just enough to press his cheek to Etienne's. *I love you*, he thought but couldn't say, not with Etienne's palm covering his mouth and his cock scattering his wits. *I love you, I love you, please fuck me—*

Etienne moved his hips in slow, carefully controlled motions, rocking in and out of Adam's body in microscopic waves. To Adam's over-sensitized nerves, every move felt like sandpaper against his skin, simultaneously too much and somehow not enough. Etienne's breathing hitched and he pushed a fraction deeper. He set a slow, steady rhythm, hips working mercilessly until Adam could feel everything all the way up into his teeth, every thrust enough to make his eyes roll back with how *good* it felt to be taken over, surrounded and invaded by this man.

Adam was dimly aware of Etienne gasping, losing his rhythm, and shuddering through his orgasm, and he clenched his body tight, taking it all, loving him fiercely and silently until Etienne sagged against him.

He didn't pull out, though. Instead he nipped at Adam's ear. "Touch yourself," he ordered in a ragged whisper. "Come with me inside you."

Adam, still gagged by Etienne's hand, didn't try to

come up with a response. He worked a hand between them, the first touch to his neglected cock making him jerk as sparks skittered through his nerve endings. Etienne lifted his head enough to see Adam's face, hips beginning to work again in tiny, fractional movements as Adam stroked himself.

In the end, there was nothing Adam could do but fall over the edge, body locking up tight and making Etienne hiss in triumph as Adam spilled between them in silent bliss.

Etienne moved his hand and kissed his jaw as Adam fell back against the covers, sucking in air. He slid out, making Adam stifle another moan, and lay down beside him, tucking Adam's limp frame in close.

"Tenny," Adam whispered. His eyes kept closing and he couldn't keep a grip on reality.

"Yeah," Etienne murmured.

"It's you," Adam managed, and let go of consciousness.

26

THE SUIT-FITTING WASN'T the torture Adam had expected it to be, with a tailor close to their ages who cracked jokes that made them double over with laughter as she measured them. Adam couldn't remember the last time he'd been this purely happy. He was at home with his family, his baby sister was marrying a good man, his career was going nowhere but up, and he had Etienne, who was currently wiping tears of mirth from his eyes.

Etienne looked up and caught his gaze, and his smile widened. Adam grinned back.

From the couch, Noemi made gagging noises. Adam flipped her off without looking.

THEY HEADED for the marina after brunch, Eli driving, Noemi off to do more wedding preparation. The rented boat was waiting for them, all the necessary gear aboard already. Adam hopped over the rail and

213

settled next to Etienne on the bench as Eli, Daved, and Morgan followed them on.

Adam had met Daved briefly a few times and liked him, with his easy, open smile and friendly brown eyes. Morgan was more reserved, saying very little, but Adam had a feeling his green eyes didn't miss much.

"Have you skied before?" Adam asked Etienne.

Etienne shook his head as Eli fired up the engine and Morgan cast off the moorings.

"I'll show you, if you want," Adam said.

Eli took the boat well past the groups of people swimming and lazing about on the water, out into the open sea. The waves were gentle, and Daved took the first turn as Adam explained the technicalities to Etienne. Eli gunned it and they were off, hull slicing cleanly through the water.

It happened fast, so fast Adam didn't have time to brace himself. One minute he was explaining how to hold the grip and leaning forward to get a beer from the cooler, and the next he was flung against the railing.

His head hit the brass with a loud crack and Adam slid to the floor of the boat, dazed, as Eli swore and killed the motor and Etienne scrambled to Adam's side.

"Are you okay? Fuck, Adam, talk to me, how many fingers am I holding up?"

Adam blinked. His vision was blurring, two and three Etiennes swimming in front of him with identical looks of worry on their faces.

"'M fine," he managed. He lifted a hand to his head, wincing as his fingers found the sore spot and Eli knelt beside them.

"I'm so sorry," he said. "There was a seal, came out of nowhere, I didn't want to hit it. Are you okay?"

Adam waved his concern off. "Help me up," he told Etienne, who hooked both hands under his armpits and easily hauled him upright. "I'm fine, really," Adam said to Eli, once on his feet. Eli looked unconvinced.

"We should go back. If I kill her brother before the wedding, Noemi will murder me."

Head throbbing, Adam didn't argue. By the time they were back at the dock, an intense headache had set in behind his eyes. He was dimly aware of Etienne calling a ride, leaning into his shoulder as they waited. When the car arrived, Etienne gently bundled Adam into the back, sliding in after him.

His fingers were careful as he examined Adam's head. "How are you feeling?" he murmured.

Adam closed his eyes. "Hurts."

"Do you think it's another concussion?"

Adam shook his head, then winced. "I don't—not sure, but I don't think so. Doesn't feel the same. It just... hurts."

"Let me see your eyes for a minute," Etienne said. He held Adam's chin in one gentle hand and used the flashlight on his phone to peer into Adam's pupils as Adam tried desperately not to flinch away. Finally, Etienne put the phone back in his pocket. "Your pupils are the same size, and they're dilating evenly. I think you're okay, but I want your mom to back me up."

AT HIS PARENTS' house, Colette exclaimed over the bump on Adam's head. Adam leaned against her, eyes sliding shut again, and Colette stroked his hair as she examined the injury and then looked at his eyes.

"Tenny's right," she finally declared. "It's a bump, but I don't think you have a concussion. Do you want to go to the emergency room?"

"*God* no," Adam said flatly. "I just want to lie down for a bit. I'll be fine, really."

Etienne followed him upstairs and Adam went not to his room but to the turret with its bigger bed. He kicked off his shoes and stretched out cautiously on top of the covers with a ginger sigh.

"C'mon," he said, face half-buried in a pillow. He felt the mattress dip as Etienne slid on and gathered Adam close to him, one arm going around his waist. Adam relaxed. "Much better," he slurred, and fell asleep.

ADAM WOKE Etienne by stretching and rolling on top of him. Etienne, flat on his back, caught Adam's hips reflexively and blinked sleep out of his eyes.

"How are you feeling?"

Adam hummed appreciatively. "I love how gravelly your voice gets when you first wake up."

"Answer the question," Etienne said, fingers tightening on Adam's hips.

"I'm fine," Adam said. "Not even a headache. And I'm really, *really* horny." He ground his length against Etienne's abdomen, making him gasp as arousal careened through him.

Still, he pushed it back to peer into Adam's eyes. "You're sure?"

In answer, Adam rubbed against him again, the

challenge clear in his eyes. Etienne swore and rolled them, pinning Adam beneath him and shoving a hand down his pants.

He jacked him hard and fast, eyes locked on Adam's the whole time, until Adam was panting and writhing, one leg thrown over Etienne's hips and silent pleas falling from his mouth.

Etienne drove him to the edge and over it, Adam locking up beneath him as he spilled wet and hot over Etienne's fist. Then he let go and straddled him, pushing his own pants down and stroking himself until he came with a shudder on Adam's perfect abs, painting them white as Adam whispered filthy encouragement.

When he settled back into his body, Adam smiled up at him, lazy and replete.

"That was nice," he murmured.

Etienne kissed him.

"Ready to go skating?" Adam asked.

Etienne jerked his head up. "You can't be serious."

"Why not? I told you I was fine."

"Adam, you just hit your head, only a few months after sustaining a fairly severe concussion. Are you sure getting on the ice the same *day* is a good idea?"

Adam scowled. "It doesn't hurt," he said mulishly. "I want to skate with you, Tens. You and Eli and the others. I miss being on the ice. Please?"

Etienne swore under his breath. "Let the record show that I am *not* in favor of this," he finally said. "But you're a grown-ass man and I guess you know your own body well enough to know if this is something you can do."

Adam's smile was almost enough to wipe away

Etienne's misgivings as he reached up and pulled Etienne down into another kiss.

HE LIKED THE SEATTLE ICE, Etienne decided. It felt smooth and sweet beneath his blades, just the right amount of grip. He circled the rink a few times, keeping a sharp eye on Adam, who'd put on a helmet without arguing and was currently warming up by going through a drill Etienne had taught him.

"More weight on your toe in that last corner," Etienne called.

Adam flipped a hand in acknowledgment and did it again, this time flawlessly, as the others stepped out onto the ice.

"Two-on-two, Eli in goal?" Daved asked Etienne.

"Sounds good to me. Adam!"

Adam sheared off his circle and skidded to a halt beside Etienne, spraying him with ice. He grinned when Etienne glowered at him.

"Two-on-two," Etienne said. "You up for it?"

Adam's grin turned hungry. "Let's do this."

ETIENNE FORGOT his concern in the sheer joy of the ice beneath his blades, the wind whistling in his ears as he and Adam passed the puck back and forth between them, keeping it away from Morgan and Daved in an effortless give-and-take down the ice. As they neared the goal, Eli crouching in front of it in all his gear, Etienne faked right and sent the puck to Adam on a drop pass. Adam caught it on the backhand and sank it behind Eli's left knee.

Etienne frowned, circling behind the net. He'd expected Adam to catch it on the forehand and put it top shelf—but Adam collided with him just then, whooping like he'd won the Stanley Cup, and Etienne laughed, hugging him back.

Five goals later, Daved called a halt, gasping for breath.

"Time-out," he panted. "It's like you fuckers are mind-melded or something."

Adam skated a lazy circle around Daved's lanky form. "When you've got it, you've got it, Davvy my boy."

Daved pulled off a glove and gave him the finger.

"Now, now," Etienne said mildly. "Don't make him feel worse about himself, Adam. It's not his fault he can't keep up."

"No, that's *my* fault," William said, stepping out onto the ice. Both Morgan and Daved stiffened.

"Hi Dad!" Adam chirped.

William fixed Morgan and Daved with a steely gaze. "Tenny here isn't even NHL yet and he's making you look like you're playing junior hockey. What happened to the conditioning drills I made you do? You forget how to play a decent defensive line?"

"Coach," Morgan protested, "did you see the way they move? It's like Tenny knows where Cary's going to be six moves ahead of time, and Cary sends the puck to him without even *looking* and Tenny puts it home, it's not *natural*."

"It's called teamwork," William said. "Something I *thought* I'd taught you."

Etienne grinned at Adam, who returned it.

"Come on," William continued. "Three-on-two, maybe we can beat them."

Adam banged his stick on the ice. "Bring it, old man!"

$$\times$$

THEY RETURNED to the house sweaty and laughing, pleasantly exhausted. Colette inspected Adam's head again but pronounced him in no danger, prompting Adam to stick his tongue out at Etienne.

"How's your vision?" Etienne asked him later, when they had a moment alone. Was it his imagination or did Adam stiffen?

"It's fine," Adam said lightly. He batted Etienne's hand away when he tried to hold up a finger. "Not doing this right now, Tenny." He looked up, into Etienne's eyes, and his voice softened. "I really am fine. I swear."

Etienne wasn't convinced but he let it go, dropping a quick kiss on Adam's forehead. "Ready for the rehearsal dinner?"

"As long as there's food." Adam brightened. "Do you think there'll be donuts?"

"You'd come back from the dead if there were donuts, wouldn't you?" Etienne said, laughing.

Adam wrinkled his nose. "Duh. *Donuts*. Come on, let's go see what Mom's making."

27

THE REHEARSAL DINNER went off without a hitch, and Etienne lost track of all the people he was introduced to. Great-aunt Henrietta, stooped and wrinkled, didn't actually pinch his ass, but did make a loud comment about how the quality of hockey players just kept improving, making Adam grin at Etienne, who couldn't help smiling back.

Etienne was an usher, with little to do except stand where they told him, but Adam was walking Noemi down the aisle, because, as she'd said, "the concept of Dad giving me away is archaic and misogynistic and I'm not his property, and besides, I want it to be you, you've always been by my side."

Etienne pretended not to notice as Adam surreptitiously wiped his eyes and hugged Noemi fiercely.

Still, for all the bustle and planning and places to be, Etienne couldn't help the feeling of—not dread, he thought, watching as Noemi discussed flower arrangements with the florist and Adam stole bites from the finger food tray he was helping prepare—but almost as though he was balancing on a precipice. Something was going on with Adam, but Adam just as clearly didn't want to talk about it with his sister's wedding less than a day away.

So Etienne waited, helped where he could, stayed out of the way when he couldn't help, and watched Adam with his family. What had he meant by "It's you" the night before? Etienne hadn't found a moment to ask him yet, with everything going on.

He wanted, suddenly, to go back to Toronto, back to his life, with his team and his friends and Adam, getting ready for the playoffs and working out together. Adam's parents had a gym in the basement but it wasn't the same. Etienne wanted to get Adam alone, find out what was wrong, and not have to worry about prying eyes.

Adam tossed a mini carrot to him and Etienne caught it reflexively. Adam winked and left the kitchen. A minute later, Etienne's phone buzzed.

Get up here.

Etienne cleared his throat and stood. No one seemed to notice as he sidled past people and out into the hall. He took the stairs two at a time up to the turret room, where Adam was sitting on the bed.

Adam held out his arms and Etienne went gladly into them, climbing onto the mattress and pulling Adam into his embrace.

"You looked a little overwhelmed," Adam murmured.

Etienne kissed the nape of his neck. "Sorry."

"*I* was a little overwhelmed," Adam admitted. "I love my sister, but Jesus. Too many people."

"What did you mean, last night?" Etienne blurted.

"When?"

"After we had sex," Etienne said, poking him in the ribs so Adam squirmed against him. "You said, 'it's you', right before you fell asleep."

"I did?"

Etienne rolled his eyes.

Adam appeared to be thinking. "I don't remember saying that," he finally admitted, and Etienne muffled a laugh against his shoulder blade.

"Idiot," he said fondly.

"But it is," Adam said suddenly, twisting so they were face to face. His eyes were serious. "It's you, Tens. It's been you since that night in the bar, there's never going to be anyone else."

Etienne's mouth went dry. "Adam—"

"I love you," Adam interrupted. "It's okay if you can't say it back, I know how you protect your heart. This isn't me assuming or steamrolling you, I swear. I just—I need you to know, okay?"

Etienne squeezed his eyes shut, overwhelmed. "Say it again," he whispered.

"I love you," Adam repeated, his voice steady.

Etienne opened his eyes, searching Adam's face. "You really do, don't you?"

Adam nodded. "Don't say it if you don't mean it," he said, running a hand over Etienne's ribs. "I can wait. I just want you to know I'm serious. About this —us. You."

"*God.*" Etienne crowded forward and caught Adam's mouth in a fierce kiss. Adam opened sweetly for him, fingers tightening on Etienne's waist. When they broke apart, Etienne pressed their foreheads together. "I love you too," he whispered.

Adam's smile was devastating. "You and me," he murmured. "Aren't we lucky?"

28

THE MORNING of the wedding was cool and clear, not a cloud in the sky. There were hordes of people in the house, and Etienne smiled and nodded to everyone and didn't stick around to make conversation. He helped Adam with his suit and fixed his tie before going downstairs and joining William, who was busy making last-minute touches to the decorations for the reception. Noemi and Colette were upstairs, getting Noemi into her dress.

"Ready for this, Dad?" Adam asked.

"Not really," William admitted. "Eli's a good kid, but—"

"I know," Adam said, bumping his shoulder. "Where is he?"

"In the den, quietly freaking out."

"I'll go talk to him," Etienne volunteered. Adam gave him a grateful glance.

Eli was pacing in front of the fireplace when Etienne slipped inside. He whirled, tense, but relaxed when he saw who it was.

"I know you don't really know me," Etienne said, closing the door behind him, "but is there anything I can do to help? Can I get you some coffee? Have you eaten breakfast?"

Eli laughed, sharp and nervous. "I think I'd throw it back up again."

Etienne studied him. Eli was in shirt-sleeves, his skin damp like he was sweating, hair rumpled and falling out of place over his brow.

"Are you okay?"

Eli shook his head, turning away. "I'm fine."

Etienne said nothing.

"I love Noemi," Eli said, spinning back to face him.

"Okay," Etienne said.

"I *love* Noemi," Eli repeated. The words sounded desperate.

"She loves you too," Etienne said carefully.

Somehow, that was the wrong thing to say. Eli's face shuttered and he turned back to the fireplace.

Etienne hesitated. "Do you need to talk? Don't you have any family here for your special day?" *Anyone's got to be better than a near-stranger on one of the most important days of your life.*

Eli shook his head. "My family's... not in the area." His mouth worked but he didn't say more.

"Friends? Who's your best man?"

"Daved. He's on his way, but he's stuck in traffic."

"Okay," Etienne repeated. "You're a really good goalie, you know." *When in doubt, talk hockey.*

Eli glanced at him, eyebrows going up. "You and Adam scored six times on me in twenty minutes, I can't be that good."

"Well yeah, but that's just... that's me and Adam.

We work really well together. I can tell you're good. How often does your own team score on you?"

Eli's face didn't move, but the shadows lying on it seemed to ease, somehow. "Not very often."

"There you go." Etienne sat down on the sofa, and after a minute, Eli joined him.

They sat quietly for a minute. Eli's feet were together, hands on his knees.

"I'm really happy for you and Adam," he said.

"Oh—thank you." Etienne resisted the urge to shift his weight. "What's your favorite thing about Noemi?"

"Her laugh," Eli said immediately. "When she's startled by something funny, it just... bubbles up, and it's so pure, I've never seen anyone *not* smile instinctively when they hear it." His face settled into lines of affection. "And *she's* funny. She makes me laugh all the fucking time."

"She's good for you," Etienne said.

"Yeah," Eli said. He squared his shoulders.

"She's nervous too," Etienne said.

Eli glanced at him. "She is?"

"It's a big step. It's normal to be nervous."

"Do you think you and Adam will get married?"

Etienne blinked. "I—we've only been together about six months. It's a little soon to be thinking about that."

"Of course." Eli ducked his head, worrying at his lower lip with his teeth.

"But I could see myself marrying him," Etienne admitted. The words made him dizzy with their truth, making him feel like he'd float off the sofa. "Don't you dare tell him I said that, or he'll be picking out matching tuxes before *your* wedding is over."

That got a ghost of a smile from Eli. "Thanks," he said.

Etienne patted his shoulder awkwardly as the door opened and Daved burst inside. Etienne rose.

"He's all yours."

As Etienne disappeared into the study, Adam's mother leaned over the balcony.

"Adam? Can you come here?"

Adam jogged up the stairs and Colette jerked her head at Noemi's closed bedroom door.

"She wants to talk to you."

"Me? Why?"

"Because you're her brother and she's having wedding jitters she doesn't want to talk about to her mother because then I might know she's actually had sex, would you please get in there?"

Adam found himself unceremoniously shoved through the door and it slammed behind him.

Noemi was sitting on the bed, head in her hands.

"Wow, you look nice," Adam said carefully, taking a step forward.

It was true. Noemi's dress was sleeveless and flared at the waist with multiple layers of some sort of gauzy material—Adam didn't fucking know fashion—that had what looked like tiny pearls sewn into it. Her hair was pulled up into a sleek chignon, a spray of white flowers at the twist, and pearl earrings.

But her eyes were red when she looked up, and Adam immediately dropped onto the bed beside her.

"Okay, what's going on?"

Noemi shook her head wordlessly and tilted

against him, head drooping on his shoulder. She smelled like honeysuckle, light and sweet. Adam slipped an arm around her waist and held on for a minute, trying to figure out what to say.

"Is Tenny the one?" she asked abruptly.

Adam took a slow breath. "I—yeah. I think he is."

Noemi sat up, plucking at the bracelet around one wrist. "What if you knew something about him that made you feel differently?"

"Like what?" Adam asked. He felt distinctly off-kilter and didn't like it at all. "There's literally nothing he could do that would make me not love him, Nomes. I mean, outside the big stuff—cheating, murder, tax fraud, that kind of thing."

That won him a ghost of a smile. "Okay, but assuming he's not cheating, he's never murdered anyone, and he always files his taxes, what if—" She faltered.

"What if what?" Adam said.

"What if he didn't want to have sex?" Noemi blurted.

Adam sat back. Noemi wouldn't meet his eyes, fiddling with her bracelet again.

"Nomes."

Noemi didn't look up.

"Nomes, are you—eugh, I can't believe I'm about to say this, but do you not want to have sex with Eli?"

"I was asking about you and Tenny," Noemi said, still not meeting his eyes. "What would you do, if you knew... that."

Adam sat still for a minute, processing. Finally he took Noemi's hand. "I would love and cherish him for the rest of his life, exactly the way I hope he'll let me do now."

Noemi looked up. Her dark blue eyes were sheened with tears. "Y-you wouldn't think it was unfair to you?"

Adam ground his teeth, searching for the words. "It's not about fair or unfair. It's not even about sex. It's…. Fuck, I don't know how to put it. I love him. If he didn't want to, you know—" He made a vague gesture and Noemi almost smiled again. "It's not a deal-breaker, I guess I'm saying. I'm in love with him, not what we do in bed. And anyone you choose to be with had better feel the same way about you, or I'll be there personally to kick his—or her—or their—ass."

Noemi's smile was small but real and she took his hand.

"This is so gross," she said. "Talking to you about —you know."

"You're telling me. Can we please be done sharing feelings?"

"Well, it was you or Mom." Noemi shuddered. "Not a conversation I ever want to have with my mother." She leaned up and kissed his cheek. "I don't know if I'm doing the right thing, Adam."

Adam swallowed hard. He was so unqualified for this conversation. "You're marrying someone you love. That's not the wrong thing. You'll figure it out. Just… you know… talk to him. And preferably not me, because I never want to think about you and—" He pretended to gag and Noemi punched his arm.

"I love you, asshole," she said.

Adam wrinkled his nose. "Disgusting, but also same."

230

NOEMI WAS STUNNING in pale ivory that left her flawless arms and shoulders bare, hugging her curves and flaring below her hips into a full train. Etienne watched, standing close enough to Adam that their shoulders brushed, as she and Eli repeated their vows to each other. Adam leaned into him just enough that Etienne felt his weight and slanted a smile at him.

Someday, he thought, and wondered if Adam was thinking it too.

After the ceremony, things devolved into controlled chaos, family and friends spilling into the Carons' backyard for the reception. Etienne and Adam were flying out that afternoon, on a flight just before Eli's and Noemi's to Hawaii for their honeymoon. Etienne drank champagne, kissed Noemi on both cheeks, and hugged Eli.

He had a game in the morning, and truthfully, he couldn't wait to get back. Adam's next game was the same day, in the afternoon. Etienne packed quickly, paying little regard to neatness as he shoved clothes into the suitcase and took it downstairs.

William and Colette were by the door. Colette pulled him into a hug immediately.

"I know we really don't know you very well yet," she said against his cheek, "but I already consider you part of this family. I hope you'll come back to visit often."

Etienne cleared his throat against the lump in it. "Any time you'll have me," he managed. "Thank you for letting me tag along with Adam for this."

William shook his head when Etienne put out a hand and hugged him instead. "Keep an eye on my son," he said in a low voice. "Something's... off."

"I know," Etienne said. "I am."

William nodded, apparently satisfied, as Adam thundered down the stairs with suitcase in tow. He kissed his mother, hugged his father, promised to call, and they were off.

SAFELY IN THEIR seats on the airplane, Adam let his head fall back with a groan. "Thank *God* that's over."

Etienne patted his leg. "Ready to get back to your superstar Wolverine lifestyle?"

Adam glowered at him. "I'm ready to go *home*. With you."

"How are you feeling?"

Adam's eyes narrowed. "Not this again."

"Humor me," Etienne suggested lightly.

"I'm fine, Tenny," Adam sighed. "Can we please stop talking about my health?"

"When I'm convinced you're healthy," Etienne said.

"Leave it," Adam warned, and his voice was tight.

"What aren't you telling me?"

The seatbelt light dinged as it turned off and Adam was up and out of his seat in the same instant, heading for the bathroom in long strides.

Etienne sat silently, fuming with worry. When Adam was still gone, fifteen minutes later, Etienne gave up and followed him. He knocked gently on the door.

"Adam?"

"Go away."

Etienne stepped sideways to let an attendant through. "No, Adam. I'm not going away."

There was a long moment of silence and then the door unlocked.

Etienne slipped through and locked it behind him. Adam was sitting on the tiny toilet lid, head in his hands. Etienne kept his back to the door, waiting.

Finally, Adam lifted his head. "It comes and goes," he said, so quietly Etienne had to strain to hear him over the noise of the engines.

Fear fluttered in Etienne's gut. "Your vision?"

Adam nodded. "It's—" He cut himself off, rubbing his face with a shaking hand. "Mostly the left eye but my right gets blurry sometimes."

"*Fuck*, Adam, we have to tell the doctor!"

"*No.*" It was explosive, hurled with enough force to almost make Etienne flinch. Adam's eyes were turbulent when they met Etienne's. "I shouldn't have told *you*," he hissed.

That *did* make Etienne flinch, and Adam was on his feet instantly, right up in Etienne's space.

"I'm sorry, I didn't mean it like that, Tenny, I'm sorry—" He touched Etienne's chest, flattening a hand across it almost gingerly. "Baby, please don't be mad at me, I can't take it if—"

Etienne folded his own hand over Adam's. "I'm not," he said. "I'm *worried*, Cary. What if something worse is going on? What if it's something bad?"

"It's not," Adam insisted. His fingers flexed under Etienne's as he chewed on his lower lip. "I've had it all my life, remember? It's business as usual."

It's not, Etienne wanted to protest. *It's getting worse, why won't you admit that?* But Adam's eyes were pleading with him not to argue, big and damp and full of unspoken fear.

The plane jostled, knocking Adam forward into Etienne's body. Etienne caught and held him when Adam would have drawn away.

"You and me," he whispered.

Adam nodded against Etienne's shoulder, arms coming up around his waist. "You and me." The words were muffled in Etienne's shirt but his hands gripped tightly.

29

THE NEXT MONTH passed surprisingly fast, both of them busy with their teams. The Wolverines were struggling, clinging to the wildcard spot by their fingernails, and Adam spent almost all his spare time watching tape, muttering about defense and forechecking, and asking Etienne to diagram plays with him. Etienne helped as much as he could, but the Freeze were rising in the standings, whispers of a playoff berth bubbling up. They were close. Really close. Etienne wanted this more than anything, and he pushed himself as hard as he could, training endlessly and reviewing his own tape, usually on the couch beside Adam.

He watched Adam's games as much as he could, although their schedules rarely aligned, and Adam himself even more closely, but they didn't speak of his vision again. Adam didn't bring it up, and he seemed to be in good spirits, so Etienne let it ride, even as dull worry gnawed at him.

Adam's playing was definitely affected, Etienne

could see that immediately. Adam's footwork was just as quick and graceful as usual, but his puck handling was more hesitant. It was measured in mere fractions of seconds, but Etienne knew what he was looking for. Adam was slower, clumsier, not as sure of himself or his surroundings. Etienne's heart hurt to watch it, but he didn't bring it up.

Toward the beginning of March, Etienne came home from an away game to his cold, empty apartment. Dropping his bags, he went into the kitchen and turned on the sink to wash his hands.

The pipes creaked and groaned and nothing came out. Etienne frowned.

The bathroom faucets gave the same result.

"Well, fuck." Had he forgotten to pay the water bill? No, he'd taken care of everything before he'd gone out of town. Etienne called maintenance.

"Oh yes," the girl at the front desk told him. "The pipes in your building have to be torn out and replaced. Didn't you check your mail?"

"I just got home," Etienne said, suppressing a groan. "I've been out of town."

"Well, it'll be at least a week before we have water in the building again," she said. "We're terribly sorry for the inconvenience."

Etienne hung up, stared at his phone a minute, and then called Adam.

Twenty minutes later, he dragged his still-packed bags down the hall to Adam's door and knocked.

Adam yanked it open and hugged him.

"Mmph—hi," Etienne said, hugging him back.

"Get in here," Adam said, pulling his sleeve.

Etienne followed him inside and put the bags down. "Are you sure this is okay? They said at least a week."

"*Yes*, I'm sure," Adam said. "Stay two weeks. Hell, stay forever."

Etienne's eyebrows shot up. "Cary—"

"Only if you want to," Adam hurried on. "But I've got the room, and I'm not much farther from the rink, and—" He broke off. "Am I doing it again?"

"Maybe a little bit." Etienne bracketed his wrist with gentle fingers, tracing over the pulse point. "Do you know what you're offering?"

"For my boyfriend who I love to move in with me," Adam said. His voice was steady but his rapid pulse gave away his nerves as he waited for Etienne's reply.

"Let's see how we do for a week," Etienne suggested. "If we suit—and you'll stop leaving your shoes in doorways—then maybe…."

Adam's eyes lit up and he leaned into a kiss. "Hungry?"

"Starving. I need massive amounts of protein and so do you."

THE FREEZE WON their game the next afternoon and clinched their spot in the playoffs. Etienne showered, changed, and immediately headed out the door for Adam's game, promising his team he'd meet them after to celebrate.

It was a disaster. The Ravens were out for blood and they got it, winning in a decisive 6-1 victory that took the Wolverines out of playoff contention. Etienne waited outside the locker room for Adam to emerge, miserable for Adam even as excitement for himself fizzed in his chest.

When Adam came out, he glanced at Etienne, his mouth tightening. "Don't say it."

"I'm not," Etienne protested. "I won't. I'm sorry, babe, I know you were hoping—"

"It's fine," Adam cut him off. "Let's go home."

"We got the schedule," Etienne told him in the cab. "I'm leaving tomorrow for the first three games."

Adam nodded.

"I'll be gone until the pipes are fixed in my building," Etienne added. "Do you want me to just go back there?"

"*No.*" Adam clutched Etienne's hand. "No, please. Tens—"

Etienne rubbed a thumb over Adam's knuckles. "You and me," he reminded him. "We'll get through this."

Adam blinked rapidly and nodded.

30

THE PLAYOFFS WERE GRUELING, everyone's expectations raised. Etienne did his level best to put his fears about Adam aside and focus on the games at hand. They made it through the first round by the skin of their teeth, but Orlov, their right-winger, cornered him after the first game away of the second round.

"What the fuck?" he demanded.

Okay, so maybe Etienne wasn't putting his personal issues away as well as he'd hoped.

"I'm fine," he said wearily.

"Like fuck you are," Orlov said. "You missed a pass from me, Jetty got clobbered because of you, and Li was right there for the layup and you didn't fucking give it to him. So I repeat—what the fuck?"

"I'm sorry," Etienne said. "Look, Orrie, I'm tired, I just got back to town and now we're on the road, and I've got... stuff going on in my personal life."

"Well, set it the fuck aside and turn the fucking key on it," Orlov snapped. "We're probably going for the Calder Cup for the first time in fifty years and I'll be fucked if you fuck it up for me, are we clear?"

"Good talk," Etienne said, and stalked away.

Still, he knew Orlov was right. It rankled at him, eating away at his core. He felt unsteady, destabilized, as if his world was going to spin off its axis at any moment.

Before the next game, he got a text from Adam.

I went for a checkup. Doc says everything is fine. Kill 'em out there for me.

Relief expanded like a supernova behind Etienne's breastbone and he took a deep breath in what felt like weeks.

They won that game and the next one, returning to the city to jubilant welcomes from the public. One more round. On the west coast, the Embers were lighting it up, advancing steadily through their division.

Etienne came home, swept Adam into his arms, and kissed him breathless. "You're sure you're fine," he said, cupping Adam's face.

Adam nodded. "Doc gave me the all clear. Are you growing your playoff beard?"

In answer, Etienne rubbed his cheek against Adam's, making him squawk and twist away at the rasp of stubble.

THEY SWEPT their opponents in the third round, sending the Blades back to Florida with their tails between their legs in four decisive games. The Embers had won their games too, and they were facing the

Freeze on the Freeze's home ice for the first game in two days.

THEY WON THE FIRST GAME, Li, Etienne, and Orlov playing a tight offensive game with no holes in it. The second, on away ice, came down to a shootout that they lost, but spirits were still high. They could do this. Their fans were excited, and that infected the players. The third game was a win. Two—or four—to go.

The fourth game, home ice, started well, Etienne focused and in his groove. Adam was in the crowd, watching him, cheering for him. Adam was healthy, he was there, and Etienne was invincible. He scored a hat trick by the end of the second period, lifting his stick to thunderous applause, flushed with victory.

They were up by one in the third period when it fell apart. Li caught a slash to the knee and went down hard. The offending player was sent to the box and Li managed to get to his feet and limp off the ice, but he was out for the rest of the game, and the coach was forced to put in the third line center, Edsel. It was a disaster. He wasn't fast enough, didn't know Etienne's body language, and hogged the puck. They lost by one, Shannon doing his best but unable to stop the winning goal.

At practice the next day, Coach Hannity gathered them around, looking somber. "Li's out," he said. The team groaned. "Shattered kneecap," Coach continued. "That means I need to do some restructuring. I want the first three lines on the ice, I'm going to try some different combinations. Tenny, I'm starting you second line next game."

Etienne nodded.

"Ordinarily," Coach said, "I'd call someone up from the Thunder. Rudy's a damn good center and I know you mesh well with him, Tens. But this is the goddamn Calder Cup and I have a different idea. I've been talking to Coach Benton."

Etienne perked up.

"Adam Caron needs some development time, Benton says. Their season's over but he's willing to send him to us for the playoffs. I understand you and he know each other, Tenny?"

"Yes sir," Etienne said, delight burgeoning under his skin and making his voice unsteady. Were he and Adam really going to get to play together? "We've skated together a lot. Mesh well."

Coach nodded sharply. "Let's see what happens. He should be here any minute."

Almost on cue, Adam appeared down the tunnel, wearing a Freeze jersey, stick in his hand. Etienne couldn't stop the smile as Adam stepped onto the ice and glided to join them.

"Miss me, boys?" he said. He was greeted with backslaps and laughter and affectionate shoulder jostlings until he'd worked his way through the team and came face to face with Etienne. The smile slid off Adam's face, leaving him looking apprehensive. "Hi," he said carefully.

Etienne grinned at him and the worry on Adam's face vanished.

"Oh, thank God," he said under his breath. "I thought you might be upset I was here."

Etienne snorted. "You ready to show them how it's done?"

"Fuck yeah."

31

Fifth game, home ice. Tied two-two, this was, many felt, the tipping point. Whichever team won this game had the best chance of walking away with the trophy.

"That's bullshit," Coach Hannity said flatly in the locker room, hands on his hips. "Even if we lose, we have two more opportunities to take this. You're going to get out there, do those attack angle drills just like we practiced, and kick their asses back to Oregon." His tone softened. "Did you think we'd get this far?"

There were a few head shakes around the room as Etienne tied his skates. Adam was pulling his gloves on, beside him.

"Well, I did," Coach said. "You have it in you. You had it in you before Cary here came along to lend a hand—" Adam flashed a brilliant grin at the room, making the players laugh. "—And you have it now. So let's go whip some Oregon *ass*."

Cheers went up around the room, sticks tapping loudly on the floor.

They took the game 5-2.

GAME SIX, on away ice, they fell to the Embers by one. Adam's playing had improved with Etienne beside him, but there was still a lag there, a feeling almost of hesitation at times. But he was healthy, Etienne reminded himself. He'd been cleared by the doctor. And Adam seemed cheerful, in good spirits, clearly determined to help the Freeze win the Cup. So Etienne put the fear away and focused on the game.

Game seven was at the Coca-Cola Coliseum, home ice. The crowd was at capacity, filling the huge arena with a buzz that reverberated in Etienne's teeth as he warmed up under the stadium in the locker room, bouncing on his toes and shadow-boxing with the wall. He went through his routine over and over until everything fell away, one by one, worries and concerns sloughing off like flakes of rust, leaving him sharp and focused, a shining steel blade made for one purpose.

He helped Adam with his gear and Adam helped with Etienne's. Before they made the trek up to the ice, Etienne caught the front of Adam's jersey and pulled him close, gently bumping their helmets together. The noise of the locker room faded away. All Etienne could hear was Adam's breathing, all he could smell was Adam's skin.

"You and me," he murmured.

Adam's smile took Etienne's breath away. "You and me. Let's do this."

THEY TOOK the ice to thunderous applause. Etienne waved at the crowd as warmups began. He kept an eye on Adam as they circled the rink, but his fears didn't surface. Adam was skating well, quick and light on his feet and easy with the puck he was currently batting around.

It was going to be a good game, Etienne could feel it in his bones. They were going to win. The ice was firm and sweet beneath his blades, the team was in high spirits, and it was one of those nights where everything fit together perfectly, each piece slotting into place with precision.

They were up by one in the second period, Etienne, Adam, and Orlov working together like a well-oiled machine through each of their shifts. Shannon blocked shot after shot as the first line worked to get the puck back in the offensive zone, but one slipped by him just before the buzzer sounded to signal the end of the period.

In the locker room, Coach paced as they sat in their stalls.

"Jetty, I want you to stay on Krzinski," he said. "He's looking for an excuse to start a fight. If he does, it needs to be with you. Keep him off the forwards."

Jetty nodded, firming his jaw.

Coach turned to Dodson, the other defenseman. "Back him up, but don't leave Orrie swinging. And for God's sake, remember your forechecking, please? I'm begging you? Tenny, remember that move you showed me a few weeks back?"

"Of course, Coach."

"They won't be expecting it from someone of your height and size. You see the opening, you take it. Cary, run it with him."

"Yes, Coach."

Coach surveyed the room. "You know what I see?"

Etienne wiped sweat off his brow as Adam leaned against him, just enough for Etienne to feel his weight.

"I see a hungry team who hasn't seen what a Cup win can do for them since before some of your parents were born. You want to see what it can do?"

"Yes, Coach!" everyone chorused.

Coach bared his teeth. "So do fucking I. Let's find out."

They banged their sticks and howled like idiots, Etienne and Adam among them, and charged back up to the ice with renewed vigor.

Waiting for their shift, they sat side-by-side, watching the play. Adam nudged Etienne with an elbow. "He's right, Krzinski's out for blood."

Etienne looked where Adam indicated. Krzinski was a huge Pole, blond and heavily muscled, with aggression oozing from his pores. As they watched, he checked Edsel into the boards and skated away laughing.

"Jesus," Etienne muttered.

"You know how you called Tibby a wrecking ball on razor blades that time? He's that, dialed up to eleven and with a bad attitude to boot."

"You're up!" Coach shouted, and Etienne and Adam scrambled off the bench onto the ice.

They hit it fast and hard, Etienne hyper-aware of Adam to his right, always exactly where Etienne needed him to be. Etienne ducked around an oncoming winger, spun and shot the puck to Orlov off the boards. Orlov caught it and they headed for the offensive zone, the Embers all over them.

Almost there, Orlov sent the puck between his skates to Etienne behind him. Adam was ahead and to his left, closer to the net, but a defenseman and the center were between them. Etienne doubled back and raced down the ice, Krzinski close behind him and the center sticking like glue to his side. Etienne sheared off before the blue line, faked right, then left, shoved the puck between the center's skates, and dodged around him. He bounced the puck sideways to Adam as the center flung out a desperate hand and tripped Etienne with his stick, sending him to the ice.

The whistle didn't blow. Etienne watched in slow-motion, belly-down on the ice, as Adam caught the puck, spun sideways past a winger on a desperate dive, and smacked it home under the goalie's reaching arms.

The buzzer sounded. The crowd erupted. The goalie picked himself back up. And Krzinski slammed into Adam from behind at twenty-five miles an hour, sending his much smaller frame hurtling into the boards.

Etienne couldn't move. Time had slowed to an agonizing crawl. He watched as Adam flew backward, helmet flying free. It soared up into the crowd on a lazy arc as Adam's back hit the boards, his head connecting with the plexiglass a split-second later, a sickening crack that Etienne heard over the screams of the crowd.

Etienne thought vaguely he might be screaming too. He didn't know. He couldn't feel anything. Somehow he was on his feet, slipping and slithering and falling in a mad scramble to where Adam lay crumpled on the ice, a terribly small, still figure.

Nonopleasenotagain—

He was dimly aware of Jetty hurtling past and

colliding with Krzinski, but Etienne didn't look. There was blood pooling around Adam's head, a slowly growing halo of crimson. Etienne went to his knees and crouched, shielding Adam with his body as Jetty and Krzinski fought just feet away, sharp metal blades gouging the ice terrifyingly close to Adam's head.

Adam's eyes were closed. Was he breathing? Etienne couldn't tell. A skate caught his sleeve and ripped it as more players joined the scrimmage.

"Wake up," Etienne pleaded. "Adam, *please—*"

Then the linesmen were there, whistles shrieking and players being dragged apart. Someone grabbed Etienne's arm. He shook them off with a snarl, hunkering down over Adam's still form.

"Medics!" someone shouted in his ear. "Let them at him!"

Etienne looked up as the stretcher and paramedics arrived. This time he allowed the hands gripping him to pull him backward. It was Jetty and Shannon, he realized vaguely. Jetty was bleeding from a cut on his temple and a split lip. There was blood on his teeth and in his beard. Shannon said nothing, but his hands were so tight on Etienne's arm that Etienne knew he would bruise. He didn't try to get away. They watched in silence as the paramedics straightened Adam's limbs and eased him onto the stretcher in one quick move.

The ice was smeared bright, bloody red, and Etienne thought he might vomit. He pulled away from Jetty and Shannon as the medics picked the stretcher up and carried Adam out of the rink.

Coach Hannity caught his arm as Etienne tried to follow. "You're bleeding."

Etienne didn't even look. "Let me go." Adam was getting farther away.

"Go with them," Coach said, releasing him. "Get stitched up and stay with him."

As if Etienne had anything else in mind. He brushed past, stooping to untie his skates, kicking them off, and then *running* down the tunnel barefoot in all his gear, shouting at the medics to wait.

They slowed their headlong pace just enough for him to catch up and scramble into the back of the ambulance, but when he tried to get closer to Adam, he was shoved unceremoniously back into place by a medic.

"Don't you dare bleed on him," she snapped.

Etienne barely heard her. His chest was in a vice, laboring for every breath. "How is he?" he managed. "Please, he's—"

The medic's face softened briefly as she motioned him backward so the other two in the ambulance could work on Adam. "Just let them work. I'm going to cut your sleeve off, okay?"

Etienne just nodded, all his attention on Adam's hand dangling over the edge of the stretcher. "He's so pale," he whispered.

"He's lost a lot of blood," the medic said. She had dark hair pulled back into a sleek, tight bun, brown skin, and dark eyes. Her name tag said ANA LOPEZ. She lifted the sodden sleeve back to reveal a deep gash in Etienne's forearm, still oozing blood, and hissed through her teeth. "So have you. How are you feeling?"

Etienne spared her a glance. "I'm fine. Just stitch me up."

"God, hockey players." Ana shook her head and reached for the disinfectant spray as Etienne willed the ambulance to hurry.

32

THEY WERE SEPARATED when they got to the hospital, despite Etienne's loud protests. A nurse and an orderly caught Etienne's arms as he tried to follow Adam's stretcher toward surgery.

"Sir, *sir*, you can't go back there. Sir, you're bleeding, we have to get you fixed up as well." The nurse was black, in her mid-forties, with hair pulled off her high forehead in a perfectly symmetrical puffball. Her eyes were sympathetic, but her tone was brisk and calm as she and the orderly nearly dragged Etienne into the nearest room and sat him down on the bed.

"I'm Tess. Are you family?" she asked, grabbing gauze and dabbing at the wound.

"I'm—yes. He's—" Etienne was swamped by a wave of dizziness. "I'm his emergency contact. Please, I'm all he has."

"He doesn't need you right now, honey," Tess said. She finished cutting his jersey off as she spoke and the orderly, apparently convinced Etienne wasn't a flight risk, left the room. "Right now he needs the best doctors in the city, and he has them. So you just sit right here and let me get you fixed up, okay?"

"He's all I have too," Etienne whispered, and tears spilled hot and stinging down his cheeks. Tess made quietly sympathetic noises as she peeled the jersey off him. When she would have cut his pads off, Etienne managed to stop her, stripping out of his gear and dropping it on the floor without looking.

"Is he alive?" Etienne asked suddenly, catching Tess's hand. "What if he—" He couldn't finish the sentence.

Tess squeezed his hand. "He's not dead. You can't think that way. He's in good hands, I promise you. Now be still."

Etienne swallowed hard and did his best to obey.

RUDY ARRIVED SOMETIME while Etienne was being stitched up. He was waiting in the hall when Etienne stumbled out, gear hanging over his good arm.

He stood when Etienne appeared, a set of pale lavender scrubs in his hands. "Give me those," he said, indicating the pads, "and take these. There's a shower just down the hall. Go get clean. I'll be here when you get back."

"Don't get the stitches wet," Tess added from behind Etienne. Her hand was warm and comforting between Etienne's shoulder blades as she gently steered him in the direction Rudy had indicated. "Go on now, honey, do what your friend says."

Etienne obeyed numbly, operating on autopilot. All he could see when he closed his eyes was Adam on the ice, haloed in blood, so he didn't close his eyes, staring unblinking at the wall as the hot spray pounded against his skin.

His arm hurt dully. Etienne embraced it, letting the pain wash through him. All that mattered was Adam.

When he came out of the showers, Rudy was waiting.

"Everyone else is in the lobby," he said. "How are you feeling?"

Everyone else? Etienne shrugged. "I'm fine."

"Oh kiddo, you're so not fine. Sit down with me a minute." Rudy guided him to the chairs along the wall and they sat, Rudy rubbing Etienne's back.

Etienne leaned forward, bracing his elbows on his knees and staring at the floor's diamond checkered pattern. "There was so much blood," he whispered.

"Scalp wounds bleed like a bitch," Rudy agreed. "He's going to be fine."

"You don't know that," Etienne said, twisting away from his hand. "You *can't* know that."

Rudy met his eyes steadily. "Have I been wrong yet?"

"First time for everything," Etienne shot back. "Fuck, I have to call his parents."

"I got your stuff from the locker room," Rudy said, and held out Etienne's phone.

To his horror, Etienne felt his face crumple as tears welled.

Rudy waited as he got himself back under control. Then he handed him the phone and took a few steps away to give him privacy.

Etienne concentrated on his breathing until he was fairly certain it would stay steady. Then he dialed Colette.

She answered on the first ring. "Tenny, sweetheart! Is the game over already?"

"You're—" Etienne swallowed. "You're not watching?"

"William's still at work, we like to watch together, so I recorded it. We're going to watch when he gets home. What's wrong, Tenny?" Her voice sharpened. "Is it Adam? What happened?"

"Don't watch the game," Etienne managed.

"Why not? *What happened?*"

"He got hit," Etienne whispered. "His head—we're at the hospital. Please… please just come."

"We're on our way," Colette said, and disconnected.

Rudy sat back down beside him. "Breathe," he ordered.

Etienne covered his face.

"You're not going to say something stupid like 'this is my fault', are you?" Rudy inquired.

Etienne dropped his hands and glared at him. "Of course not." But a worm of doubt niggled under his breastbone. *Could I have done more? Pushed harder for him to take it seriously?*

"He's a grown man," Rudy said. "He knows the risks."

"We all do. It doesn't stop us."

"Exactly." Rudy patted his knee. "Now come on, everyone wants to see you."

Etienne followed him out to the waiting room, which was filled with very large, very worried hockey players. He stopped dead, scanning faces. Logan, Theo, Johnny and Liam, even Broussard was there. Beside and around them stood the Freeze, almost the entire team. Jetty's face was no longer bloody, although bruises were developing quickly around his eye and on his forehead. Shannon was next to him, quiet and unwavering as ever. Even Li was there, balancing on his crutches on Jetty's other side.

"You guys are… here for Adam?" Etienne managed.

Rudy gripped his shoulder. "We are, but we're also here for *you*."

As if on unspoken cue, everyone crowded forward until Etienne was surrounded, held tight in the middle of the circle. He found his forehead on Liam's shoulder, Logan pressed up against his side, Rudy's hand on his back, and if a few more tears fell, no one commented on them.

"How is he?" Jetty asked when Etienne had himself under control again and they'd moved back to give him some room.

Etienne shrugged helplessly. "No one will tell me anything. I don't *know*."

The glass doors whooshed open and Coach Benton, Jake Kano, and Hideki strode through. Benton zeroed in on Etienne.

"How is he?"

A tall man in scrubs came through the door behind them before Etienne could answer.

"Etienne Brideau?"

Etienne whirled. "Me—that's me."

"I'm Dr. Arenesche. I understand you're Adam Caron's emergency contact?" The doctor had black hair and coppery skin. His eyes were tired but clear, his handshake firm when he took Etienne's hand. "Would you come with me, please?"

Etienne cast a quick glance at the team and

followed Dr. Arenesche into the hallway. "Is he—" He couldn't finish the sentence.

"He's out of surgery and resting comfortably," Dr. Arenesche said.

Etienne put a hand on the wall to steady himself. "Can—can I see him?"

"He's still asleep, and likely to be for a while. He has a broken wrist, two broken ribs, and he sustained a severe concussion. We had to operate to relieve the swelling on his brain."

Etienne swallowed hard. "Will he... be okay?"

"The operation went smoothly," Dr. Arenesche said. "His vitals are good. There's no reason to suggest he won't make a full recovery."

"When can I see him? Please, I need to—" Etienne clamped his mouth shut before he did something he regretted, like falling to the floor and clutching the doctor's knees as he begged.

"He's in recovery. As soon as he's moved to a room —which should be soon—I'll have you brought back. Does he have any other family in the area?"

Etienne shook his head. "His parents are on the way but they're in Seattle."

Dr. Arenesche nodded. "I'll make sure you're allowed in as soon as possible."

"Thank you," Etienne managed. "For—thank you."

"We'll send for you soon."

33

SOMETHING WAS BEEPING. It filtered into the fog in Adam's head, down through the waves where he floated, suspended and at peace. It *hurt*. He tried to move and discovered he couldn't. The beeping was strident, piercing his skull like a cleaver. He moaned.

"Get the doctor," someone said.

Adam was pulled under again before he could protest that he didn't want the doctor; he wanted Etienne.

When he woke again, the beeping was gone and someone was holding his hand. A thumb traced patterns over Adam's knuckles. He knew that thumb, that touch. Adam turned his head on the pillow, wincing against the pain that raked dull claws through the back of his skull and down his ribs at the movement.

"Adam?" That was Etienne's voice.

Adam's mouth was so dry. He opened and closed it, eyes still shut. Something small bumped his lips.

"It's a straw, baby," Etienne said. His voice was rough, raw like he'd been crying. "It's water."

Adam opened his mouth and Etienne slipped the straw between his lips. Adam had never tasted anything so sweet as the cool water sliding down his throat. He whimpered a protest when Etienne pulled it away.

"Shh," Etienne said, a hand ghosting over Adam's jaw. "Not too much at first."

"Tenny—" Adam turned his head into Etienne's palm. "What...."

"You were hit," Etienne said. He stroked Adam's cheekbone and Adam sighed, melting into his touch. Nothing hurt as long as he didn't move. "Krzinski—you scored and he checked you into the boards. Y-your helmet came off—" His voice caught.

"'M okay," Adam slurred. "Did... we win?"

Etienne's breath hitched. "Yeah, baby," he managed, laughter and tears choking his voice. "Yeah, we won."

Adam opened his eyes. The room was dark, a jumble of blurred objects, Etienne's broad shoulders just barely visible through the gloom.

"Why're... the lights off?"

Etienne's thumb, still stroking Adam's cheek, stopped.

"Tens?"

"Adam, can you see me?"

"Yeah," Adam slurred. "You're right there. Why's it so dark?"

Etienne let go of him and fumbled with something on the bed. Someone answered, tinny over a speaker, a few seconds later.

"Get the doctor in here *now*," Etienne said. Adam

had never heard his voice like that, brittle and stretched thin with fear, and he struggled to sit up, to figure out what was wrong, but his joints weren't working, ribs stabbing him with every breath.

"Tenny, *what*—"

"Don't move," Etienne said. He gripped Adam's shoulder, gently pinning him to the bed. "Don't move, Adam, please—"

"You're scaring me."

Etienne's hand tightened as a door to Adam's left opened and closed, sound from the hallway momentarily filtering in and then silenced again. Footsteps approached.

"Mr. Caron, good to have you back with us," a soothing voice said. "I'm Dr. Wilson, the attending on call. How are you feeling?"

Adam squinted through the dark. He could just make out a shape to his left, short and plump. Cool fingers touched his arm and he jolted.

"Easy," Dr. Wilson said. "Just taking your pulse."

"Turn the lights on," Adam said. "Tenny, tell her to turn the lights on."

Etienne's hand on Adam's shoulder tightened almost to the point of pain but he said nothing.

The doctor cleared her throat. "I'm going to touch your face, Mr. Caron. Open your eyes wide for me."

Adam struggled to obey through the haze of panic as she gripped his chin, turning his head this way and that.

"Can you see anything?" she finally asked.

"Shapes," Adam said through his teeth. "What's going on?"

Instead of answering, Dr. Wilson put her hand on

his left cheek, holding his eyelid open. "Can you see that?"

A faint ray of light sparked through the gloom, there and gone again.

"There," Adam said. "I think—what was that?"

"I just shone a flashlight in your eyes, Mr. Caron," Dr. Wilson said.

Adam shook his head. "No. *No.* The lights are off, it's just dark. Tenny, turn the lights on. Tell her, Tenny, tell her I'm not blind, she's wrong, *I'm not blind*—" He heaved for air, biting his tongue so hard bitter copper flooded his mouth. He couldn't breathe, couldn't move, as the panic welled inside him and drowned out the voices that were suddenly shouting.

It was a mercy when the abyss closed over his head, dragging him down into the deep.

34

WHEN HE WOKE UP AGAIN, his mother was talking in that cold, clear, tightly controlled voice she only used when pushed to the limits of her considerable patience, but he couldn't quite understand what she was saying.

"Mom—" Adam's throat closed up. Even to his own ears, he sounded like a child, helpless and terrified. Was she really there?

"I'm here," Colette said immediately. A door opened and closed and her voice drew nearer. "I'm here, sweetheart, can you see me?"

Adam shook his head, reaching desperately in the direction of her voice and the vague shape of her, and Colette caught his hand.

"*Mom*," Adam repeated. Tears prickled his eyes and he wanted nothing more than to bury his face in her stomach, the way he had as a child. "I can't see, Mom, I can't—"

"I know, baby," Colette said, wiping away the tear that escaped Adam's eye. She sounded on the verge of tears herself. "You're going to be okay. I'm here. So is Dad. He's getting coffee."

"Where's Tenny?"

"He's asleep on the couch beside you." Colette's voice gentled with affection. "He called us after the game. He hasn't left your side."

"How is he?" Adam whispered.

"Worried about you, sweetheart. But he's okay."

"Is it permanent, Mom?"

Colette drew a breath, and all of Adam's fears welled in a stifling wave.

"Don't lie to me," he gritted out.

"We don't know," Colette finally said. "They're still doing tests."

"Adam?" That was Etienne's deep voice. Adam turned to him instinctively, reaching for him and wincing when the movement jostled his arm. "Don't move," Etienne said. Adam heard rustling, then footsteps. His voice was much nearer when he spoke again. "How are you feeling?"

"I'm fucking great," Adam snapped. Silence followed the outburst and he bit the inside of his cheek. "I—"

Colette squeezed his hand. "I'm going to find your father."

There was more silence after she left, until Adam took a shaky breath and scooted himself slowly, agonizingly, to the edge of the mattress.

"Cary, *stop*." Etienne sounded distressed but he didn't touch him. Adam ignored him.

He was trembling when he was done, pain vibrating through him, but he didn't care.

"Tenny, please—"

Etienne made a small, hurt noise and then he was

there, crawling onto the bed beside him. He settled his big frame in carefully, curving himself protectively around Adam's body in a long, warm line.

"I'm sorry," Adam whispered.

"Don't," Etienne said, breath stirring Adam's hair. "It's okay, baby, I know."

"I'm so scared," Adam managed. He squeezed his eyes shut against the tears.

"I know," Etienne said. "I am too. But we'll figure it out." He stroked Adam's hair off his forehead in slow, rhythmic movements.

"What if—"

The door opened, cutting him off. Etienne tensed as if to move.

"No, Tenny, stay there," Colette said. "Adam, I found your dad."

"Hi Dad," Adam said, aware of the wobble in his voice. His parents were almost formless shapes against the gloom. The larger of the two took a shape forward.

"You know we'd have come to visit if you'd just asked," William said. "You haven't had enough of us yet?"

Adam hiccuped an almost-laugh and his father took his good hand.

"What day is it?"

"Sunday morning," William said. "We got here last night but you've been out cold."

"How—" Adam swallowed. "How'd you get here so fast?"

"Your mother chartered a jet," William said.

"I know where you got the genes for being extra," Etienne murmured in his ear.

Adam actually laughed at that. "Ow, ow, *don't*. How much of me is broken?"

"Ribs, wrist, and another concussion," Etienne said. His voice was steady, but his arm tightened around Adam's waist. "They operated to relieve the swelling on your brain—does your head hurt?"

"Everything hurts," Adam said. "Although the drugs are good. As long as I don't move, it's not too bad. I just—" *My eyes.*

"The doctor will know something soon," Colette said. "You should rest."

Adam didn't want to rest. He wanted his eyes back. He wanted to be on the ice. But he could feel exhaustion tugging at him.

Etienne kissed the nape of his neck. "Sleep," he murmured.

Adam had no choice but to obey.

35

ETIENNE USED the time while Adam was asleep to go back to Adam's apartment and pack clothes and necessities for a week. He ignored the throbbing of his arm as he shoved clothes into a bag, but he couldn't as easily ignore his phone when it rang.

"How is he?" Rudy asked.

"Awake and lucid," Etienne said. He sat down on the bed. "He... he can't see right now."

Rudy's breath was sharp. "At all? He's blind? Do you have a prognosis yet?"

"No. He can... he can see shapes. Dimly. I'm at his place packing clothes for both of us."

"And how are you?"

Etienne rubbed his eyes. "Tired."

"Are his parents there yet?"

"Yeah."

"Then you should get some sleep."

Etienne snorted. "I'll sleep when I get back to the hospital."

"Tenny—"

"Leave it, Rudy," Etienne snapped. "I'm not sleeping without him, okay?"

"Okay," Rudy said gently. "But you need to take care of yourself. You're no good to him if you collapse. Have you eaten?"

Etienne sighed. "I'll eat when I get back. I promise."

"When can we visit?"

"I don't know," Etienne said. "I'll ask. Rudy—"

"Yeah?"

"Thanks. For—well, everything."

"Logan sends his love too," Rudy said, and hung up.

He took the side entrance to avoid the reporters camped out in the lobby. Adam was stirring when Etienne got back to the room. Colette was leaning over the bed, holding his hand and talking gently to him. She looked tired, Etienne thought.

"Why don't you go back to Adam's place and get some rest?" he suggested, dropping the bag in the corner. "I'll call if Adam needs you."

Colette dropped a kiss on Adam's forehead and straightened. "If you're sure."

But the door opened before she and William could leave, Dr. Wilson stepping through. She looked momentarily taken aback at the number of people in the room, but recovered quickly.

"Mr. Caron, how are you feeling?"

"Do you have news?" Adam asked. His fingers were white-knuckled on the bed frame, and Etienne skirted the bed, resting a hand over his. Adam twisted his wrist and clutched at Etienne's hand but said nothing, his attention focused in the direction of the doctor.

"We have the results of the CT and MRI," Dr. Wilson said. "I understand you've had some mild vision impairment all your life?"

Adam lifted a shoulder. "Very mild."

"But it's gotten worse lately," Etienne interjected. "After he hit his head a few months back the first time, he lost about forty percent in his left eye, but it came back within a few days. And then in Seattle in January, he bumped it again. It wasn't a concussion that time, but he told me his vision started blurring in and out after that."

Adam grimaced but said nothing.

Dr. Wilson looked disapproving. "And you didn't get it checked at that time?"

Etienne glanced at Colette and William, who both looked unhappy but not surprised.

"Have you ever met a hockey player?" Adam snapped.

"Wait, you said," Etienne interrupted. "During the playoffs, you told me you went to the doctor and he gave you the all clear."

Adam hunched his shoulders.

"Did you lie to me?" Etienne asked.

"*No*," Adam said. He tucked his chin, that habitual gesture of his. "I... didn't give the doctor the whole story, though."

Dr. Wilson sighed. "At any rate, the scans revealed something. A small mass—very small—the size of a pea, probably."

"A mass," Adam repeated flatly. His face was

expressionless, but his hand was suddenly punishingly tight on Etienne's.

"It appears to be benign," Dr. Wilson continued. "It's likely you've had it all your life and it's what's caused your vision impairment in the past. The concussions caused your brain to swell, pushing the mass into your optic nerve."

Adam didn't move. Etienne watched him anxiously. He doubted the doctor could see the beginnings of distress in Adam's face; the tiny muscle twitching in his jaw, the stress around his mouth. But Etienne could see it, and he wanted to wipe it away, make it better, chase the doctor from the room. He said nothing, though, shifting his weight and keeping his grip on Adam's hand firm.

"So what does that mean?" Adam asked. "Will I see again or not?"

Dr. Wilson cleared her throat. "Well now, we can't be sure."

Adam's breath hitched, so quiet Etienne almost missed it.

"We have a few options," she continued. "One— we let the swelling in your brain go down, leave the mass alone, and hope your vision returns on its own. It has in the past, it may well do so again. Even if it does, I doubt you'll recover enough to play hockey again. You may regain up to sixty percent of your vision, but it will likely still be compromised, and another hit could cause permanent damage."

"And the other option?" Adam was keeping his voice steady with an almost visible effort.

"Surgery," Dr. Wilson said baldly. "Remove the mass."

"Would that work?"

Dr. Wilson hesitated.

"The truth, Doctor," Adam spat.

"It's in a tricky spot," Dr. Wilson said. "Even if we get it all, the optic nerve could be damaged beyond repair. You could be permanently blind." The words hung in the air, hard and uncompromising. *Permanently blind.*

Adam was going to leave bruises, Etienne thought distantly, but it didn't occur to him to let go.

"What are the odds with surgery?" Colette asked, her voice wobbly.

"It's always hard to say," Dr. Wilson said.

Adam made a noise in the back of his throat.

"I would say you have a forty percent chance of full recovery with the surgery. If it fails, however, you would more than likely be permanently completely blind."

The bones in Etienne's hand creaked with Adam's grip on them.

"Can you give me a minute?" Adam said, deathly quiet.

The doctor nodded. "Of course. There's no rush to decide—we can't operate until the swelling goes down anyway. I'm on call if you need me." She left the room on silent feet.

Colette glanced at William and then Etienne. "Adam, honey, do you want us to stay?"

Adam shook his head. "Please just—" He snapped his mouth shut.

"We'll go back to your apartment, then," Colette said gently. She hesitated. "We love you, baby."

Adam nodded, lips clamped.

Etienne waited until the door shut behind them. "Do you want me to go too?"

In answer, Adam clutched at him. "Don't leave me, don't leave, don't—Tenny, *please*—"

Etienne slid onto the bed and gathered him into his arms. Adam's breathing was harsh, rattling in his chest. "I'm right here," Etienne said. "Breathe, love, I'm not going anywhere."

Adam heaved a sob and buried his face in Etienne's throat. "I can't—I don't know what to *do*."

"Okay, you don't have to decide this minute," Etienne said soothingly, rubbing Adam's back in long, comforting sweeps.

"It's not fair," Adam managed.

"I know."

"It's not *fair*." He sounded like a little kid, bewildered at the cruelty of the world, and Etienne's eyes stung at the hurt in his voice.

"It's okay to be angry," Etienne said.

"I *am*," Adam said, lifting his head. "All I want to do is play hockey and be with you. And I'm *losing* that. It's not fucking *fair*."

Fear flashed through Etienne. "You're not losing me," he said.

Adam said nothing, ducking his head again.

Etienne drew away enough to put a finger under Adam's chin, lifting his face. "You're not losing me," he repeated. "Adam? Do you hear me?"

Adam pulled away. "I will," he said, voice muffled against Etienne's chest.

"Why? Help me out here. Why are you going to lose me?"

Adam jerked a shoulder, not lifting his head. "You'll… get tired of it. Of me. If I'm—"

Etienne let go and rolled off the bed. Adam didn't move, except to press his face into the pillow. From what little Etienne could see, his expression was resigned.

"Hang on," Etienne said. "Let me get this straight. You think if you're blind, or you can't play hockey, or you're not a hundred percent the person I fell in love with, that I won't want to be with you? That I'll just, what? Walk away? Tell you to have a nice life and leave?" He barked a sharp, angry laugh, dragging hands through his hair. "Christ, Adam, what do you think of me?"

Adam mumbled something.

"What?"

Adam lifted his head. "I said, what else *is* there?"

For a moment, all Etienne could do was stare at him, jaw hanging. Then he took a quick stride and crawled onto the bed again. This time, though, he straddled Adam's hips, careful not to jostle his broken ribs, and bent to cup Adam's face in both hands.

"I love you, Adam Alexis Noah Caron," he said, enunciating each word. "I would love you no matter what happened. Whether you're blind or not, even if you never set foot on ice again, I love *you*. Not your ability to shoot a puck or anything else you seem to be grading your self-worth by. You think *that's* what I fell in love with? Your face or your body or your... slap-shot or something?"

Adam's lips trembled. "I don't know what else there is," he whispered. A tear slid down his cheek, and Etienne wiped it away with a thumb.

"There's your heart," he said quietly. He kissed the track the tear had made. "There's your quick mind. Your sense of humor. How kind and generous you are." He kissed Adam's eyelid. "There is so much about you to love." He kissed Adam's other eyelid. "This doesn't make you less, my love. Just different."

"But what about me?" Adam said, pushing away. Etienne let him go immediately. Adam's eyes, dark blue and lovely as ever, were wide and unfocused. "What if I *am* blind forever? I'll never see the sun again. I'll never see a cute kitten again and send you a picture of it." Tears spilled down his cheeks and his face crumpled. "*I'll never see your face again.*"

Etienne slid to the side and gathered him in as Adam sobbed, tucking his face into the crook of his neck. "Breathe," he whispered. He closed his eyes and held on until the worst of the tears had passed and Adam was limp against him, hiccupping occasionally. Finally, Etienne disentangled himself enough to reach for a tissue. "Listen to me," he said, wiping Adam's face. "You think blind people can't find joy in life? You're doing them a disservice. So you might have lost your sight—that doesn't mean you're never going to be happy again. Besides, you can still see me."

"*How?*"

Etienne caught Adam's good hand and lifted it to his face. "Like this." He pressed Adam's fingers to his forehead and down, tracing over his eyes and the jut of his nose, then across his mouth. "I'm right here," he whispered. "See?"

Adam's eyes were still unfocused, but he kept his hand on Etienne's face when Etienne dropped his, exploring with fingertips soft as a butterfly's wing.

"Oh," he murmured.

Etienne turned his head enough to brush a kiss across Adam's palm. "Oh?"

"You're still beautiful," Adam husked.

Etienne's breath caught. "You and me, baby." He pressed their mouths together, tasting the salt of their mingled tears as Adam clung to him.

36

"THERE ARE A MILLION REPORTERS DOWNSTAIRS," Etienne told Adam later. The nurse had been in and out, giving Etienne in the bed a disapproving glare but not making him relocate. Etienne intended to take advantage of that. He traced lazy shapes on Adam's arm above the fiberglass cast. "I've been sneaking in and out the side exit but at some point we should probably make a statement."

Adam grimaced. "Not yet."

"No, of course not."

"But—" Adam looked thoughtful. "I think… it's time."

Etienne stiffened. "Really?"

"When better?" Adam said. "Rhetorically speaking. I got injured, you won't leave my side—people are going to talk anyway. They're gonna want to know what's going on. Coach Benton is ready, so are my teammates. When it's time, we can call a press conference and just… get it all done at once. Over with."

"So romantic," Etienne teased, but kissed him

quickly so Adam would know he wasn't serious. "Are you sure, though? This is your career on the line. What if you lose signing opportunities?"

"What if I never play again?" Adam countered. "I want to stand beside you, hold your hand in public. But are *you* sure? Even if I don't ever play again, you still have *your* whole career ahead of you. I'll never forgive myself if—"

Etienne put a finger over Adam's mouth. "I don't give a flying fuck if I never go further than the Freeze, as long as I have you."

"That's not true," Adam said against his finger.

"No, you're right, it's not. But I *do* love you more than hockey. And as long as I can play, and you're with me, I *will* be happy. I promise."

"I don't want the surgery," Adam said abruptly.

Etienne hesitated. "Are you—sure?"

Adam nodded, but his mouth was set in an unhappy line. "It may come back, right? I don't want to take the chance that I'll lose it for good." He reached up, tracing a line down Etienne's cheek. "I want to see you again," he whispered.

"You'd—" Etienne stopped to swallow. "You probably won't be able to play hockey again if you don't get the surgery, baby."

"I know." Adam looked miserable but determined. "I *know*, Tens. But what are my choices? Have the surgery and risk being permanently blind, therefore no hockey, or don't have the surgery, a slim chance of hockey, and maybe I'll be able to see your face again."

Etienne closed his eyes as tears sprang to them. "Adam… are you really choosing the possibility of seeing me again over *hockey*?"

Now Adam looked mulish, that stubborn expression Etienne knew so well and secretly loved.

"I love your face," he said. "I love *you*. I love looking at you. I'd only have hockey for about ten more years anyway, but you—I want to look at you for the rest of my life."

"*God.*" Etienne crowded forward, cupping Adam's cheek to press their mouths together as the tears spilled down his cheeks. "Adam, God, I love you *so much*—"

"I love you too," Adam managed between kisses. There were tears on his face too, and Etienne kissed them away tenderly.

"Okay," he finally said.

"That's it? You're not going to try to change my mind?"

"It's your body," Etienne said, capturing Adam's wrist and pressing a kiss to each fingertip in turn. "Your decision, your future. I'll support you no matter which way you go."

Adam's mouth wobbled briefly, then firmed. "You and me?"

"Always," Etienne said, and kissed him.

THEY SENT Adam home from the hospital with strict instructions to rest and allow his broken bones to heal. Adam bore it with ill-hidden frustration. He wanted to be *gone*, out of the smell of disinfectant and sick people, back to his own place with Etienne.

His sight returned in agonizingly slow stages, the gloom lightening almost imperceptibly every day, until he had about sixty percent vision in his right eye and twenty percent in his left. No matter what he did, though, it was blurry and dark, details lost to obscurity even in blazing sunlight.

He developed a ritual. Every morning, Etienne got up first and drew the blinds so sunlight enveloped the room. Adam stayed in bed, eyes closed, and counted backward from a hundred. When he opened his eyes, he told himself, he'd be able to see.

Every morning, he opened his eyes to the same dim gloom.

EVERYONE CAME TO VISIT, of course, in pairs so perfectly coordinated that Adam suspected Etienne and Rudy of organizing it. He didn't ask. Rudy and Logan were first, Rudy translating for Logan as they talked about how close they'd come to the Kelly Cup that year. They didn't mention Adam's eyes, or his plans for the future, and Adam forced himself to listen and make appropriate responses.

Hideki and Jake brought flowers and pizza. Johnny and Liam brought their Playstation and played NHL 19 while Adam listened to their cheerful chirping of each other. Hunt brought Adam an album he'd been listening to that he thought Adam would enjoy. Claude Latour told him the story of how he'd nearly lost his career due to a severe concussion. Coach Benton stayed for over an hour, talking about the Wolverines' need for better defense.

"I'm just saying, we can't expect you guys to score all the time and hope that makes up for a defense with holes in it, you know?"

Adam made noises of agreement and didn't

mention that he wasn't going to score ever again anyway.

Through it all, Etienne stayed with him, waiting on Adam's every need until Adam got tired of the hovering and pushed him away, a month after his release.

"I'm not a *child*," he said, and heard Etienne take two quick steps back. Adam swallowed guilt, lifting his chin. "Stop treating me like I'm going to break. I can walk on my own."

"I know," Etienne said. "I'm sorry."

"Don't," Adam said sharply. "Stop apologizing and just—" He turned away, groping along the wall until he found the door to the bathroom. Slipping inside, he shut it behind him with a final click.

ETIENNE CAME to bed that night silently, climbing in his side and turning off the lamp without a word. Adam lay quietly, guilt and shame tangling under his breastbone in knots.

The room was still, Etienne's breathing slow and steady. Adam rolled over, careful of his still-healing ribs.

"I'm working out with Jetty and Orlov tomorrow," Etienne said. "Will you be okay on your own?"

Adam nodded.

"Is there anywhere you'd like to go?" Etienne asked.

"Like where?"

"I don't know." The sheets rustled as Etienne shifted to get comfortable. "I just—you've been stuck in the house for weeks now. You need to get out. Get some fresh air."

Adam drew away. "There's nowhere I want to go."

Etienne took a breath. "Adam—"

"Leave it alone."

"We need to talk about it," Etienne insisted. "You need *something* to do, Cary. Are you just going to be my house-husband, staying at home all day with no hobbies, nothing to do except twiddle your thumbs? You know I can support you and I *will*, but this is about you. *You* need this, for your own sanity."

"And what *can* I do?" Adam shot back, sitting up. "I can't play hockey, I can't coach if I can't see the fucking players; I can't even be an announcer. What am I supposed to *do*?"

"Lots of things," Etienne said. The nearness of his voice said he'd sat up as well. "Your life isn't over, Cary, there are so many things you can still do. You could teach. You could write. Hell, you could go to law school or become a sports agent—there are *so* many options!"

Adam snorted derisively. "Because a blind agent is going to inspire all kinds of confidence."

"Don't," Etienne said. "I know you're depressed, but don't just shut down my suggestions." His voice gentled and Adam felt a hand on his knee. "It's still you and me, baby. I'm right here and I'm not going anywhere."

Adam fought the sting of tears and crawled into Etienne's arms. He didn't miss the tiny hitch of Etienne's breath as Adam curled up, head under his chin.

"I'm sorry," he whispered.

Etienne curved his arms around Adam's waist, holding him tight. "We'll get through this."

Adam rubbed his cheek against Etienne's chest, then pushed until Etienne got the hint and lay down so Adam was sprawled over him.

"You've been so busy taking care of me. When's the last time you were taken care of?"

Etienne cupped Adam's cheek. "I'm fine."

In the dark, Adam might as well have been fully blind. He couldn't even see Etienne's face, barely a foot away. But his voice was soft and full of affection, so Adam bent and kissed him. Then he slid backward until he was straddling Etienne's thighs.

He didn't need his eyes for this. He could do this one thing, at least, by feel and sound alone. He savored the tiny noises and stuttered breaths, the salt on his tongue as Etienne surrendered to his touch, body going limp against the mattress even as his cock hardened in Adam's mouth.

I love you, Adam told him silently with every stroke, every flick of his tongue. *I love you, I love you, I'm sorry.*

Etienne made a muffled noise and caught at Adam's hair, hands clutching tight as he emptied down Adam's throat. Adam swallowed it all, easing Etienne through it until he sagged back into the pillows with a choked noise. Then he pulled off, wiping his mouth.

"Come here," Etienne murmured.

Adam obeyed, but pushed Etienne's hand away when he tried to reach for him. "I'm okay."

"Are you sure?"

Adam rubbed his nose against Etienne's shoulder. "This was for you."

Etienne sighed and pressed a kiss to Adam's hair.

ADAM WOKE up the next morning as Etienne drew the blinds and the sound of his footsteps retreated into the bathroom. The shower started. Adam rolled onto his back, feeling the sun's rays on his face, and began to count.

When he opened his eyes, he told himself, he'd be able to see. He'd be able to get on with life. Coach, or be an announcer. Do *something* other than sit around and be useless.

Three, two, one.

He opened his eyes.

Etienne came out of the bathroom. "Morning," he said. His voice was muffled—probably drying his hair.

Adam blinked back tears and sat up, holding out a hand. Etienne crossed the bedroom and knelt in front of him, taking Adam's hand. Like this, in full sunlight, Adam could just make out the jut of Etienne's nose, his striking eyes shrouded in shadow. He traced the curve of Etienne's lips with a thumb.

"I miss your face," he whispered.

Etienne's mouth drooped under Adam's touch. "I know, baby. I'm still right here."

"But if I get the surgery and it doesn't work, I won't even have this much," Adam managed. He brushed Etienne's cheekbone. "I'll have *nothing*."

"That's not true," Etienne said, catching Adam's hand and pressing it to his cheek. "You might not have your eyes but you still have everything else. You have *me*."

"Do you want me to have the surgery?" Adam asked abruptly.

Etienne was quiet for a long moment. "I want you

to do what you feel you need to do. Whatever that is, I'll support you."

"But you want me to."

Etienne sighed, breath warm on Adam's fingers. "I want you... out of this stasis. I hate seeing you like this. But it's not about me. It's your choice."

Adam leaned forward until their foreheads were pressed together. "I'm scared."

"I know."

"I need more time."

"Okay," Etienne said immediately. "Are you hungry?"

Adam nodded and followed him to the kitchen.

37

A WEEK LATER, Etienne woke Adam up in the middle of the night.

"What time is it?" Adam asked through a yawn.

"About midnight," Etienne murmured, kissing him.

Adam made a sleepily pleased noise and tried to pull Etienne on top of him, but Etienne slithered out of his hands.

"Get dressed."

"What? *Why?*"

"It's a secret," Etienne said. The noises suggested he'd gotten off the bed and was putting his shoes on.

Adam sat up. "But it's *midnight.*"

"I'll make it worth your while," Etienne said. Something hit the bed. Adam's shoes.

Adam scowled but he swung his legs out of bed. "Find me something to wear, then."

Dressed and still complaining, Adam followed Etienne out the door. He held Etienne's hand tightly as they walked down the hall, the dim lighting no match for Adam's limited vision.

They rode the elevator down and Etienne took Adam outside. A car door opened in front of them.

"Watch your head," Etienne said, guiding him to the opening.

Adam slid carefully inside. Etienne shut the door behind him but was around the other side and crawling in beside him almost immediately. The car started without a word.

"Where are we going?"

"You'll see." Etienne took Adam's hand.

Adam scowled but didn't pull away. When the car stopped, he got out at Etienne's prompting, shivering in the night air. Etienne just took his hand again and started walking. Adam followed, feeling cobblestones under his feet. Etienne would tell him if there was a step or something in his path.

Keys jingled. A lock turned. Etienne opened a door and they stepped through.

Adam stopped dead just inside as the familiar smell of the rink hit his nose. He could smell stale popcorn and spilled beer, rubber and concrete and cleaning chemicals, and underneath it, cold and sweet in his lungs, the smell of the ice.

"*Tenny*—"

Etienne said nothing, locking the door behind them. Then he stepped close, into Adam's space. "Do you trust me?" he murmured.

Adam swallowed hard. Of course he did. But was he strong enough to step out on the ice when he could barely see? The reminder of what he'd lost cut him to the quick. But he trusted Etienne. He *loved* Etienne, and Etienne would never hurt him willingly.

He nodded and was rewarded with a quick kiss. Then his hand was back in Etienne's, and they were walking down the hall. Adam trailed his free hand along the cinder block wall, over the bumps and ridges. He knew the way by heart, knew the way the locker room door creaked when it opened, the feel of his footsteps on the hard rubber floor mats inside.

Adam sat where Etienne put him, fear and antici-pation choking his breath. He accepted the skates Etienne put in his arms and bent to put them on. This too, he could do without sight, his fingers swift and sure on the laces. When they were on, Etienne handed him a helmet.

"Ready?" he said softly.

Adam nodded again, still unable to speak. They went up the ramp to the ice hand in hand, Etienne making a quick detour to flip on the lights. Adam almost smiled, remembering how he'd done the same thing after the disastrous visit to Etienne's father.

"Is this our thing?" he asked when Etienne returned.

"What?"

"Making things better by getting on the ice."

Etienne led him through the box. "Get on the ice and tell me if it helps. If it does, then yeah, it's our thing." There was a smile in his voice.

Adam huffed an almost-laugh and obeyed. His eyes stung at the familiar glide, the *shing* of the blades on the ice, the wind in his face as the smell and feel of the ice rose up and enveloped him. The lights blazed above them, providing just enough illu-mination that Adam could see the boards to his side and angle his direction to keep from running into them.

He struck out, picking up speed, keeping a yard or so between himself and the boards as he circled the rink. He was panting and out of breath by the second lap and he skidded to a stop, doubling over and putting his hands on his knees.

Etienne laughed, somewhere across the rink. Adam held up a middle finger in the direction of his voice, making him laugh harder.

"God, I'm already gassed," Adam panted. Etienne's skates got louder and then stopped near him.

"You've been off the ice for over two months, of course you're out of condition," he said. He put a warm hand on Adam's back. "I want to try something. Listen, okay?"

Something fell on the ice.

Adam cocked his head. "A puck?"

"Good." Etienne put a stick in Adam's hands.

Adam ran his hands along the length of it. The blade wasn't quite as curved as he liked, but it would do. He put it on the ice, blade down, and swung it back and forth just to hear the sound it made. He couldn't help his smile.

"Where's the puck?"

"I'm gonna give it to you," Etienne said. "You just listen, okay?"

Adam closed his eyes. It was easier to focus when he wasn't distracted by the shadows in his vision. This way, he could hear the scrape of Etienne's blade on the ice, a few feet away. The puck made a rasping noise as it skidded toward him and Adam moved on instinct, stopping it with his stick.

"*Good!*" Etienne said, clearly delighted. "Send it back to me now."

Adam fired it in the direction of his voice and Etienne laughed as he stopped it.

"Again. Listen for it."

They passed it back and forth, over and over, until Adam could track the sound of the puck sliding across the ice and stop it nine times out of ten.

"Okay, now let's do it while moving."

Adam tensed. Batting the puck back and forth while stationary was one thing. Doing it in motion?

"I'll tell you if you're too close to the boards," Etienne said. His voice was warm and comforting, so rock-steady in his belief that Adam could do this that Adam nodded in spite of himself.

He pushed off, opting for quarter-speed and listening for Etienne. He wasn't far away, his blades a comforting noise against the ice, the click and scrape of his stick alerting Adam just before the puck slid toward him. Adam reached out, fumbled, and missed.

"That's okay," Etienne said. He peeled off and retrieved the puck as Adam stopped. "Let's do it again. We still have half the rink."

He stopped talking and Adam began moving again, straining to hear. This was Etienne, he reminded himself. He knew Etienne, how his mind worked, how he operated. He liked to keep the puck ahead of himself, where his superior reach worked against his shorter opponents. His passes were sharp and crisp, calculated on the fly for the perfect angle—Adam moved without even thinking and the puck connected with his stick with a solid smack.

Adam laughed out loud in delight and sped up, keeping the puck on his stick by feel alone. He could sense Etienne close to him, and he ducked around him, dropping the puck between his feet. He fumbled finding it again but Etienne caught him instead, spinning him around on the ice and pulling them both to a stop.

Adam clung to him, joy suffusing him. Etienne's face was in shadows, but Adam knew he was smiling down at him, knew his slate-blue eyes were warm with love and concern.

"You're right," Adam said. He grabbed Etienne's head and pulled him down into a kiss.

"Mmph—I didn't say anything," Etienne protested.

Adam kissed him again. "We both know why you brought me here. You're right. I have to try. I can't keep being paralyzed by fear."

Etienne tightened his arms. "I'm with you no matter what."

"I know." Adam put his cheek to Etienne's chest, closing his eyes. "It's the only way I'll have the courage to do this." He pulled back suddenly. "This doesn't mean I love hockey more than you."

Etienne's laugh was startled. "I know that, you idiot."

"As long as we're clear," Adam said, and pulled him into another kiss.

38

THE LAST THING Adam remembered before they wheeled him into surgery was Etienne pressing their mouths together and whispering, "You'll see me soon." Then he was rolled down the hall and put on the table, and someone asked him to count backward from ten.

BEEPING WAS the first thing he heard when he woke up. Adam lay very still, eyes closed, and listened. The doctor had warned him that his vision, if it came back at all, would be blurry at first. It would take some time for his eyes to refocus and function properly, weeks, even.

He was afraid. Hell, he was terrified. He could admit that. What would he do if he opened his eyes and couldn't see anything at all?

You'll get on with living, he told himself sternly. *You'll figure it out. At least you'll have Etienne and your family. The rest will follow.*

Adam listened to the soft noises around him. There was a monitor beeping from somewhere on his left. Out in the hall, he could hear footsteps passing and voices calling to each other in quiet tones. Inside the room, to his right, he recognized Etienne's breathing—slow, deep, and steady. He was asleep then, probably conked out on the couch beside Adam or sprawled in a chair so he'd be close.

Adam was seized with a deep and terrible affection. Whatever happened, he had Etienne. Nothing else really mattered.

He opened his eyes.

It was dark in the room, and Adam had a heart-stopping moment before he realized the shades were drawn, the sun down outside. The lights really *were* off, but when he looked up, he could see the running lights above the bed, blurry and indistinct but definitely there. Even in the dim room, with unfocused vision, he was still already seeing better than he had before.

Adam didn't try to stop the tears of relief that sprang to his eyes. He held up his good hand and inspected it, spreading his fingers wide, wiggling them, smiling foolishly through the tears as he watched them obey his commands. He groped for the bed's controls, squinting at the buttons until he figured out how to raise the bed so he was sitting partly upright.

There. Now he could see Etienne—sound asleep on the couch, his long limbs trailing off the ends. Adam almost made a noise to wake him when his attention was caught by something on the table at the end of the bed.

He leaned forward and grasped the corner of the

box, pulling it off the table and into his lap. He flipped the lid up and looked inside.

When Etienne woke, Adam was sitting up in bed, a box of strawberry glazed donuts in his lap, smiling at him, his eyes fixed on Etienne's face.

Etienne rolled to his feet so fast he nearly fell.

"You brought me donuts," Adam said.

"Had to think of some way to make sure you came back to me," Etienne said, matching his smile.

Adam hiccuped and wiped his face, then held out his arms. The donuts got pushed to the side, unheeded, as Etienne crawled into the bed to kiss away the tear tracks on Adam's cheeks.

"Can you see me, baby?" he whispered.

Adam nodded, arms around Etienne's neck. "You're blurry. It's—I can't focus. But I can see you. I can—I missed your face *so much*." He ducked his head, burying his face in Etienne's shoulder, and Etienne held him tight.

EPILOGUE

ADAM WOKE up early and rolled out of bed silently so as not to wake Etienne. He used the bathroom, then tiptoed back to the bed. Etienne stirred when Adam slipped under the covers, one long arm snaking around Adam's waist.

"Go back to sleep," Adam whispered.

Etienne opened an eye and looked at him. "Why are *you* awake?"

A month of his vision returning steadily, details coming more into focus every day, and Adam still wasn't prepared for the way Etienne took his breath away, sleep-rumpled and languorous as he smiled at him.

He pecked him on the nose. In response, Etienne reached out and pulled Adam on top of him, tugging his head down so their lips could meet, wet and filthy. Adam groaned into it as Etienne's hands began to roam, slipping under Adam's soft sleep pants to cup his ass.

"*Fuck*," Adam said, breaking away to gasp for air. "It's been almost a year, why is that still so good?"

Etienne grinned, opened his mouth to answer, and Adam's phone rang.

Adam moaned, pressing his forehead to Etienne's chest. "Ignore it."

"Could be important. It's pretty early."

Adam wriggled against Etienne's hands. "*Ignore it.*"

Etienne laughed silently and squeezed his ass, then reached out and scooped Adam's phone off the nightstand.

I hate you, Adam mouthed as Etienne hit Answer.

"Adam Caron's phone." He listened and his brows went up. "Yes sir, he's right here." He held the phone out to Adam. "It's Coach Benton."

"You're not out of the woods yet, pal," Adam told him as he put the phone to his ear and rolled off Etienne's body to sit up. "Coach?"

"Adam, how are you feeling?"

"Good, sir, thank you."

"How's your vision?"

"Better every day. The doctor has faith in a 100% recovery."

"Fantastic news!" Benton said. "I'd like to talk to you today. Can you come in for a meeting?"

Adam sat up straight. "I—yes sir. What time?"

"Make it nine."

"See you then." Adam hung up and looked at Etienne, still flat on his back with his hands behind his head.

He raised a brow. "What'd he want?"

"To talk to me. This morning. In—fuck, an hour and a half!" He nearly fell out of bed in his scramble for the bathroom. Halfway there, he spun. "Will you come with me?"

"I can't be in a confidential meeting between you and the head coach of the Wolverines," Etienne pointed out, propping himself up on his elbows.

Adam waved that off. "No, I know. But you can wait for me outside. Please?"

Etienne's face softened. "Yeah, of course I will. Go shower."

ADAM WAS a bundle of nerves in the car on the way to the stadium. Finally Etienne took his hand.

"Breathe," he said. "You look nice."

Adam glanced down at his fawn suit, smoothing his free hand over the lapel. "What do you think he wants to talk to me about?"

"You're a grown man," Etienne said. "Use your head and think about it."

Adam narrowed his eyes at him. "Maybe I want to hear you say it."

"Maybe you shouldn't get everything you want," Etienne countered, and laughed at the scowl on Adam's face. He pulled him close, tucking him in under his arm. He smelled wonderful, his aftershave piney and sharp, and Adam took a deep breath. "You're on your way to a full recovery. You've been working out with me and getting back in shape all summer. The doctors are all saying that you've made incredible strides in healing and your vision will be as good as before—better, even, since the blind spot is gone now. So what do *you* think he wants to talk to you about?"

Adam groaned. "Okay, don't say it, I don't want to jinx it."

He felt Etienne press a kiss to his hair. "Superstitious idiot."

"Like you're any better," Adam countered, sitting up and poking Etienne in the ribs just to hear him squawk.

HE LEFT Etienne in the front office and made his way alone down the halls to the conference rooms. Coach Benton rose and greeted him with a big smile.

"Adam, you look great!"

"Thank you, Coach," Adam said, shaking his hand. "Grace, you're here too?"

His agent rose from her seat, smiling at him. "Good to see you looking so well, Adam."

"Have a seat," Benton said. "Donut?" He pointed at a box.

Adam groaned. "That's a very mean question, Coach. I'm trying to get back into skating shape. Donuts aren't part of that."

Benton grinned like Adam had passed a test. "Let's just cut to the chase then, shall we? We want you back, son."

Adam took a careful breath, relief making his joints weak.

Grace slid a sheaf of papers across the table to him. "Read it over," she suggested. "It's a two-year contract and the terms are very generous, in my opinion."

Adam rifled through the pages. The proposed salary made his eyes widen, but he kept going, reading the fine print and then looking up at Benton, who was waiting patiently.

"You really think I'm worth this?" he asked.

"I think you're going to be worth a lot more, sooner than you might expect," Benton said. "But it's a good starting place. Take some time, think it over. Talk about it with your boyfriend—how's he doing?"

Adam couldn't help the smile. "He's good. I don't need to—we already talked about it. My options, I mean." He picked up the pen and signed, his eyes stinging.

"One other thing," Benton said as Adam put the pen down. "I called a press conference to announce your return, I hope you don't mind. It's in fifteen minutes."

The laugh bubbled up before Adam could stop it. He pressed a hand to his sternum, grinning. "Pretty ballsy of you, Coach."

Benton inclined his head, eyes gleaming. "I had a hunch."

An idea occurred to Adam and he hesitated. "Coach, can I—"

Benton made an encouraging noise.

"You know what we talked about last season, before... everything?"

"I just mentioned your boyfriend," Benton said, lips quirking. "I remember our conversation."

Adam took a deep breath and flattened his hands on the table. "Can I... use the press conference to come out?"

Benton's brows went up. "Now who's ballsy?"

Adam hunched his shoulders. "It's just—I mean. I'm tired of hiding it. I want... I think it'd be a good time, if the Wolverines want to show they support me, you know?"

Benton nodded thoughtfully. "Good point. Alright. Give me an hour, then. Scott needs to write a statement for you and you'll need to approve it. You sit tight."

He and Grace left and Adam was alone, sitting at the table with hands that wouldn't stop trembling. Was he doing this? He was doing it. He'd re-signed with the Wolverines, he had their support, and he was about to come out to the country. He was… going to throw up.

He was kneeling over the trash can in the corner of the room when the door opened and then Etienne was there, rubbing his back with a warm, comforting hand.

"Hey, hey, breathe," he murmured.

Adam clutched at him blindly. "I signed," he choked out. "I signed and I'm going to come out and —" His stomach twisted and he heaved again.

Etienne held him as he shook, murmuring to him. "You're doing so well," he said, over and over. "You're being so brave. I've got you. You can do this. You and me, remember?"

"People are going to be *shitty*," Adam managed, sitting back on his heels.

"Yeah," Etienne agreed. "And you know how much you're going to help kids who think they'll never be able to play a pro sport because they're gay?"

Adam looked up at him. "Yeah?"

Etienne's eyes were warm with love. "If someone like you had come out when I was a kid, it would have meant the world to me. So focus on the people you're helping, and let the other shit roll off your back. You've got me, and your team."

"Do I, though?" Adam said, grabbing Etienne's

sleeve. "*Do* I have the team? I know I told them, but then everything happened and—what if some of them have a problem? What if—"

"*Stop*," Etienne ordered. "You've got Jake, don't you? And Hideki, and Victor, and Claude. Who else?"

"Hunt. And Coach." Adam took a shaky breath. "They have my back."

"Exactly."

The door opened again and Scott stepped through. His eyebrows climbed toward his hairline at the sight of them crouched in a corner, but he just held up a piece of paper.

"I've got your statement. Want to go over it with me?"

Etienne patted Adam on the back and helped him stand. "I'll go find you a toothbrush or some breath mints." He dodged Adam's half-hearted swing, grinning, and nodded at Scott before leaving.

It took about twenty minutes to revise and amend the statement until it read like him. Adam murmured the phrases to himself, committing as much as he could to memory, letting the repetition ground him as Etienne sat beside him, a solid, reassuring presence.

Five minutes before time, Benton put his head in the door. "Adam, can you come out here for a minute?"

Adam threw a baffled look at Etienne and stood. He stepped out into the hall and the question died in his throat as a cheer went up and he took in all the faces grinning at him. Jake was in front, bouncing on his toes with excitement. Beside him was Hunt, his eyes calm and a smile curving his mouth. Victor, Hideki, Claude, and the rest of the team clustered behind them. Some of them had reservation in their eyes, their smiles not as warm, but they were *there*.

"You—" Adam stopped, unable to get words past the boulder in his throat. "You guys... are here for m-me?"

Jake rolled his eyes. "Duh. You don't get to hog *all* the spotlight!"

"We wouldn't make you do this alone," Hideki said. He gripped Adam's hand, and as if that was a signal, the rest of the team crowded around, sweeping Adam up in the middle of a breathless hug.

Adam, torn between laughter and tears, looked for Etienne over their heads. He found him off to the side, smiling so hard his face had to hurt. Adam put out a hand without thinking and Jake reached out, grabbing Etienne and dragging him into the middle of the scrum until he and Adam collided.

Adam closed his eyes, pressing his face into Etienne's shoulder.

"Ready?" Etienne whispered in his ear.

Adam took a deep breath and nodded. Behind them, Coach Benton swung open the doors to the press room, and Adam turned to face his future.

Keep reading for a sneak peek of Odd Man Rush, a Seattle Kingfishers novella and the next hockey romance from Michaela Grey!

ACKNOWLEDGMENTS

Thank you to everyone on Twitter and Tumblr who helped me shape this book and bring the characters to life. Special thanks to Sarah, who is responsible for the cover and helping me with formatting, promotion, and sales. I literally couldn't have done it without you and I'm so glad we're friends.

ABOUT THE AUTHOR

Michaela Grey told stories to put herself to sleep since she was old enough to hold a conversation in her head. When she learned to write, she began putting those stories down on paper. She resides in the Texas Hill Country with her cats, and is perpetually on the hunt for peaceful writing time.

When she's not writing, she's watching hockey or blogging about writing and men on knife shoes chasing a frozen Oreo around the ice while trying to keep her cat off the keyboard.

Tumblr: greymichaela.tumblr.com
Twitter: @GreyMichaela
Facebook: www.facebook.com/GreyMichaela
E-mail: greymichaela@gmail.com

ODD MAN RUSH

CHAPTER ONE

When Rune Hedaya walked into the Sirens' locker room, dread crawled inside Eli McKenna's chest and curled up there.

Practice hadn't started yet, everyone still busy getting their gear on, and the room was the usual raucous mess of stick tape and balled up socks being hurled around, chirps and rude comments and bragging blending seamlessly into white noise that Eli effortlessly filtered out. He focused on getting his own gear in place, buckling his pads on and keeping his breathing slow and even.

He was shrugging into his chest protector when William Caron, their head coach, had ushered the tall stranger inside, a hand on his shoulder. It was a measure of the respect Caron commanded that the room immediately quieted, although maybe they were just curious about the newcomer. He was strikingly handsome, dark brown hair shaved close to the sides of his head and left long on top, with olive skin and sharp eyes that surveyed the room.

"Boys, this is Rune Hedaya," Caron announced. "He comes from the Otters. He's a d-man, and we're gonna try out some pairings today."

The captain was the first to greet him, because there was a reason he was captain. "Seth Williams," he said, holding out his hand.

Rune took it as others crowded around.

Eli breathed through his nose, in and out, not looking over. He stood, gave himself a once-over, and then bounced on his skates several times to make sure everything was settled and secure. When he glanced up, Rune was walking toward him.

"Hi," he said, hand out. "Rune."

Eli accepted the hand, hoping his hesitation hadn't shown. "Eli," he said. "Um. Goalie."

Rune's eyes creased with amusement. Up close, they were a striking blue-green. "Is *that* why all the gear?"

He had a faint accent, but Eli couldn't place it. It sharpened the corners of his words, made them crisp and clear. He was grinning, waiting for a response, and Eli just shrugged awkwardly.

"You know what they say about d-men," he said. "Can't read a clue to save their lives, let alone a play. I was just helping you out."

Rune's eyebrows shot up and he burst out laughing. "*Ouch*! Guess I'll just have to prove you wrong, huh?"

Eli found himself smiling back without meaning to, and he ducked his head, breaking eye contact. "Yeah, sure."

"Rune," Seth said, appearing at Rune's elbow. "Come meet Ilya and Josh. Couple of our d-men."

"Nice to meet you, Eli," Rune said. "See you out there."

He let himself be pulled away and Eli took another deep breath, rolling his shoulders and letting the tension flow from him on the exhale.

Daved was watching him when he turned for the door. Sympathy, visible only to Eli who knew him so well, glimmered in his eyes.

Don't, Eli warned him silently, and Daved just nodded and pulled the door open for him.

ON THE ICE, it was better. But then, it was always better on the ice. Here, between his pipes, he knew what was expected of him. *Stop the puck.* That's all he had to know. All the training, all the discipline, all the stretching and exercising—it all came down to that.

He shaved down his crease methodically, breathing loud inside his helmet, as the rest of the team, roughly half in black jerseys and the other half in gold, spilled onto the ice and spun out into broad loops and circles, cheerfully calling abuse at each other. Eli let it wash over him, in it but not of it. He went through his warmup routine, counting each part off in his head, until Coach blew his whistle.

"Eli against Väinö," he said. "Eli, you're gold team. Vinyl, you're black, obviously."

"No, Seth is," Jay pointed out, causing a wave of snickers.

Coach gave him an unimpressed look and Jay grinned, cheeky and unrepentant. "Here are the pairings," Coach continued. "Black with me, gold with Rob."

Rob, the assistant coach, held up the whiteboard by his side and Eli scrutinized it. Rune had been paired with Josh. They were talking quietly off to the side, heads together. Eli didn't try to listen in. He read the rest of the lines and headed back to his crease.

The first few minutes were a burst of frenetic activity, the players all coming off a two day break and more than ready to get back into action. Eli stayed loose and ready in his crease, watching the play like a hawk.

Jay tried a sharp angle shot off him and Eli blockered it away with ease. It was scooped up by Rune and dumped into the far end. Eli watched as they gave chase. Rune was a good skater, fast and balanced, with an agility that belied his size. He crashed the scrum in the far corner and flipped the puck out to Josh, who sent it backward to Seth.

Ilya picked Seth's pocket before Seth could make a move toward goal, though, and then they were all heading back toward Eli, Ilya on a breakaway out in front. Eli floated forward to the edge of his crease, watching Ilya bear down on him. He knew Ilya well enough by now to know when he was going to make his move. He always dropped his right shoulder, *there* —Rune came out of nowhere just as Ilya fired, hurling himself to the ice in front of the puck.

It hit him in the bicep and Rune grunted and slid in a sprawl of long limbs through Eli's crease. Eli caught his arm, stopping his forward motion, as Ilya skidded to a halt in shock and the others caught up.

"Is *practice*," he said accusingly. "Coach is kill me if

I hurt new d-man in very first practice! Why you so stupid?"

Rune grinned up at Eli, still flat on his back. "Thanks for catching me. You're not too bad at this goalie thing."

"Yeah well, you're a lot bigger than a puck," Eli said, pulling off his blocker and extending a hand. "Slower, too."

Rune laughed as he took his hand, grip firm, and let him pull him to his feet. "Are you always this mean?"

"I'm honest," Eli countered, but he couldn't fight the smile on his face.

"Whoa, did you just make Reaper smile?" Jay demanded.

Eli rolled his eyes. "I smile, Davo. If I don't smile at you, it's because you're not funny."

"Does that mean I *am*?" Rune asked.

"Jury's still out," Eli retorted.

Coach blew his whistle. Rune winked at Eli and skated away.

So it went for the rest of practice. Every time anyone with the puck got close to Eli, Rune was there first, breaking their shot, spoiling their aim, sometimes straight out slapping the puck off their stick. He was as fast as he was agile, not afraid to use his size but also careful not to make unnecessary contact.

"Why the fuck did the Otters let you go?" Eli overheard Josh demand during a lull.

Rune shrugged easily, his reply inaudible.

After the first ten minutes or so, Coach switched it up, putting Rune with Ilya. Their chemistry was obvious from the beginning, working off each other's passes seamlessly. Rune shot Eli a blinding smile as he swept by him at high speed, gone before Eli could even smile back.

At least he's having fun, Eli thought, but something prickled under his skin at the thought of Rune and Ilya being friends. He shut that thought down before it could really form, turning his focus back to the practice. Daved was barreling down on him with the puck and Eli knew from experience just how hard he was to stop at that speed.

IT WASN'T that he didn't want Rune to have friends, Eli told himself in the shower. He didn't even *know* Rune, it was ridiculous to be concerning himself with Rune's hypothetical relationships.

Eli turned his face into the spray and closed his eyes.

He'd just found himself watching for Rune's brilliant smile, wanting it turned on him, wanting Rune's attention, his focus. On him.

But he couldn't want that, he reminded himself, and turned the shower off.

He came out of the shower to find the room deserted. Not surprising—he'd taken awhile. He dropped his towel and stepped into his underwear, pulling them up over his hips.

"Why do they call you Reaper?"

Eli spun.

Rune was leaning against the door, ankles crossed, turning his phone over and over between long fingers. He raised an eyebrow when Eli didn't immediately answer.

"Oh, uh—" Eli struggled to marshal his thoughts, reaching for his pants. "It's stupid."

"Try me."

Eli zipped his pants and picked up his shirt. "Because I don't have a sense of humor and I'm lethal between the pipes."

It didn't take Rune long. "So you're the grim reaper. I like it." That bright smile spread across his face, making Eli feel like he'd been punched in the gut. He covered by sitting down to put his socks on, focusing hard on what he was doing.

"What—why are you still here?" he asked without looking up.

"Oh, group of guys wanted to take me out for lunch at some place called Savour? They said it's the team's favorite restaurant. I thought I'd see if you wanted to come with us."

Bad idea bad idea bad idea.

Eli shook the thought away and stood to step into his shoes. Going out to eat once with his team and the new guy wouldn't hurt anything. There was nothing *to* hurt. Rune was just being friendly.

"Sure," he said, and Rune's smile widened until Eli couldn't breathe.

"Awesome! Well, I don't have a car, so… any chance of a ride?"

Eli had the sinking sensation that he'd bitten off more than he could chew. He was helpless to do more than nod and grab his keys off the shelf.

Rune followed him out of the rink, keeping pace easily. He looked around, taking in the rain-soaked pavement and the trees that crowded above them, forming a lacy, green-shaded cover over their walk to Eli's car.

"Sure is pretty out here," he remarked.

"Could be worse," Eli allowed. "Could be east coast."

"Hey, east coast is gorgeous—oh, you're teasing me. Who says you don't have a sense of humor?"

Eli shrugged, unlocking the car. "People who think fart jokes are funny."

"Ah," Rune said, sliding into the passenger seat. "Jay."

"Among others."

The car fired up smoothly and Eli rubbed the leather steering wheel with one thumb. "So why *did* you get traded?" he asked as he left the parking lot. "If you don't mind saying."

Rune stretched his long legs out as far as they would go, lacing his hands over his belly. "That's classified," he said comfortably.

Eli felt the flush all the way up to his ears. "Right. Never mind."

"Oh hey, no!" Rune said, sitting up. "That was a joke, I'm sorry. A stupid joke. Not funny."

The flush burned hotter. Eli hunched his shoulders, clutching the wheel tighter, and said nothing. Now Rune would see exactly how humorless he was.

The pause was awkward and Eli didn't know how to fill it.

"I, uh… I didn't fit in with the Otters, I guess," Rune said suddenly. He scratched his nose. "I didn't like how they relied on muscle and heavy hits to get the job done. They wanted me to be more aggressive. I just wanted to play."

Silence fell in the car as a pop singer crooned on the radio.

"My first year in juniors," Eli said after a minute,

"my coach made me loosen one of my pipes. If anyone bumped into it, it would pop off immediately and I'd get a whistle."

"Oh," Rune said. "That's...."

"Yeah." Eli took a slow breath. "Dirty. Or at least weighting the game in our favor. It made me—it made me sick. I didn't want to cheat to get a win. If I didn't win clean, what was the point?"

"Yeah," Rune said softly. "I'm sorry."

Eli shrugged, turning the corner toward the restaurant and looking for a parking space. "It's over and I survived. So did you."

"Will they let me play hockey here?" Rune asked, and for the first time he didn't sound confident and sure of himself.

Eli parked and took a moment to gather his thoughts. "I think so," he finally said. "Cary—Coach —he may want you to hit someone sometimes, shake 'em up and put a little fear of God and the Sirens into them, but he'll have already seen your talent. You're not just big dumb muscle to him."

Rune was watching him when Eli looked at him. "You like him."

"And respect him," Eli said. "He's a great guy. He'd open a vein for us and every single one of us would do the same for him. You'll see."

Rune's eyebrow went up. "Damn. So what do you like to do for fun?"

Eli blinked at the sudden shift in topic. "I mean, normal stuff," he hedged. "Why?"

"Just curious. You're so quiet. I wanna know what makes you tick."

"We should go inside," Eli said abruptly, and unbuckled.

Rune didn't move, watching him with narrowed eyes. "You like to drink? Party?"

"No," Eli said, startled into truth. "I'm boring. I like to read. I don't go out unless the team drags me out." He fidgeted with the seatbelt. "Why do you *care?*"

"Why do you think?" Rune asked cryptically. He pushed his door open and stepped out before Eli could answer, leaving him to swear and scramble after him.

The guys were already in the back of the restaurant at their favorite booth when they showed up, and they were greeted with cheers and chirping over being late.

They settled in, Rune right next to Eli on the bench, and Eli picked up his menu, determined not to notice how solid and warm Rune's thigh was pressed up against his own. He almost managed it until Rune nudged him with his knee.

"What's good here?" he asked under the chatter of the table.

Eli forced himself to focus. "The beef au jus is nice. Or they have an Italian sub that's not too far off our diet plan, especially if you get it with all the vegetables."

Rune smiled at him and when the server came by, he ordered the beef au jus. "So," he said once she was gone. "What's there to do around here, boys?"

"Webber will show you all the best coffeeshops," Jay said. "'Specially the ones with cute baristas. You got a girl, Runer?"

"No girl," Rune said equably, leaning back against the seat and spreading his arms along the spine. His fingers brushed Eli's shoulder and Eli forced himself not to react. "No guy, either."

The booth went momentarily still.

"That gonna be a problem?" Rune said. His voice was utterly calm.

"We see you play, you fuck anyone you want," Ilya said into the fraught silence. "You're not hit on me though. I have girlfriend. Very beautiful. You want see?" He was digging out his phone before anyone could stop him, thumbing through pictures and then holding it out so Rune could see.

"She *is* beautiful," Rune agreed. "What's she doing with your ugly ass?"

Ilya cackled. "NHL player, baby. Lots of money!"

Eli focused on the air entering his lungs, trapping it there, then letting it out slowly. Rune wasn't straight. Rune had been—possibly, unless Eli's wishful thinking had clouded his vision—hitting on him.

Rune's fingers brushed his shoulder again and Eli turned to look at him. Up close, Rune's smile was somehow even more beautiful, his striking eyes crinkling at the corners.

"We good?" he murmured under whatever Ilya was saying.

Eli took a breath. Another one. Rune waited.

"Yeah," Eli said. He mustered a smile, even though it wasn't very big. "Of course. So where are you from, anyway? I can't quite place your accent."

"Germany by way of Syria," Rune said. "My parents wanted a better life for their kids. Papa's an engineer and Mama's a doctor. Hey." He leaned closer and lowered his voice. "Do you wanna maybe hang out later? Just the two of us?"

Eli froze. Was he asking what Eli *thought* he was asking? The look in Rune's eyes said maybe, just maybe, he was.

He opened his mouth to say something and his phone rang, cutting off his answer. *Shit.*

"Sorry," he muttered, dragging it from his pocket. "I have to get this."

"Is that Noemi?" Jay demanded, and Daved elbowed him in the ribs. "Ow! Tell her I said hi, Reaper. *Ow*, Davvy, stop it!"

"Who's Noemi?" Rune asked.

"Um." Eli slid from the booth, the phone still ringing. He glanced at Rune, looking up at him with nothing but friendly curiosity in his eyes, and back down at the phone. "My wife. Excuse me."

He hit answer and walked away without looking back.

Preorder Odd Man Rush today!